THE THING ITSELF

D1630795

A Selection of Recent Titles by Peter Guttridge

The Brighton Mystery Series

CITY OF DREADFUL NIGHT *
THE LAST KING OF BRIGHTON *
THE THING ITSELF *

The Nick Madrid Series

NO LAUGHING MATTER
A GHOST OF A CHANCE
TWO TO TANGO
THE ONCE AND FUTURE CON
FOILED AGAIN
CAST ADRIFT

* *available from Severn House*

THE THING ITSELF

The Third Brighton Mystery

Peter Guttridge

This first world edition published 2012
in Great Britain and in the USA by
SEVERN HOUSE PUBLISHERS LTD of
9–15 High Street, Sutton, Surrey, England, SM1 1DF.
Trade paperback edition first published
in Great Britain and the USA 2012 by
SEVERN HOUSE PUBLISHERS LTD.

British Library Cataloguing in Publication Data

Guttridge, Peter.
  The thing itself.
  1. Brighton (England) – Fiction. 2. Detective and mystery
  stories.
  I. Title
  823.9'2-dc23

ISBN-13: 978-0-7278-8081-9 (cased)
ISBN-13: 978-1-84751-437-0 (trade paper)

All Severn House titles are printed on acid-free paper.

Severn House Publishers support The Forest Stewardship Council [FSC],
the leading international forest certification organisation. All our titles that
are printed on Greenpeace-approved FSC-certified paper carry the FSC logo.

Typeset by Palimpsest Book Production Ltd.,
Falkirk, Stirlingshire, Scotland.
Printed and bound in Great Britain by
MPG Books Ltd., Bodmin, Cornwall.

To the late, great Geoff Wyatt, SGI (1951–2011)

'If only he had been able to breathe in more air. If only the road were less steep. If only he were able to reach home.'

Ivo Andric, *The Bridge Over The Drina*

'To Brighton, to Brighton,
Where they do such things,
And they say such things,
In Brighton, in Brighton,
I'll never go there anymore.'

Music hall song, 1934

PROLOGUE

June, 1934

I was sitting in my suit in a corner of the room when she came home. *City of Dreadful Night* lay open in my lap. My father, a sunless man, had given me the bleak Victorian poem for my twelfth birthday. The gas jets were lit and the one behind my head cast my elongated shadow across the room.

'You startled me,' she said, her mouth somewhere between a smile and something more nervous. 'I didn't expect to see you today.'

I was sitting, left leg crossed over right, trousers on the left leg pulled up to avoid bagging at the knees, a narrow band of lardy, hairless leg between turn-up and sock.

'Where have you been?' I said.

'To Hove – to that doctor we heard about. It's all set for next week.'

I knew my temper scared her. I saw she was avoiding looking at my face, her eyes fixed instead on that narrow band of bare leg. Her eyes were still focused there when I stood. She looked up and saw my face. I moved towards her.

I felt I was in a cathedral or some vast building where the silence buzzed. That strange susurrus of sound that pressed on my ears. Then I realized the dim roar was inside, not outside my ears. My blood pumping through me in sharp surges. I checked my pulse with a finger on my wrist. My heart was beating quickly but not as rapidly as I expected.

I looked around me. Everything neat and in its place. I glanced down at my suit. I saw a dark spot on my waistcoat. I took my handkerchief from my pocket and rubbed at the spot. It didn't budge, although there was a blossom of pink on the white cloth.

I needed to still my ears. I walked to the radiogram and turned it on. The bulb glowed red. I recognized the music that grew louder as the radio warmed up. Ketèlbey's *In a Monastery Garden*.

I picked up the packet of Rothmans on the table beside the sofa. I smoked two cigarettes, listening to the music, looking everywhere but at her. She lay face down on the floor, blood in a spreading halo around her head.

I should have felt regret. I knew that. But long ago, in Flanders, my emotions had been cauterized. I had returned unable to feel. Besides, the carcass lying splayed on the carpet was not the woman I had desired and, in my way, loved.

I'd explained the rules right at the start of our relationship. It was just a bit of fun. I would never leave my wife. I said things, of course. The things women liked to hear. But she knew – she must have known – that was just pillow talk.

I had been intoxicated by her. In bed there was nothing she wouldn't do. Things my wife would never contemplate. Soiling things. I was shocked by some of her suggestions – she could be coarse, using phrases I'd never heard before – but I had enjoyed what she did with me, there was no doubt about that.

I tolerated her wish to be seen out in public. In the best places, places I had never taken my wife. A part of me liked being seen with her – she was as beautiful as a movie star – whilst another part worried about being seen. Especially as she laughed in a ribald way. She was loud and vulgar. In private, I accepted it. In public, I was faintly embarrassed.

For me, the life had gone out of her weeks before I'd killed her. It had drained away the day she said: 'There's something I have to tell you. It will come as a surprise to you – as it did to me.'

I knew she didn't know about me. How could she? And so when she told me she was pregnant, she saw the immediate change in me but misunderstood the cause.

She sensed my heart harden but thought I was worried about a scandal. She promised to get rid of it but I could see she hoped to keep it.

It wasn't the scandal. She didn't know the reason. How could she? An abortion would make no difference.

I went to the kitchen and took her apron from behind the door. I put it on. I bent and opened the cupboard beneath the sink. I took out the toolbox. Removed the short saw.

I crossed to the window. I had a coppery taste in my mouth. All I'd asked of her in return for this flat, the money, the expensive meals was fidelity.

I knew the baby wasn't mine. It couldn't be. My inability to give my wife a child had been a heavy burden for many years. It wasn't that I couldn't do the deed. It was that nothing ever came of it.

The day outside went on, unconcerned. Nothing in the street had changed. *In a Monastery Garden* was drawing to a close. It reminded me of the beautiful ruined frescoes I'd visited some months earlier in the churches on the South Downs whilst we were staying in Brighton.

I moved from the window to stand over her, the saw in my hand. The music stopped and there was silence. For a moment.

And then a hammering on the door.

I tilted my head. Silence, then the hammering again. A voice, faint through the solid wood. I strained my ears. I thought for a moment. I put the saw down. Though my hands were clean, I wiped them on the apron and walked to the door. I lifted the latch. I opened the door wide and half-turned.

'Excuse the mess.'

PART ONE
God's Lonely Man

ONE

Twenty years earlier

August 1914, and I was upstairs on the front seat of a London double-decker bus a few yards behind a Waring and Gillow pantechnicon. We should have been on Oxford Street but we were jostling along a cobbled road in northern France, lined by cheering peasants throwing flowers. In the narrow seats behind me in the scarlet bus, tired soldiers dozed on each other's shoulders. I didn't have a shoulder to sleep on but I couldn't sleep anyway, despite my exhaustion.

In the past week 80,000 of us – the British Expeditionary Force – had been mobilized and shipped over to fight the Bosch. A year earlier I'd lied about my age to enlist. In a couple of years other men would be lying about their ages to get out. But for the time being everyone was gung-ho and keen to get at the Hun, who was bayoneting Belgian babies and raping nuns and Red Cross nurses.

I'd been infected by Rudyard Kipling. Until 1910 I'd been at preparatory school in Rottingdean, outside Brighton, with his son Jack. Jack got a good-natured ribbing every May when we had to memorize and recite his father's poem, *Children's Song*, about our duty to the Empire. Personally, I believed the sentiments.

I liked Jack. We'd started chatting first when he'd seen me reading *City of Dreadful Night* and thought it was his father's Indian story with the same title. We'd lost touch but I'd heard Jack had tried to get into the war in 1914 – his father had pushed him forward – but he was as blind as a bat so would be useless in battle.

Not that I'd had battle experience. I was wet behind the ears. Even so, I was a professional soldier, a Tommy Atkins. Kitchener's amateur army came the following year.

I was in the Royal Sussex. Good lads but not all from Sussex. I'd palled up a bit with three ex-weavers from somewhere up north. Cousins: Jim, Jack and Ted. A salty bunch. Ted and Jack were both married men with two young ones apiece but they'd been reservists. All three men reckoned the war would be over by Christmas and they'd be home war heroes with the chance of better jobs.

A whole panoply of boats, steam whistles screeching, left Southampton and took us to France one night. We'd crossed the rough and tumbling channel on a civilian ferry like holiday-makers. Holidaymakers who could fire fifteen rounds a minute in three clips of five.

There were six divisions in the BEF and we knew we were just a gesture of support for the French. Although we wanted to, we didn't expect to get stuck in.

There was a remote possibility. The French had a million men mobilized but they were in the wrong place. There was a danger of them being outflanked by the German army coming through Belgium. Our job was to plug the gap if need be.

At dawn we were steaming up the Seine to Rouen. People lined each bank, cheering and waving tricolore flags. Rowing boats tried to keep up, people standing unsteadily in them, throwing fruit and flowers, toffees and rosettes.

We were mobbed in the narrow streets of Rouen. People were hanging out of windows, children running alongside waving flags. Our buttons were ripped off our jackets as souvenirs by screaming women. Hardly anybody hung on to their cap badges. A lot of us lost our caps altogether.

For other regiments that was pretty straightforward, but we in the Royal Sussex had the Roussillon plume as part of our cap badge. The regiment had got it at the battle of Quebec decades earlier when we had wiped the floor with the soldiers of the French Roussillon brigade and ripped the plumes off their helmets.

When asked about the plume by curious older men in Rouen, I simply said the French brigade had given it to us in recognition of our bravery in battle. Others, stupidly, told the truth in gory detail. The welcoming crush turned into a near-riot.

It was a hot afternoon and marching on cobbles, buffeted

at every turn, was no picnic. By now our uniforms were hanging mostly buttonless. We stumbled finally into a large park where we were bivouacking for the night. I wandered down to find my Lancashire mates at one of the beer tents. I'd managed to get some local currency early on. Just as well – there were long queues outside the Paymaster's as soldiers changed coppers and threepenny bits so they could get a tuppenny pint.

I found Jim, Jack and Ted and we sat together eating our iron rations – biscuits and bully beef – then Jim was lured away by the siren sounds of girls calling from outside the park railings. Some just wanted to flirt, others had a more professional purpose. The warm evening got hotter.

'Not interested?' I said to Jack and Ted.

'I love my wife,' Ted said.

'And you made her a promise.'

He shook his head.

'Didn't need to. It goes without saying.'

I sipped my beer.

'What about you, Jack?'

'Didn't you read that note from Kitchener?'

We all laughed. Kitchener had put a note in every kit bag: 'Do Your Duty Bravely, Fear God, Honour The King.' It also said: 'In this new experience you may find temptations both in wine and women. You must entirely resist both temptations, and, whilst treating all women with perfect courtesy, you should avoid any intimacy.'

'You?' he said.

'Nobody back home waiting for me or worried about me.' I gestured towards the railings. 'But I'm not interested in that.'

'You've got family at home, though, worrying over you,' Jack said. 'A mum and dad.'

'Neither.' I smiled. 'I'm God's lonely man.'

Ted clapped me on the back.

'Jesus, lad – that's a bit bleak for your age. Wait until you go home the conquering hero – the girls will be all over you.'

We marched fifteen miles north the next day. We were billeted in the evening in school rooms, village halls and, in my case, a big barn stinking of cow dung. We were supposed to stay there a few days, so the next day we helped with the harvest – the grain in the fields was ripe and high. Grateful women kept us supplied with buckets of home-brewed cider.

We cheered when on the lane beside our field we saw a line of bright red London double-decker buses led by a van with an advertisement for HP Sauce plastered on its side. Posters on the side of the buses advertised West End plays – Shaw's *Pygmalion* and a comedy with Sir Charles Hawtrey at the Coliseum. The sight of them tugged at my heart.

We didn't cheer quite so much when the next day we had to get in the buses for the journey up to the Mons–Condé canal. We bumped and shuddered and listed for mile after slow mile through the French countryside.

It was hard to think about fighting alongside the French, not against them. I had an ancestor who had fought and died at Malplaquet. The Roussillon plume in my cap was a constant reminder of our former enmity.

On Thursday, 20th August, the Belgian army was forced to abandon Brussels and withdraw to Antwerp after eighteen days resisting the Germans. The Belgians were poorly trained and ill-equipped but clearly brave – it was only later, when we came face-to-face with the mass of the German army, that we realized they must have been outnumbered a hundred to one.

On the 22nd we had our first sight of the enemy. We were on the undulating Nimy Road and a German cavalry patrol trotted over the brow of the next hill, bold as brass on their big horses, spruce in their grey uniforms and polished helmets, long lances held upright. The commander was puffing on a cigar. They were a shock, I can tell you. A few of us opened fire.

We set up quite a racket but we were too far away to hit anything. The horsemen wheeled in an orderly manner and trotted back over the brow of the hill, leaving us pocking only the bright blue sky.

TWO

We'd heard that we weren't going to attack the Hun army until our commander, Sir John French, was sure of its size and disposition. But the sighting of the cavalry must have startled him because suddenly we were out of the buses and marching double-time to the Mons canal in torrential rain. When the rain stopped, the sun came out and hit like a hammer. The dust kicked up. Then more rain, more sunshine.

We started out, as Robert Service had it, battle-bound and heart-high, singing *It's A Long Way To Tipperary*. But by the time we'd covered forty kilometres my uniform was so soaked in sweat and rainwater I could have wrung it out. Some of my companions didn't make the forty kilometres. They had new boots they hadn't yet broken in. A lot of old stagers were sitting at the roadside nursing blistered feet.

The first night, we camped in a field with no fires or lights. We were not much more than a stone's throw away from Malplaquet. The field was open but we were in the Black Country. There were slag heaps and coal mines, chemical plants, glass works and factories, and sooty washing on the lines in the back gardens of grubby villages.

Ted closed his eyes and breathed in.

'Smell that slag heap. You could imagine you're in Accrington.' He laughed. 'I'm not saying that's a good thing, mind.'

Next day we hobbled into Mons during a big market. We sat on the cobblestones in the sunshine, bedraggled, steaming like horses. We got our rations: a big loaf of bread between us four and tins without labels, some rusted, probably dating back to the Boer War. It was pot luck what was in them. Mine had stewed apple, Jimmy had pilchards – we put them together. The locals gave us cheese and sausage, apples and pears. I stuffed my knapsack full for later.

We went for a walk. Got hauled into cafés for beer. Hauled into a hairdresser for a haircut. Given cigars and cigarettes. A photographer pulled us into his shop and out into his muddy back yard for a photograph against a bit of tarpaulin. Jack scribbled on a piece of card 'Somewhere in France' and propped it against a barrel next to us. We each got a print of the snap.

When we got back to the square, our regiment was lining up. We marched on to Nimy to take up position on the bank of the canal.

'Bloody hell, this is a bit bigger than the Leeds and Liverpool,' Jim said, looking across the wide expanse of water. 'I wonder if we can have a dip?'

'If you don't mind having your bare white arse shot off,' Ted said.

It was cold and wet on the canal bank, especially after a thunderstorm at ten. We couldn't use our bivvies so we'd done our best to make trenches in the scrubland behind the canal. It was misty. There was some heat gusting from the blazing barges on the canal – we'd set them alight so they couldn't be used for makeshift bridges across the canal.

We were told we were going to engage the enemy the next day. That night our morale was good. Nevertheless, everybody wrote their notes to their loved ones back home. Gave them to friends, stuck them on the end of their bayonets with their wedding rings.

Ted spent some time beside me writing a note in pencil. When he'd done, he folded it round a small photo. He held out the package to me.

'Just in case.'

'What if I get a packet?' I said.

'I'll carry yours for you.'

'I didn't mean that. I've no one to write to.'

Ted proffered the package again. I shook my head.

'I mean who'll deliver your message if I get a packet? Best you keep it with you. I promise that if I come through and you don't I'll get it from you.'

Ted tucked it into one of his breast pockets.

'Fair enough. You sure there's no one you want to write to?'

'Nobody. I told you. I've been orphaned for five years and there's no sweetheart with her nose pressed to the windowpane pining for my return.'

At six a.m. on Sunday, 22nd August, the bells of Nimy church rang for mass. Smoke was coming from the chimney of a cottage about a hundred yards away and it was so quiet I could hear someone riddling the fire and adding more coal.

At nine a.m. the Germans started shelling. It lasted an hour but they couldn't get the range. All the shells fell short, into the canal. Made our ears ring, though. We were waiting for our guns to reply but they didn't.

The German infantry started forward soon after, a solid mass of grey. It gave me a jolt to see them coming, roaring and bellowing. My arms were shaking as I raised my rifle but then I realized we couldn't miss. They came over a bank directly in front of us and as soon as they topped it we let them have it. The range was seventy yards, so we were firing our fifteen rounds a minute at them point-blank.

They outnumbered us three to one but it was exhilarating to see what kind of devastation concentrated firepower can wreak. Horrible too, by Jove. Legs, arms and heads were flying all over the place. One minute the Hun was there, the next they were all dead. We absolutely smashed them.

I glanced at Ted, Jim and Jack beside me. Their eyes were burning as bright as mine.

I heard later the Hun was convinced we'd mowed them down with machine-gun fire but it was our musketry training coming through.

Then they got their machine guns into action and at that distance we were now the sitting ducks. We had to get out of it pretty sharp. That's when Jack and Ted copped it. I didn't see Jack die but Ted was right next to me.

One minute we were clambering up the canal side together, the next he'd fallen across me, his brains blown out through the back of his helmet. I scrabbled in his pocket, taking out the few things I thought he'd want his wife to have in addition to the

package and his wedding ring. I found another piece of paper
with his home address on it.

I looked at what was left of his face. From human being to
lifeless thing in an instant.

Jim went ten minutes later. I dug in his pocket for Jack's
stuff and his own.

I had a warm time of it the rest of that day. There were
exploding shells, shrapnel in the air, machine-gun bullets.
Eventually, German buglers sounded the ceasefire. Then,
drifting down the lines, we could hear German voices singing
'Deutschland, Deutschland über alles'. Made my blood boil.

There was no respite that night. The guns pounded away.
Villages and farms were on fire in front of us, and behind us
factories and towns blazed with light.

The next five days seemed to last five years as we retreated
under the unrelenting racket of big guns and machine-gun fire.
It rained still more, and withdrawing through villages I slipped
and slid as the coal dust on the cobbles turned to slime.

On the last day, 26th August, at a place called Le Cateau,
I had my first taste of hand-to-hand combat. Well, bayonet-
to-bayonet, really. I was the lucky one in that encounter. Lucky
in the battle altogether. We suffered 8,000 casualties on that
last day alone. Everyone I'd known in the Royal Sussex had
died. I hadn't got a scratch.

THREE

In 1915 I got my first Blighty leave. I stepped off the train
in Brighton, in a uniform still splattered with mud from
the front, surrounded by Tommies just as muddy but all
carrying rifles.

I'd heard stories of men returning home earlier than
expected, finding their wives or girlfriends messing about with
some man in essential work and putting one of the King's
issue bullets into each of them. The whole affair hushed up
and the soldier sent back to the Front.

I visited Jack and Ted's wives to deliver the final letters, wedding rings and other stuff, including the photographs taken in Rouen. I substituted my copy of the photograph for Ted's. Mine was crumpled and muddy but his was stained with blood. Both wives were working to make ends meet. Jack's wife was a tram conductor, Ted's was working as a dance teacher three afternoons a week and as a hostess in a dance hall in Gloucester Place for two evenings. Men paid fourpence a dance and she got a ticket for every dance they had. At the end of the session she got twopence for each ticket. She was a pretty woman and I regretted I wasn't much of a dancer.

I stayed in Brighton for my leave. Every day on the seafront I could hear the sound of the big guns across the Channel; distant booming in the bright blue air.

Brighton was the recuperation centre for men who had lost limbs during the war. Hundreds of men thronging the promenade without legs or arms, in wheelchairs and on crutches. Those who had lost all their limbs were carted around in big baskets. Basket-cases they were called.

On my last day of leave I was walking down near the West Pier by the bathing machines when the guns started up again. There was a gang of limbless men huddled together near the gents' toilet. One with no legs perched in a wheelchair; several with one leg and crutches. They were watching the young women come out of the machines with their buckets and spades. The girls screeched and giggled as they paddled into the cold water.

I threaded between the sailboats drawn up on the shingle between the huts.

'Someone's copping it,' I said to a man with no arms. He ran his eyes over my stained uniform and gave me a nod. He saw me looking at his empty sleeves.

'I had to go into no-man's-land to cut a bit of wire,' he said. 'So that our major could show it to his old woman. I knew the idea was she would be so proud of his bravery she would let him have a bit of grummer.'

'"Grummer"?' I said.

'That's what some Irishmen call the "blow through".' I still looked puzzled. 'Sex, man, sex.'

'Of course,' I said. 'Sorry.'

'I hope he's like me, and when she's on her back waiting for him to up her, he won't be able to get a hard-on.'

He spat next to his polished boot. I nodded to him and walked on, past barrows loaded with herring, twenty-four for a shilling. They stank but it was a better stink than I was used to.

I was thinking I wouldn't mind a bit of grummer myself, but wondered if I'd be able to manage.

I stepped aside for big, lumbering horses pulling carts piled with tradesmen's wares and a coal cart pulled by the biggest horse I'd ever seen. I was surprised these animals weren't at the Front.

On the King's Road there was a hubbub. Khaki-clad troops marched by, their uniforms spick and span. I heard someone say that the fresh-faced youth at the head of the march was Prince Edward. They were singing *Sussex by the Sea* and then *Tipperary*. I looked back at the group of limbless men and shrugged.

Someone screamed and I looked around, then up. There was a Zeppelin, cutting lazily across the sky. It was too high to see the crew leaning over to toss out the bombs, but I saw a dozen or so explosives drifting through the air before they plummeted sharply, growing larger as they fell to earth.

The explosions were loud. The sound bounced off the tall buildings. Ten minutes later I reviewed the damage. The Grand Hotel had taken a hit and a tram had come off its lines. A motor car swerved by it, throwing up dust on the dirt road.

The hit on the Grand would cause panic right enough. I'd been in there the day before for afternoon tea. It was stuffed with people who had left London for fear of air raids. Members of the royal families and the aristocracy of Britain and Europe rubbed shoulders with theatre and cinema stars, wives of bankers and industrialists, profiteers and more obvious London crooks like the Sabinis, who ran the rackets at the racecourse.

Most German Zeppelin attacks on the coast had been in the east, in Suffolk and Kent. German warships had shelled the east coast. In consequence, those people taking holidays flocked to Brighton rather than Broadstairs.

I thought about going out into the country, maybe down to

Black Rock. But I also had the address of a brothel. It had been given me by a man who died beside me at Le Couteau. He joined up in 1912 at Preston barracks, just outside Brighton. His father had taken him there when he turned sixteen. His father had kept the shilling his son was paid as a new recruit. He was with the Second Sussex. He told me he was a virgin but he'd been given this address and on his first Blighty leave he was going to see to that. He died an hour later without ever knowing a woman.

I looked across the road at the slums that came right down to the sea. I could find some girl in there who'd do it for a penny and a tot of gin but I was mindful of disease.

Ted's wife had asked me if I'd go to see a friend of the family, who was invalided up on the Ditchling Road in a school converted into a hospital. She said he was very low. A grenade blast had caught him, splintered his right arm, blinded him in his right eye; crippled him.

I went there now. It continued to be a hectic day. There were a lot of men in the hospital coughing up their lungs from the poisoned gas. More Zeppelins soughed over, bombs falling out of the sky. They were trying to hit the munitions factory in Hove. I came away not knowing which of us had tried harder to be cheerful.

FOUR

I didn't get a scratch in the Great War. Not even a Blighty wound for me. I knew a lot of men who prayed for that wound serious enough to earn them a ticket home without being life-threatening. Some men tried to inflict it on themselves. One man shot off his toes and then had to hobble unaided to the post where a firing squad was waiting to shoot him for cowardice.

As the war ground us ever more finely, I knew many men become so desperate to get out they would happily sacrifice a limb. Two limbs. Maybe some of the men I saw in Brighton did the same.

Men put their hands up above the trench parapets to have them shot by the Germans. Soaking a gunshot wound in a filthy pond would ensure a worse injury. Some faked abscesses by injecting paraffin or turpentine under the skin. One man drank petrol to make himself ill but he drank too much of it and died.

The authorities came down hard on malingerers. They got field punishment number one, morning and night for up to twenty-one days. It didn't hurt but it humiliated them. They were tied to a wheel by their wrists and ankles. From a distance, they looked like they'd been crucified.

I don't know many survivors of the Great War willing to talk about the horror of those four years. I'm not the man to describe it. I will say that I never saw a bayoneted baby. I will say that I never would have imagined the many ways in which Humpty Dumpty can be taken apart, with no hope of him ever being put back together again. I will say that we played football with the Hun in no-man's-land on Christmas Day, but on Boxing Day we were sticking German heads on poles all along the top of our trench.

Sigmund Freud might fruitfully have explored the effect of that close confinement in the stench and ooze of the trenches on the libido. It destroyed the urge for many. But just as the devastation wrought by pipe grenade and machine gun and howitzer shell blurred what it meant to be human, so the edges of sexuality dissolved for others.

A batman I knew called himself his colonel's slut. Married men openly comforted each other in the most physical way imaginable. Men with sweethearts at home loved other men. Less welcome – but unsurprising, given the darkness at the centre of all our beings – men raped other men.

You won't read about that kind of behaviour in the poems of Mr Sassoon or the memoir of Mr Graves.

At Mons, where the battle was ghastly beyond description, I saw acts of tenderness amid the horrors. I saw Ted's brains blown out, but further down the line I also saw two men going over the top hand in hand. In the calm after that phase of the battle I saw a Royal Sussex man I vaguely knew cradling his dying mate in his arms.

'I'll give you your mother's kiss, Bob,' I heard him murmur. 'And one for me.'

He kissed him twice on the brow.

I saw men cry all the time. But then there were no words to describe what we were experiencing. Later I realized that the only true account was the thing itself.

I was raised in pessimism and sorrow. After Jim, Jack and Ted all copped it I steered clear of pals. I decided I could not get too close. I know comradeship is one of the great themes of the Great War. At the time, the authorities pushed the idea of the Pals battalions – friends from before the war fighting side by side. But it was a lie.

What was the point of making pals who would be dead within the week? Once, we were playing marbles in our trench and someone straightened up and was shot through the head. At Mons, in those tremendous twenty-two hours, the deaths of my fellow men seemed a very small thing. Why, in the first thirty minutes I saw two thousand gallant men lay down their lives.

I learned not to stop to help wounded men and I was not alone in that.

The years passed. Every day I expected to be killed. Every winter I expected to freeze to death. I began the war in fear. Shuddering, corrosive fear. I was surprised at how long a man can live in fear. But then I decided I was going to die and I accepted it. Fear replaced neither by fatalism nor resignation but by certainty.

In that I was wrong. I lived. But at what price? I have not shed a tear for twenty years. I am unable to feel anything except self-loathing. My body is not my own. I came back from the Great War cut off from everything and everybody. I pretend, of course. I make a facsimile of living.

I survived the war: the Hun couldn't kill me. But the Spanish flu almost did. The pandemic. Millions died – more than in the Great War. I was laid low in a hospital in London for months. I recovered, although I didn't know until later that it had made me sterile.

I resumed a life. Of sorts.

FIVE

After the war I had an appetite for the ladies and the money to feed it. Then, in 1925, up at the racecourse, I met a young woman and her swaggering brother. The young woman took a shine to me, her brother less so. They were both cockneys but were Italian by descent. The brother worked for the Sabini family, who controlled the rackets on many racecourses.

The young woman worked in Liberty in London. I was footloose. I moved up to London. She held out for marriage. In a moment of foolishness – she was a beautiful woman and lust was about the only emotion I was capable of feeling – I married her.

We honeymooned in Siena, her family's city of origin. She hoped for children but it didn't happen. The Spanish flu. I joked it could be worse. I knew of people who had contracted sleeping sickness through the influenza and hadn't woken up yet. She didn't find me funny. She got depressed. Blamed me. Blamed herself. There were rows. She had a fiery temper.

Oswald Mosley founded his fascist party and I joined straight away. I wore the blackshirt uniform with pride. I was interested in a better Britain. My wife and I visited Italy when we could. Mussolini was doing great things. He was keeping the Socialists down. The trains ran on time.

Her brother was wary of my uniform but reluctantly accepted me when he discovered we had something in common. Hatred of kikes. The big Jew and the small Jew, as Sir Oswald described it. I hated them for bringing our country down. My brother-in-law hated them because the Italian gangs were at war with Jewish ones for control of Soho and the racecourses.

Her brother warmed to me further when I saved him from a beating at Brighton racecourse. He was openly a gangster now. I happened to be around when a man came at him with an open razor. Man? He was little more than a teenager but with an evil face – a long razor slash down one side of it. I knocked him to the ground without really thinking twice, but he had two older men nearby who I could tell knew how to handle themselves.

We squared off but then it all drizzled away.

My wife put on weight as only Italian women can. Screamed at me. I took mistresses. One in particular. She knew the Chinese method. It was whispered Wallis Simpson knew it too. If it made a king abdicate, what chance did I stand?

My brother-in-law saw us together one day. I was expecting a beating – knuckledusters and coshes.

'The racecourse thing?' he said. 'We're even.'

I killed my mistress for her infidelity. There was a knock on the door. I let my wife in. I didn't ask what she was doing there. I'd long suspected she was having me followed.

She stood by the radiogram looking at the body on the rug, the blood thickening around it. She pointed at the saw on the table.

'What were you intending to do with that?'

'What do you suppose?'

She looked at me for a long moment. Looked at the apron covered in bright red flowers.

'And then?'

I raised my shoulders slowly. Let them fall.

'I hadn't thought that far.'

She nodded.

'Do you have any knives? Kitchen knives?'

'A set,' I said.

'Good. But we also have to do some shopping.'

'What are we buying?'

'We're buying a trunk.'

My wife and I were standing looking down on the open trunk and the body beside it, the knives and the saw on the table, when the apartment door opened. Her big and burly brother entered.

'I asked him to help,' she said.

He was carrying a parcel of brown paper wrapped in twine and a large can of olive oil, presumably from one of the Sabini brothers' restaurants.

'Let's get to it,' he said, scarcely glancing at the body.

Later, on the drive down to Brighton, I asked him: 'What's the plan?'

He smirked.

'You're mine now.'

We were trying to get the trunk out of the car, parked on the cliff edge across the road from the racetrack, when I spotted a middle-aged couple watching us suspiciously.

'Change of plan,' he said, pushing the trunk back into the boot and slamming it closed.

When I got home, late in the evening, my wife was waiting in the kitchen with an open bottle of Chianti. She handed me a glass.

'Welcome home,' she said.

I drank the wine. It tasted coppery.

'Keep the apartment on for another six months,' she said. 'I'll take the legs and feet in a suitcase to King's Cross luggage office tomorrow. When it's discovered, the police will think it's the White family's handiwork.'

The White family ruled Islington and King's Cross, though it also had a piece of Soho.

'Then our life can resume.'

I put my glass back on the table. I had to ask.

'What did your brother do with the head?'

SIX

When the trunk was found at Brighton left luggage office, the press dubbed it 'The Brighton Trunk Murder'. A few weeks later there was a second so-called Trunk Murder. That had nothing to do with me.

By then there had been a knock on my own door. A routine

enquiry from a bored local policeman. The people near the racecourse had noted the registration of my car. I expected this. My brother-in-law had tutored me.

I told the bobby my car had been out of my possession at the time. Stolen. The policeman was satisfied with my answer. He did not even ask to see the vehicle.

It was the last I heard from any policeman. The torso was never identified. The murder was never solved.

For the next three years I devoted my life to my work but my wife and her brother ruled me. Then my wife and I went on holiday to Italy. We visited her family in Siena. We never went back to England. My wife never went anywhere again.

A terrible accident, I told the *polizia*. Horrible, I said. I had actually photographed it, I said.

We had gone to Spoleto, set among high, wooded hills, for me to see the magnificent fresco cycle by Fra Filippo Lippi in the cathedral. Such things did not interest my wife so her mood was not of the best, especially after an uncomfortable drive. After a late meal in our hotel dining room, we had slept in separate beds, though in the same room.

The next morning, I suggested we ignore the extensive Roman ruins in favour of the medieval aqueduct. She was interested in neither but reluctantly agreed to my plan.

We went to the east of the town and up a steep cobbled street. It was a hot morning and we moved slowly through promenading family groups.

We walked through a crumbling Roman arch and followed a path round the town's curtain wall. The ground fell steeply away into a deep wooded ravine. It was spanned by the Ponte delle Torri, the half-mile-long bridge and aqueduct.

My wife peered down at the silvery thread of water in the very bottom of the ravine among a dense growth of ilex. I knew it to be a 300-foot drop.

'Quite a feat of engineering,' I said, squinting down the length of the bridge to a tower among the trees at the far end. I looked at the dozen thick pediments that held up the bridge and down at their foundations so far below.

'Fourteenth century but built on Roman foundations,' I said, though I knew my wife wasn't interested. Her feet hurt from walking on the cobbles in her high-heeled shoes. I pulled my camera out of my bag. 'I want to get a picture from the other side.'

'I want to go back into town,' my wife said. 'It's not like you to be so interested in taking snaps.'

I gestured at the bridge.

'It's spectacular. Look – there's a walkway along the side. You want to come with me?'

'I'll wait here.'

'Come on – I need you in the picture for scale.'

The bridge was essentially to carry a water pipe, which was cased in a ten-foot-high wall of brick. The walkway to the left of this casing was about four feet wide. As protection for people on the walkway, there was a low wall topped by a rail. The wooded ravine was an almost perfect V.

We had scarcely gone more than hundred yards when my wife, glancing down at the trees and the river so far below, lurched.

'Vertigo?' I said with concern.

'I'm not going any further,' she said. 'This wall is too low.'

'"Have ye courage, O my brethren? He hath heart who knows fear but vanquishes it, who sees the abyss but with pride."'

My wife looked at me as if I was mad.

'Nietzsche,' I said. She snorted.

A couple of giggly teenage girls were approaching from the other side. I moved back against the iron rail and my wife flattened herself against the aqueduct wall to allow them to go by.

The walkway was now deserted beyond us. My wife began to perspire, craning her neck to look down again. It was a dizzying drop. I liked the feeling of walking in space. I took a couple of snaps.

'Can we go back now?' my wife said sharply.

'I'd like a picture from the other side. Wait – I'll be back soon.'

'Wait for you?'

But I was already striding off.

'Come back!'

I waved.

'Five minutes.'

I disappeared behind the tower at the far end of the bridge. As I did so, two men in dark suits stepped on to the walkway and set off briskly towards the centre of the bridge. I followed a rough trail up through the trees. I could still glimpse the aqueduct with the town above it.

I saw my wife start to totter off the walkway. I found a spiral staircase pretty much intact in the tower. I went up two steps at a time and came out on to a magnificent view. From this height I could see the snow-streaked mountains rising behind the sprawl of Spoleto.

My wife had stopped on the bridge, facing the two men in dark suits whose laughter I could hear from the tower. She was standing a little stiffly, looking everywhere but down into the ravine. I took her picture.

I trained my camera on her as the two men purposefully approached.

My wife stepped back to let the two men go by. They didn't go by. I had paid them well. They lifted my wife into the air and out over the parapet. There was nothing but air between her and the silver thread of water. The men dangled her over the parapet, her skirt falling down over her head. They let her go.

I took her snap. Arms flailing, she fell to the river so far below.

I telephoned her brother.

'You're a dead man,' he said.

'I'm staying in Italy for a while.'

'That won't save you.'

'You know that Mussolini hates the Mafia? Most of the Mafiosi here are either dead, in prison or in hiding. I don't recommend you do anything rash.'

'I can wait,' he said.

'You're going to have to.'

I gazed at the wall in front of me. It was as blank as my heart.

We give ourselves airs. Significance. Every life is sacred.

No, it isn't. After the Great War only an imbecile would believe that.

Life is nothing. We are animals, and animals die. When the spark dies, you become a thing. What are we, after all? Bone and gristle. Meat and muscle. Is a knee joint sacred? Has a shoulder blade a soul?

Life is not sacred, although it is perhaps a gift. You have it and it is snatched away as I snatched away the lives of my mistress and my wife.

As mine will one day be snatched away.

PART TWO
Charlie Laker

SEVEN

Today

Detective Sergeant Sarah Gilchrist was reading the *Guardian* with increasing irritation when her phone rang. She ignored it, focusing instead on the offending article, from the newspaper's crime correspondent. The headline read: 'No Action To Be Taken Against Police Officers Involved In Milldean Massacre.'

The article went on:

> The Police Complaints Authority today announced that no action is to be taken against any officers from the Southern Police Authority in connection with the so-called 'Milldean Massacre' in which four people were shot and killed in a police raid on a house on the Milldean estate, Brighton, last year.
>
> A spokesperson said that whilst a report from the Hampshire police, who had investigated the incident, was 'highly critical' of the system that was in place for armed response operations in the Southern Police Authority, it had been unable to conclude exactly what had occurred during the operation and thus was unable to assign blame.
>
> The spokesperson added that the Hampshire police regarded this as 'highly unsatisfactory' but felt unable to say whether the officers involved were being deliberately obstructive or were just responding to the chaos of such an operation. An additional problem was that only one of the dead people had been identified: Stephen Strong, known as Little Stevie, a male prostitute.
>
> Since the massacre two of the officers involved have died in suspicious circumstances, one has committed suicide and three have retired due to ill health. Only

one – Detective Sergeant Sarah Gilchrist – continues as
a serving police officer, though she will never again be
part of an armed unit.

The only scalp taken as a consequence of the Milldean
Massacre was that of high-flying Chief Constable Robert
Watts. The morning after the killings he defended his
officers in terms that were felt to prejudice the official
investigation beginning that day.

Watts – a much-decorated former army officer and the
youngest chief constable in the country – had been generally regarded as a poster boy for modern policing. Married
with two children, he refused to resign for his error of
judgement but did so when newspapers published
accounts of his affair with Detective Sergeant Sarah
Gilchrist.

Whilst there was no suggestion that he was protecting
DS Gilchrist, who has been fully exculpated by the
inquiry, the revelation of the affair and her proximity to
the massacre was regarded as significant.

The violent robber Bernie Grimes, the man the armed
police were attempting to detain, remains at large. Indeed,
it is speculated that he was never in the house that was
raided. The Police Complaints Authority, Hampshire
Police and Southern Police have all declined to answer
accusations that the armed raid was actually on the wrong
house.

Commenting on the fact that the report will remain
confidential, Southern Police's Chief Constable Hewitt
said: 'There is nothing to be gained by publishing the
report. The killings were a tragedy but we must put the
past behind us. We now have systems in place to ensure
that such a terrible error does not occur again.'

Sarah Gilchrist dropped the newspaper on the low table beside
her. Bastards. She hated that nothing had been resolved, that
she was no nearer knowing exactly what had happened.
Especially given all that it had sparked: the arrival of Balkan
gangsters, grotesque medieval deaths, a bloodbath in the Grand
Hotel and another in a village outside Dieppe. John Hathaway,

Brighton's crime king for the past four decades, left to die, stuck on the end of a pole on a cliff-top.

She shuddered at the thought of her own close encounter with the psychopathic Bosnian torturer Miladin Radislav, also known as Vlad the Impaler. He'd come for her as part of his vengeful rampage through Brighton. She vividly recalled his grey face and his cold eyes as he bore down on her on the beach whilst she was embroiled with a gang of feral girls. The irony was that his arrival had saved her from them.

She swallowed bile and lowered her feet from the wrought iron framing the balcony and looked down on the pretty garden below her. She had liked it here at first in Clarence Square. It was central – the shops were just up the road, the sea just down it – and it had been a little oasis of sunny quiet. In the daytime at least.

The small hotels on either side of her did get noisy on summer nights. Especially when those dirty weekenders who had balconies and had their French windows open moaned, groaned and bellowed into the square through the night.

But now it was an oasis no longer. Noisy lovers were the least of it. She felt exposed, vulnerable. The journalists had been bad enough. As the time had approached for the Police Complaints Authority to make its announcement, she had avoided the balcony because of the journalists harassing her. Some threw notes up. Others shouted her name repeatedly from the street below.

Only a few days earlier one had taken a room in the hotel next door and climbed on to her balcony to photograph her. She'd freaked out when she'd heard him tapping on the window. When the photo appeared in several newspapers the next morning, she thought of complaining to the Press Complaints Commission. Then she discovered the chair of the PCC was the editor of one of the papers that had splashed her all over its front page.

But her fear now was that if a journalist could get easily get close, so could Miladin Radislav.

She was standing near her balcony when the phone started again. It was DI Reg Williamson, her sometime partner, recently promoted to be her acting boss. The promotion was

hers by rights, but she'd had no rights after Milldean.
Williamson was conscious of that and never pulled rank on
her, treating her as a partner in exactly the same way as before.
Indeed, usually deferring to her.

'Reg,' she said. 'Why is it I know you're not calling for
anything good?'

'Experience?'

'That would do it.'

'Actually, it's not so bad. Wanted you to check on that girl
you rescued on the beach. She should be about ready to give
a statement about those girls who attacked her.'

EIGHT

At the hospital Sarah Gilchrist went to the private room
occupied by the girl she'd rescued from a stoning on
the beach. She'd seen a group of teenage girls attacking
her at the water's edge, photographing their assault. When
Gilchrist got to her, she found her bloodied, bruised and unconscious, water swirling round her.

The girl was the only child of a single mother who lived
on the Milldean estate. Her name was Sarah Jessica Cassidy
and she was thirteen. She'd been in intensive care for days,
her distraught mother hovering, but now had been moved into
this private room. She had no memory of the incident and,
miraculously, no permanent physical scarring or damage. She
was, however, black and blue all over, with three broken ribs,
her left arm in a cast and all the fingers on her right hand
taped up.

Gilchrist visited her in her civvies – jeans, white T-shirt and
leather jacket. She asked the WPC keeping guard on the door
to step inside to witness their conversation.

'How are you?' Gilchrist said.

'You a copper?'

Gilchrist smiled.

'Is it that obvious?'

Cassidy's head had been shaved to get at half a dozen or so cuts and gashes on her scalp. Underneath the bruising she was a pretty girl but she had a sullen mouth.

'When you know what you're looking for.' Cassidy gestured at the WPC. 'Plus, she's a bit of a giveaway.'

'I suppose she is,' Gilchrist said.

Cassidy examined Gilchrist's face.

'You the one who found me?'

Gilchrist nodded.

'They said it was a hefty woman.'

'Hefty?' Gilchrist said, glancing at the WPC, who was pretending not to hear.

The girl smirked.

'Have you caught them?'

'We've been waiting to talk to you. What do you remember?'

'Nuffink.'

Gilchrist nodded.

'OK. What's the last thing you remember?'

'You walking in and sitting down.'

'I mean before you were on the beach.'

The girl looked at the ceiling for a minute.

'Having a McDonald's.'

'What time was that?'

'Don't know.'

'Were you alone?'

'Don't know.'

Gilchrist sighed.

'Who are your best friends at school?'

'Don't have any.'

'A loner, are you?'

'Suppose I must be.'

'Are you popular?'

Cassidy gestured at herself with her taped fingers.

'Doesn't seem like it, does it?'

'Do you have particular enemies?'

'No.'

Gilchrist glanced again at the WPC who was staring blankly at the opposite wall.

'Do you have a boyfriend?'

Cassidy twisted her mouth into a sneer.

'Did. You lot put him away.'

'In a youth detention centre?'

Cassidy shook her head. A look that might have been pride came on to her face.

'In prison.'

Gilchrist sat back.

'He's in prison? How old is he?'

A smug expression crossed the young girl's face.

'Twenty-two.'

'And you are?'

'Coming up to fourteen.'

Gilchrist pursed her lips.

'What's he in for?'

Cassidy's expression changed to something less certain. Something confused.

'Killing his best friend.' Gilchrist stared at her. 'Then chopping him up.'

Gilchrist started.

'Your boyfriend is Gary Parker?'

The look of pride came back on to Cassidy's face.

'You've heard of him?'

Some months earlier Gilchrist had taken a call from a man saying that his friend, this Gary Parker, had phoned from Hove to brag he'd just killed his flatmate and dismembered him. Gilchrist had gone to the scene and found the remains of a dead man with various body parts strewn around the flat. An arm had been discovered in a children's paddling pool on the seafront and Parker had been found sitting under the Palace Pier, cradling his friend's head in his lap.

Gilchrist found it hard to keep the revulsion off her face as she looked at this young girl bragging that the creature Gilchrist had unfortunately encountered professionally was her boyfriend. She needed to get out. She stood.

'OK, well, that will do for now. If anything comes back to you before we visit again, just give us a call.'

Gilchrist turned for the door.

'Have you heard of him?' Cassidy said.

Gilchrist nodded without looking round.

'I've heard of him.'

As Gilchrist reached the door, Cassidy called: 'Don't worry about whoever did this. My dad'll sort 'em.'

Gilchrist turned.

'Who's your dad?'

Cassidy had the smirk on her face again.

'They'll wish they'd never been born.'

'So you do know who they are?'

'I told you I didn't.'

'Then how is your father going to sort them if you don't know who they are?'

Cassidy gave a little shrug.

'Does your father live in Milldean?'

Cassidy shook her head.

'Sarah Jessica, who is your father?'

'Who said you could use my first name?'

'Names, actually, Miss Cassidy, names. And, incidentally, if I hadn't come along when I did, you would quite probably be dead now.'

As she stalked down the corridor, Gilchrist regretted saying that. Her mind was reeling with the thought of this girl with Gary Parker. She was curious about the identity of Cassidy's father. But most of all, as she glanced at her reflection in the windows she passed, she was thinking of one thing.

'*Hefty?*' she muttered.

On the way out of the hospital Gilchrist bumped into a hard-faced blonde who'd clearly had a boob job and wanted everyone to know it, judging by the amount of cleavage on display.

'Mrs Cassidy,' Gilchrist said. 'Could I have a quick word?'

'I've already told you I don't know nothing,' Cassidy said, in a cigarette-wrecked voice.

Gilchrist ushered her over to a bench. When they were seated, Gilchrist said: 'It's about her boyfriend.'

Cassidy fished out a cigarette from her coat pocket.

'My daughter is very independent for her age.'

'You didn't mind her going out with a twenty-two-year-old man?'

'She goes her own way.'

'You didn't mind she was probably having sex with a twenty-two-year-old man?'

'Look, dear, I don't know about you but I lost mine when I was twelve. To my dad. He'd been poking about before then but he'd always said he'd wait until I was a woman – you know, until I'd started my periods – before he gave me a proper seeing to. And I know you're not supposed to say this these days about whatchamacallit – incest? – but he was quite good at it. I'd much rather a twenty-two-year-old who knows a bit than a pimply thirteen-year-old who can't find the right hole to stick it in.'

'Even if he murders and cuts up his flatmate?'

Cassidy adjusted her left breast unselfconsciously, lifting then releasing it.

'Yeah, well, that came after.'

'But he's clearly a psycho.'

Cassidy thrust her face at Gilchrist.

'Look, dear, I don't know what la-di-da men you knock about with but we live on Milldean. Different world, different rules. All I've ever known is violent men. He was a bit rough round the edges but until he did what he did he seemed normal.'

Gilchrist slid back along the bench a few inches.

'So you accept that what he did wasn't normal?'

'Course I bloody do – I'm not touched, you know.'

Gilchrist cleared her throat.

'Who is Sarah Jessica's father?'

Cassidy narrowed her eyes.

'None of your fucking business; excuse my French.'

'Sarah Jessica said he'd sort out her attackers.'

'He probably will.'

'So you know who they are?'

'I've already said I don't.'

'But Sarah Jessica does?'

'She says not.'

'How long were you married? Were you married?'

Cassidy waggled her right hand. On her second finger she had an engagement ring and a gem-clustered wedding band.

'Some detective you are.'

'When did you last see him?'

'My Sarah Jessica's expecting me.' She stood. 'If you'll excuse me.'

NINE

t didn't take Sarah Gilchrist long to find the name of Donna Cassidy's husband through her marriage certificate and Sarah Jessica's birth certificate. She blinked at her computer screen.

'Listen to this, Reg,' she called across the office to DI Williamson, standing by the open window with a mug of coffee in his hand. He was peering intently down at something on the street outside, but she was pretty sure he was really standing there because he'd had a curry the previous night and they'd both been suffering the consequences. 'Donna Cassidy's husband is one Bernard Edward Grimes of Lewisham. Stated occupation "handyman".'

Williamson turned to look at Gilchrist and raised an eyebrow.

'Actual occupation "scumbag". Last heard of in Milldean en route to the south of France.'

He walked over to peer at Gilchrist's screen.

'How the bloody hell did everyone miss that?'

The Milldean armed intervention that had gone so disastrously wrong the previous year had been designed to apprehend Bernie Grimes, dangerous armed robber. He was believed to be staying in a house in Milldean prior to taking the ferry to Dieppe en route to his hideout in the south of France.

He was not in the house they'd stormed. Other people were. These people had been shot and killed, though by exactly which of Gilchrist's colleagues it was still not clear. There was no trace of Bernie Grimes in the house or any indication that he had ever been there.

'The bastard wouldn't need to stay in that house given his ex-wife and kid were living down the road. You and your guys were truly shafted.'

'What's her address – maybe it's similar to that of the house we raided?'

Gilchrist tapped some keys, shook her head.

'Nope. Donna Cassidy's address and that of the house we raided are nothing like each other.'

'How the bloody hell did everyone miss that?' Williamson repeated. 'I mean that's major information.'

Gilchrist phoned the Met Police and after being passed around eventually reached a serious crime unit that had a particular interest in Grimes. She spoke to a detective sergeant for ten minutes, Williamson back at the window.

When she put the phone down, she walked over to join him.

'They don't have any information about Grimes having a wife and child – and certainly not one living in Milldean,' she said.

Williamson gave her a long look.

'They've got a rat in their unit, deleting stuff.'

'That's what the detective sergeant was realizing.'

'So they'll be heading down here.' He reached for his jacket. 'We'd better get to her first.'

Donna Cassidy was not pleased to see Gilchrist and Reg Williamson on her doorstep in Milldean.

'I'm just going out,' she said, her voice even throatier than Gilchrist remembered from the hospital.

'We can do this down at the station if you want, love,' Williamson said.

'Who the fuck are you calling "love", fatso? And stop staring at my tits.'

Gilchrist knew that Williamson was always imperturbable when faced with insults, especially about his paunch.

'I'll take that as an invite to enter the premises, shall I?' he said, stepping forward.

Cassidy gave him a hard stare, then barked a laugh.

'I'm not making you a bloody drink, though,' she said, moving back into her entrance hall. They squeezed by a table piled with opened and unopened mail, past the open sliding door of a toilet under the stairs and into a large square living room.

'You'll know why we're here,' Gilchrist said as Cassidy walked over to a pink sofa and plonked down.

'You've found the little monsters who tried to kill my daughter?'

'We've found out who you're married to,' Williamson said, from the middle of the room.

'I knew I'd said too much at the hospital,' Cassidy said, glancing down at her breasts pushing out of her blouse.

'We're not interested in catching him,' Gilchrist said. 'Though there'll be others coming from London to question you, I've no doubt, who will have other ideas. We just need to know when he was last in Milldean.'

Cassidy turned to look at her and almost snarled: 'And you think I'll tell you that?'

'OK, not that,' Gilchrist said. 'Look, we're not out to get him or you. But you know that Milldean thing last year?'

'When you lot shot a house full of innocent people?'

'We were there to arrest Mr Grimes.'

'Shoot him more like, if what actually happened is anything to go by.'

'Definitely not,' Gilchrist said. 'I was there. I was downstairs when it happened. I want to find out why and how it happened.'

'And you want me to help how exactly?'

Gilchrist stepped closer.

'We heard your ex-husband was staying in Milldean in that house en route to the south of France. Was he? Or was he staying with you? Or was he not in Milldean at all?'

'Why should I tell you something like that?'

'Because you owe DS Gilchrist the life of your child,' Williamson said. 'As does Bernie.'

Cassidy looked at him.

'How do you reckon that, fatso? She just found her and called for help.'

'It were a bit more than that—'

'Reg—' Gilchrist said.

'Those girls were still attacking your daughter when DS Gilchrist, off duty, passed by. She saw off ten of them on her own, out of uniform. If she hadn't, your Sarah Jessica would be dead.'

Cassidy looked at Gilchrist.

'That true?'

'Something along those lines,' Gilchrist said. Thinking: if you miss out the bit where the three Balkan gangsters turned up and scared the bejesus out of the kids, then tried to kidnap me.

Cassidy looked off to one side for a long moment.

'And you're not going to try to hang something on Bernie?'

'It's other people we're after,' Williamson said, unconsciously stroking his paunch. Cassidy watched his circling hand.

'He was in Milldean and he was with us, and the next day he did go off to France,' she said. 'He never went anywhere near that house.'

'Did he know about it?' Gilchrist said.

Cassidy gave her a sharp look.

'That sounds like the start of a new line of questioning.'

'Or a way of clearing him of all suspicion of complicity in what happened,' Williamson said.

'You'd have to speak to him about that,' she said, with an odd twitch of the lips.

'Love to,' Williamson said. 'Can you give us his number? Or, better still, his address? I'm fond of the south of France.'

'I think it's time you went,' Cassidy said. 'I think you've already got more than you deserve.'

'Was that a loo down the hall?' Williamson said. 'Do you mind if I use the necessities?'

'On your way out,' Cassidy said.

'Well, DS Gilchrist has just one final question for you,' Williamson said, striding off down the corridor.

Gilchrist, startled, smiled uneasily at Cassidy.

'Er, I just wondered when Sarah Jessica was coming home from hospital?'

Cassidy gave her a calculating look.

'End of the week, they think.'

'Remembered anything more?' Gilchrist said.

Cassidy shook her head, looking beyond Gilchrist as

Williamson emerged from the downstairs loo, his jacket over his arm.

Gilchrist followed her look.

'Right then,' she said. 'We'll be off.'

Cassidy followed her down the corridor. Williamson was on the doorstep.

Gilchrist joined him and turned back to Cassidy.

'By the way, I found your marriage certificate and I found your daughter's birth certificate. But I couldn't find your divorce registered anywhere.'

Cassidy looked from one to the other of them, smiled slowly then closed the door.

TEN

'Y ou're looking pleased with yourself,' Gilchrist said, glancing across at Williamson as they drove back into Brighton from Donna Cassidy's house in Milldean.

'Fancy getting a quick half somewhere?' Williamson said.

They parked in the small courtyard of a thatched pub opposite the youth hostel at Stanmer Park.

'OK – what have you been up to?' Gilchrist said as they sat down with their drinks – pints not halves. 'You're looking insufferably smug.'

He tapped his glass against hers.

'Did you see that pile of mail? On the table by the front door? There was a phone bill.'

'Jesus, Reg – you didn't? They could hang you up by your balls for stealing that.' Gilchrist stuck her hand out. 'Let's see it, then.'

Williamson shook his head.

'I didn't take it; I just borrowed it for a couple of minutes. It was already opened.'

'And?'

'I got a mobile number she phoned a lot lately and a foreign landline number that I hope is in France.'

'Did you memorize them?'

Williamson looked at her over the rim of his beer glass.

'I scribbled them down.'

'Jesus, Reg. With your handwriting we're fucked.'

Williamson took a crumpled piece of paper from the top pocket of his jacket. He tossed it on to the table.

Gilchrist spread it between them.

'Did you use a spider instead of a pen?'

'Give me a break. I was in the loo scribbling it down as fast as I could.'

'What's that – a two or a five?'

'Pass.'

'And that?'

'Look, we can try options, Sarah. Don't be a pain in the arse.'

Gilchrist patted his hand.

'Only kidding, Reg. This is great – but what the hell can we do with it?'

'What do you mean?' Williamson said.

'Well, if we pass it on to the Met, we've got to explain how we got the numbers. Same if we try to do anything with them.'

'Bugger that,' he said. 'We track the locations down and worry about the legalities later.'

'You want us to go down there? How? How can we justify it? Plus, he's a very dangerous man.'

'What about Bob Watts and his mate, Jimmy Tingley?'

'You're suggesting we use vigilantes?'

Williamson looked at her again over his glass.

'Let's see what the numbers show us, then decide.'

Sarah Gilchrist bumped into Philippa Franks coming out of a café in the North Laines. Franks had been a member of the armed response unit that had killed the apparently innocent citizens in Milldean.

'How's retirement suit you, Philippa?'

Franks, along with several others, had taken early retirement on the grounds of ill health to avoid any possibility of criminal proceedings. Gilchrist was sure Franks knew much more than she was letting on.

Franks shuffled a little.

'I'm retraining to be a social worker,' she said.

'You'll be good at that,' Gilchrist said.

'Terrible what's going on at the moment.' Franks gave a little shudder. 'That man impaled on a stake on the Downs as a warning. John Hathaway over in France. They're saying he was done the same way.'

She looked intently at Gilchrist. Gilchrist nodded.

'He never had much chance, Hathaway,' Franks said. 'Having the father he had.'

'You knew his father?'

'I know I'm not looking great but do I look that old?' Franks smile was tired. 'My father knew them both. He used to run a pub that Dennis Hathaway "protected". Then John took over the collecting when he was still a teenager. He was in a band. Charlie Laker was the drummer. Dad said it was God-awful but they got all these bookings in Brighton because everybody was frightened of his father.'

'The men who killed Hathaway thought he had something to do with the Milldean thing. It was in revenge for that couple in the bed. You remember, Philippa – the two people that were shot to death by policemen in your presence.'

Franks looked down at her feet.

'I don't know anything about that.'

She kept looking down, but Gilchrist stared at the top of her head until she looked up.

'I think you do. Don't you think it's time you told?'

Franks started to walk past her.

'Not as long as I've got my kids to protect, Sarah.'

Gilchrist watched her go. When Franks was about ten yards down the street, she called after her: 'We've located Bernie Grimes.'

Franks seemed to falter for a moment then carried on. Without looking round, she raised her hand in a little wave.

ELEVEN

Charlie Laker was having an early fish supper in a restaurant on Whitby harbour front when his phone chirruped. It was a new phone and he hadn't got round to changing the ringtone – he'd had a busy few weeks – but he winced every time it rang because it sounded like a bird choking.

'Yeah?' he said, his mouth full of Dover sole.

'Bernie Grimes, Charlie.'

'Bernie – how's the south of France?'

'Sweltering. Charlie, I need a favour.'

'Well, I owe you one for your help with that Milldean thing.'

Laker reached for his glass of wine. Muscadet. The best the restaurant had to offer. It was OK, actually.

'My wife tells me some gels have been picking on my daughter.'

'Didn't know you had a daughter. Or a wife, for that matter.'

'The missus and me aren't living together any longer. You know how it is. You can't live with 'em and you can't kill 'em.'

Laker gave a quick snigger to show willing.

'And she brought up your daughter?'

'Sarah Jessica. Lovely girl. Goes off the rails sometimes but a good kid.'

'And these girls been picking on her?'

'They overstepped the mark. Big time.'

'And you want my people to have a word.'

'More than that. They almost killed her. Stoned her on the beach.'

Laker reached for the bottle and poured a big glug into his glass.

'Jesus, Bernie, I'm sorry to hear that.'

'You have contacts moving girls, don't you?'

Laker frowned.

'Yeah, but they're coming in, Bernie. These girls are already here, aren't they?'

'I want them working in some hovel of a brothel in some cesspit of a port town in some cancer of a country for the rest of their hopefully short lives.'

'You do want revenge, don't you? How old are they?'

'Twelve, thirteen, fourteen. Some of them won't have been plucked yet.'

'This is a pretty big favour you're asking, Bernie. Massive, in fact.'

'I know that. I'll owe you.'

'How many girls you talking about?'

'Ten.'

Laker got a coughing fit as his Muscadet went down the wrong hole.

'Ten?' he spluttered. 'Are you mad? We can't lift ten.'

'Sure you can. It's Milldean. I hear it's chaos down there at the moment with that hoodlum Stevie Cuthbert missing, presumed dead. I don't know if that was down to you or John Hathaway, but with the crime boss of Milldean out of the way after all these years, who's going to stop you?'

'But ten all at once, Bernie. One missing kid is bad enough but a third of a class – that'll definitely be noticed when they take the register.'

'So what? They'll be gone by then. Disappeared. I was thinking Africa – the Congo or somewhere?'

'Lot of HIV down there, Bernie. Place is rife with it.'

There was silence on the end of the phone for a moment.

'All the better,' Bernie Grimes said.

'Well –' Laker said, distracted by the sweet trolley going by. He fancied the look of the Black Forest Gateau – 'they're always complaining class sizes are too big.'

Next morning, Laker sat on the bench below the statue of Captain Cook and looked across to the ruined abbey on the opposite headland. He could picture the plague ship coming into the harbour below, the navigator strapped to the wheel, all the crew dead and drained of blood. Dracula lying in the dank hold of the ship, in his coffin of Transylvanian earth.

Laker's car idled behind him. A handful of his men were spread across this headland keeping an eye on the people climbing up from the harbour and passing beneath the arch of the whale jaw cemented into the ground at the top of the incline.

Charlie Laker looked out to sea, squinting behind his sunglasses against the glare of the sun on the water. He disliked the sea but only because he wasn't good on it. He'd never had sea legs.

The irony was he'd run pirate radio stations off ships for Brighton gang boss Dennis Hathaway back in the sixties. But in the three years he'd done it he'd never once set foot on the rusting hulks they were using.

Laker had never wanted to be a gangster when he was growing up. He wanted to be a pop star. But then his little brother, Roy, died and everything changed.

He thought about Roy almost every day. Charlie Laker had never forgiven himself for his brother's death. He knew Roy hero-worshipped his Teddy-boy older brother. That's why he'd allowed Roy to come with their friend, Kevin, up to the bonfire that fateful November day in 1959.

'Let me get in the den, Charlie. I can be the guard.'

The den was in the middle of the bonfire. Charlie tousled his brother's hair.

'OK – but keep close watch.'

It was fucking freezing in the wind. It took Charlie and Kevin a good five minutes to light their fags.

'Fancy a cup of tea?' Kevin said. Charlie looked at his brother, who was grinning to himself as he explored the narrow space inside the rough pile of wood.

'Back in five,' Charlie called as he and Kevin hurried down the street to the café on the corner.

They stayed ten, maybe fifteen minutes. It wouldn't have been that long if Kevin hadn't fancied the girl behind the counter. She wasn't even that good-looking.

'We've got to get back to Roy,' Charlie said.

Reluctantly, Kevin followed him out. They saw the bonfire burning at the top of the street.

'Fuck.'

Charlie set off at a run.

Telling his parents was the worst thing ever. His father was too upset even to give him a hiding. His mum had been the one to offer violence, smacking him across the face and punching at his chest, screeching, until his father pulled her off.

Roy had always been her favourite – because he was the youngest, of course – and she never forgave Charlie for not looking out for him.

When Charlie saw *On The Waterfront* on the telly, he broke out into a sweat when Brando was in the back seat of the taxi with Rod Steiger, who played his older brother, Charlie.

'You should have watched out for me, Charlie. Just a little bit.'

It was like hearing his grown-up brother's voice.

His mother scarcely said two words a year to him for the next ten years. And his father didn't even have the energy to beat him up again.

He went to work for his dad at his garage out of guilt. Sometimes he'd catch his dad staring at him, a perplexed look on his face.

His parents seemed to take it for granted the police investigation got nowhere. The life had been sucked out of them. In the evenings they'd sit in front of the telly, side by side on the sofa, morose and blank. Both chain-smoking. Both dead of lung cancer before they were sixty.

Now, a tap on his shoulder. A voice in his ear.

'Boss? A call for you. From Italy.'

TWELVE

'Charlie. It's Crespo di Bocci.'

'Greetings from windswept Whitby, Crespo.'

'There's an Englishman coming here. Signor Jimmy Tingley. He is looking for Drago Kadire. Some of my family have a grudge against him, as you know. But I also know you are connected to Drago. What shall I do?'

Laker thought for a moment. When he'd made his play to take Brighton away from his former friend, John Hathaway, he had known the risk he was taking bringing in the Balkan gangs. Especially Drago Kadire, the Albanian sniper, and Miladin Radislav, who rejoiced in his nickname of Vlad the Impaler.

Laker had taken control of the Palace Pier through cut-outs but the local guys weren't really up to the job of toppling Hathaway. That required people without conscience. Subhumans. That required Miladin Radislav.

But the danger had been: if he got them in, could he get them out? Not without pissing off his friends in the Italian mafia – quite aside from other Balkan guys running rackets in England.

Laker knew about Tingley. Ex-SAS. Handy. Tingley might offer a way out. Unconnected. Doing his 'Man With No Name' routine. Charlie idly wondered whether that ex-cop, Bob Watts, was with the old soldier. He knew they were friends. Laker didn't think Watts was up to the job. Wasn't certain Tingley was, either.

Kadire and Radislav. Get rid of them and the Balkan invasion would stall long enough for Charlie to sell up and get back to America. Once he'd done that, he didn't give a toss what happened to Brighton. Oh, he had UK plans but they were bigger. Legit. Well, almost.

'Let them fight it out,' he said.

Laker had made Whitby his temporary HQ for sentimental reasons. When he was a kid, before he became a Teddy boy, he'd been in the boy scouts and they'd come north from Sussex on a camping trip to Whitby, Scarborough and Robin Hood's Bay. In those days, the mid-fifties, their scoutmaster had managed to arrange for them to camp inside the ruined abbey. It was scary and it pissed down, and nobody slept very much, but they all loved it.

Now he was waiting in his suite for a couple of girls to arrive from Harrogate, the nearest place to Whitby you could buy quality arse. Not that he would be paying.

He was thinking about his late wife, Dawn. John Hathaway's

sister. He'd got her pregnant, some forty years earlier. Her father, Dennis Hathaway, had given him a choice. They'd been in the chilly wooden hut Hathaway used as his HQ behind the firing range on the West Pier in Brighton.

Dennis Hathaway. Jesus. Burly, friendly-faced and vicious as fuck.

That day Hathaway had handed Laker a whisky – Canadian Club, naturally – and said: 'Here's the choice, Charlie. You can go against my wishes and marry Dawn and have the kid. But you're out of the business. I don't want my Dawn involved in this.'

'Or?' Laker said, feeling the whisky burn his throat.

He could tell Dennis Hathaway didn't take to his tone but Laker couldn't help it. He'd never been good at being told what to do.

'Watch your lip, Charlie. It's your future we're talking about. The alternative is that you persuade her to have an abortion, you finish with her and you continue your career with me and you thrive.'

Hathaway scrutinized Laker.

'I think you were made for this life. I hope John is going to come through, but you – I see it in you.'

Hathaway swigged his drink.

'You lost your brother, didn't you?'

Charlie nodded.

'Burned alive, wasn't he?'

Charlie nodded again.

'Gives a man a bit of impetus.'

'What do you mean?'

'Did the coppers ever get whoever did it?'

Laker shook his head.

'No clue.'

Dennis Hathaway, still staring fixedly at Laker, nodded slowly.

'Sorry,' he said.

Laker started to say, 'It's OK—'

'I'm going to need a decision from you this morning.'

Laker liked Dawn. Lusted for her. But he wasn't father material. He knew that.

'I'm Catholic,' he said.

'Lapse,' Hathaway said without missing a beat. He raised his glass. 'What's it to be?'

Laker raised his own glass.

'OK,' he said in a low voice.

'OK what?'

Laker leaned over and chinked Hathaway's glass.

'You get your way.'

Laker could see that Hathaway couldn't hold back.

'I usually do.'

That was meant to be that but Charlie Laker couldn't get Dawn out of his head. He was getting plenty of women but there was something about her. He saw her after the abortion, from time to time, and she was dispirited and listless. Although Laker had insisted she have the abortion, she knew her father was behind it.

'I wish I'd been able to stand up to him,' she said. 'But I'm just a coward.'

'You're no coward.'

'Aren't I? To let him kill my child.'

'We'll make another,' Charlie said, on absolute impulse.

She smiled then and took his hand.

'Over my dad's dead body,' she said.

Which is the way it worked out.

Charlie decided to kill Dennis Hathaway for many reasons. For Dawn, yes, but mainly because he was ready to take over Brighton. He knew he would have to kill the enforcer, Sean Reilly, too. He would probably have to kill his mate and rival, John Hathaway.

He bided his time. He thought their joint trip to Spain in 1970 would be a good opportunity. As it turned out, John Hathaway thought the same – and then some.

One minute, they were sitting around getting pissed on Sangria and whisky, Sean Reilly standing at the edge of the terrace looking out into the mountains. The next, John Hathaway shot his own father in the head and was about to do the same to Laker.

'Goodbye, Charlie,' Hathaway said and Laker closed his eyes, resigned, knowing this was payback for him executing Hathaway's girlfriend. He'd been ordered to because she'd witnessed something she shouldn't have, but he didn't blame his old friend for not understanding.

'Don't,' Sean Reilly said, suddenly beside them.

That Reilly had stepped in to save Laker's life had surprised him. It was no surprise that Reilly told him to leave that night. Before Laker left, Reilly gave him the deeds to a couple of clubs in Ibiza and Majorca.

'To help you start up on your own,' he said. He handed Charlie £10,000, too. A fuck of a lot of money in those days.

Charlie kept to himself that Dennis Hathaway, as part of their deal over Dawn, had given him two clubs on the Costa del Sol, the pirate radio stations and cash in a Jersey bank account.

THIRTEEN

Charlie Laker went to Ibiza first. Set up a drug deal on his own with some Sardinian mobsters who provided the link through to the same Moroccan gangs Dennis Hathaway and now John were dealing with. It cost more to go through the middleman but it kept his name out of it.

He stayed in Spain for a couple of years. Dawn moved into the house Dennis Hathaway had been building. Her brother had given it to her, without saying why. Charlie saw to the laying of more concrete in the bottom of the swimming pool. They chose turquoise tiles for the pool bottom.

Charlie never swam. Told Dawn he didn't know how. She swam there all the time. Her mother came to stay just twice. Bewildered, strung out on the Valium wonder drug she'd been prescribed a couple of years before. She was devastated by her husband's abrupt disappearance.

'I know Dennis must be dead,' she said once, in a rare lucid moment. 'I just want to know where he's buried.'

Charlie watched her slow breaststroke across the pool, neck stretching out of the water, mouth pursed and eyes closed, swathes of her swim-dress floating behind her. And he wondered if he should tell her that with each length she was passing just four feet above her husband, buried underneath the tiled bottom of the pool.

The clubs and the drugs were complementary and provided a regular flow of money into his Jersey account. The system pretty much ran itself.

After two years, Charlie sold out his businesses to his Sardinian partners. He got a good price, not a great price, but he was pragmatic. He knew eventually they would have simply taken them from him.

He'd sold off the pirate radio stations to Keith Jeffery, a manager on the make with a club in Majorca. Jeffery was getting as bad a reputation as Charlie once had in the pop music business.

Charlie made a deal with him over his own roster of groups. Jeffery ostensibly took them over but Charlie remained a silent partner and occasional enforcer. He still liked getting his hands bloody.

His trips to England were rare and he always made sure he stayed under the radar. More frequent were trips to the US to handle Jeffery's burgeoning business there.

He got involved with the Mafia, who controlled transportation, backstage and technical stuff on pretty much all the pop tours.

He supposed the rumour that he had offed Jimi Hendrix came about because he was a bit of bogeyman in the business. He still smiled at it.

Dawn and he had been trying for another child. After her mother's death, they had been trying with increasing desperation. Dawn was still in touch with her brother. John Hathaway never asked about Charlie. Just in case he changed his mind, Charlie was armed at all times. Sean Reilly phoned from time to time, kept him vaguely informed.

Dawn went to see doctors in Spain and England. They said

the same. The abortion had been botched. It was possible she was now unable to conceive.

Laker told Dawn how her father died soon after her mother passed. He didn't tell her where he was buried – thought that would totally freak her out – but he did tell her that John Hathaway, her brother, had shot her father in the head.

He didn't know exactly what process of osmosis went on in her mind, but the death of her mother, the discovery she could not bear children and the revelation about her father's death gave her a single focus. Her brother, John Hathaway, was responsible for fucking up her life.

She never spoke to him again. She wrote him a letter saying she was cutting all ties with him. Didn't really explain why. She and Charlie moved to America. New York, though the music business was booming in California.

He did go to the west coast from time to time. He bumped into Dan, the lead singer of his old group, The Avalons, a couple of times, but they had little to say to each other. They'd been in a band together but they had never been close.

He had good contacts in the US Mafia. There were cousins of the Sardinian guys who were cousins of other families in the US. They got fed up with Jeffery. Some unspecified offence. Told Charlie how Jeffery had been ripping him off. Told him about Jeffery's secret accounts in the Bahamas. Asked Charlie if he felt up to taking over?

Three months later, Jeffery was dead, killed in a plane crash. Three months after that, Charlie and Dawn were living in LA, next door to Cary Grant no less.

And it was Charlie's turn to have his emotions undergo osmosis.

One drunken evening by the pool, the lights of Los Angeles carpeted below them, Dawn told him about an evening back in 1959 when John Hathaway had come home with burned hands and singed eyebrows, the smell of petrol strong on him. She tended to him with butter from the larder and snow from the back garden. Didn't get much sense out of him.

A couple of days later, it was in the local papers a little boy had been burned to death in a bonfire maliciously set alight. The police were assuming it was manslaughter not murder, but they wouldn't know for sure whether the arsonist knew the little boy was hiding in the bonfire until they tracked him down.

'Did John know my brother was in the den?' Charlie croaked.

'He didn't say,' Dawn said.

Charlie remembered the conversation he'd had with Dennis Hathaway when they did the deal over Dawn and the abortion.

'Did your dad know what John had done?'

She pursed her lips.

'Oh yes.'

FOURTEEN

Reg Williamson was in the office hunched over his computer when Gilchrist walked in. He clicked his mouse, then slid from behind his desk and hurried over to her.

'Bingo. Bernie Grimes. Place called Homps on the Canal du Midi. Not far from Carcassonne.'

Gilchrist looked at him.

'Fantastic, but you're saying those place names as if they should mean something to me. I'm a Brighton girl. I've never heard of them.'

'Carcassonne is this medieval walled town in the south of France. Looks just like it should – they used it for that Kevin Costner Robin Hood film donkey's years ago. Reason it looks so Walt Disney perfect is that it was actually rebuilt in the nineteenth century. So it's kind of a recreation.'

'You've been there.'

Williamson looked away.

'Me and the wife. Before . . .'

His voice trailed away. Gilchrist realized she didn't know anything about Reg's private life.

'Your divorce?'

Williamson flashed a look at her.

'Our David killed himself.'

Gilchrist was swept back to a conversation she'd had in the car with Reg, it seemed an age ago now, about suicides off Beachy Head.

'Reg, I didn't know. I'm so sorry.'

Williamson worked his jaw.

'His own daft fault. Drugs.' Gilchrist saw tears in Williamson's eyes as he turned away. 'Anyway, we know where Grimes is. We now have to decide what we do about it.'

Gilchrist reached out and gave his arm a quick squeeze.

'I don't even know your wife's name – I'm sorry.'

'Angela.' Williamson looked down. 'Lovely lass but she's suffering. Every day I see her sink further down. Don't know what to do.'

He worked his jaw.

'When I left for work this morning, she didn't even have the energy to say goodbye.'

He gave an awful false smile.

'Ay well, I'm sure it will all work out for the best.'

Gilchrist nodded uncertainly.

'So what next?' he said.

'I bumped into Philippa Franks. Mentioned Bernie's name.'

Williamson cleared his throat.

'And?'

Gilchrist shrugged.

'Nothing, really, but I have the feeling it shook her a bit.'

'OK, we need to find a way to put pressure on her,' Williamson said, all business again.

'And I think I know where Charlie Laker is going to be in a while.'

'Well done.'

'Not really. He's made a reservation at the Grand.'

Charlie Laker sat in the back of his Bentley heading south, his phone clamped to his ear. Time to move things up a notch. He looked out through tinted windows and made a series of calls. As the rugged northern landscape softened towards

Nottingham, he put his phone away and closed his eyes. Thinking back. Again.

He'd vowed he wouldn't do anything to John Hathaway for the sake of Dawn. But he'd planned. And prospered.

Dawn coped with her depression with therapy three times a week and cocaine every day. Charlie worried that the cocaine would trigger in Dawn the mental instability that had afflicted her mother, but he didn't know what to do about it.

Charlie, in his mind having let down his brother, then been abandoned by his parents, valued loyalty. He would never leave Dawn, although that didn't mean he didn't have women on the side.

Dawn wanted him to get into films. It was a source of private humiliation for her that they lived next door to Cary Grant but had never met him, even over the back fence.

She expected Grant to throw lots of parties but she never heard a sound from the house. She read in some of the gossip rags that he had a reputation for meanness.

'You'd think he'd like fellow English living next door,' she said plaintively to Charlie when Grant's secretary politely declined the latest invite to one of Dawn's parties.

'But he must be in his eighties,' Laker said. 'Old codgers don't always like parties.'

When Grant died in 1986, all Dawn said, glumly, was: 'That's that, then.'

In the late eighties, comedy became the new rock 'n' roll and he opened a cross-country chain of comedy clubs. Pretty much legit, though the alcohol came in the front door and went out the back and he couldn't remember the last time he'd paid retail price for a delivery of ciggies.

His management company looked after a few acts and that parlayed into TV productions on cable. And all the time he kept a distant watch on John Hathaway's upward progress through life. Pondering how he was going to take his revenge on him.

FIFTEEN

Kate Simpson, radio journalist, daughter of former government spin doctor William Simpson, was walking home when she saw the long, skinny man coming towards her on the narrow pavement. A man who'd frightened her months earlier in the cemetery beside the grave of the Brighton Trunk Murder victim. As they drew closer, he smiled at her in that same malevolent way.

She crossed the street and he stopped and watched her go, still smiling, slightly bent in a kind of half-bow. She looked back repeatedly as she hurried home but he didn't seem to be following her.

She checked behind her before she opened the main door to her block. Checked it had closed properly behind her. She went up the stairs at a run.

She was out of breath at her own door and fiddled with the security locks in her nervousness. She got in and slammed the door, bolting it and turning the key, then leant against it for a moment.

She let out a long breath, dropped her bag and walked into her bedroom. A different man was waiting there.

Squat, broad-shouldered. He grabbed her round the waist, swung her off her feet and in a wide arc hurled her on the bed. She hit the bed hard, face down and bounced straight off.

As she sprawled on the floor, winded, he grabbed her ankles and dragged her back to him then hooked his forearms under her armpits, lifted her and threw her on the bed again.

'Please,' she gasped as he tore at her clothes.

'It's not you, sweetheart. It's your father. He's not picking up his messages. So this is a special one.'

'Please,' she moaned as he fell on her with all his weight. 'Don't.'

'No chance of that, darling.'

His accent was northern. His breath smelt of alcohol. That

much she took in. He clawed at hcr underwear. She managed to take a breath. Got a hand under the pillows. Touched plastic.

'OK, OK. Do what you want but please don't hurt me. I won't resist.'

His expression changed and for the first time she felt him really press against her. He slapped her face. Hard.

'You won't resist? Where's the fucking fun in that?'

Ex-Chief Constable Bob Watts had been at his father's house in Barnes Bridge on and off for days. His father, Donald, better known as the thriller writer Victor Tempest, had suffered a stroke.

Watts was sunk in his father's wingback chair gazing blankly out of the long window above the Thames when his phone rang. He glanced at the name on its screen. Sarah Gilchrist.

'Sorry, Bob, but I thought you'd want to know. Kate Simpson has been attacked. She's in hospital.'

Watts swallowed.

'How bad is she?'

'Bad. Attempted rape. Badly beaten.'

Watts clenched his jaw.

'Who did it?'

'Nobody she knows but she does know why.'

Gilchrist seemed to take forever to continue.

'And?' Watts said.

'It was a warning to your old mate, unemployed former government spin doctor, William Simpson.'

Watts walked over to the window. A fog lay over the Thames, obscuring Barnes Bridge entirely.

'Bob?'

'I'm here,' he said, pressing the tip of his nose against the cold glass and closing his eyes.

'She killed the guy who attacked her.'

Watts sighed.

'How did she kill him?'

Gilchrist was silent.

'Sarah?'

'A volt gun.'

An old man pushing a pram hobbled through the mist on the other side of the road. Watts frowned at the odd sight.

'A what?'

'A rather more lethal taser. But not usually a death-dealer.'

'How did she get that?'

Gilchrist was silent again.

'Fuck,' Watts said.

'I had a bad time once.' Gilchrist sounded defensive. 'Saw the need for protection. When I was staying with Kate, I told her about it. Left it with her.'

'So she killed this creep with an illegal weapon.'

'It can be handled,' Gilchrist said. Watts said nothing. 'It can be handled,' she repeated.

'I wasn't thinking that,' Watts said.

'What, then?'

'Killing someone is a hell of a thing to deal with.'

'You and Tingley don't seem to have any problems.'

'I can't speak for Tingley,' Watts said shortly. 'What can you do for her?'

'Sorry I said that,' Gilchrist said. 'We should meet.'

'Of course,' Watts said. 'I'm on my way to Brighton.'

'Not just about this. We've found Bernie Grimes.'

The mist swallowed the old man.

SIXTEEN

B ob Watts walked along the towpath from his father's house to Hammersmith Bridge. He'd run the distance there and back at six that morning. Now he passed the odd dog-walker as joggers passed him, but for the most part he was alone with his thoughts.

Not long before his father had fallen ill, Watts had confronted him about his womanizing past. Watts had realized that William Simpson, his erstwhile friend, was his half-brother. Kate Simpson was his niece. He had been

puzzling over when – or whether – to tell her. Now was
certainly not the time.

He was aware of the screeching of the parakeets high up
in the canopy of trees that arched over the path. Escapees, it
was said, from some 1940s film made at Twickenham studios.
He saw a grey heron, neck elongated, standing still as a statue
in the shallows.

He took the tube to Victoria just in time for the fast train
to Brighton. He'd left his car at the station a couple of days
earlier. He'd forgotten where, of course, but after five minutes'
wandering he located it.

There was an old Archie Shepp CD on the stereo. *Goin'
Home*, with Horace Parlan on piano. Watts liked dissonance
in music. Anarchy, really. That's how he'd first got into Shepp
and his crazy tenor sax. But this was sweet, old-time blues,
more Ben Webster than Ornette Coleman. He turned it up loud
as he drove to the hospital.

Gilchrist was waiting for him in the foyer. They hugged
briefly, awkwardly. Since their brief fling, he knew she felt as
unsure as he did about how to be with each other.

She took him in to see Kate Simpson. Her face was broken
and bruised.

He thought she wouldn't want any man near her, but Gilchrist
nudged him forward and Kate raised a shaky hand for him to
take. Tears welled from her eyes as she held his hand fiercely
for a moment before her grip relaxed and her eyes closed.

'The drugs,' Gilchrist murmured.

Watts clenched his jaw.

They hugged again when they parted half an hour later.
Gilchrist had filled him in on Bernie Grimes and the south
of France. Watts was fired up about that but mostly he was
thinking of Kate Simpson. Her broken voice. The cuts and
the swellings. The tears welling from her eyes as he held her
hand.

Watts had been living in an odd little house in the centre
of Brighton for a couple of months now. It was one of a
handful of cottages around Brighton that had been built by
French prisoners during the Napoleonic wars. It was local flint
and brick that had then been tarred black. It was on a terrace

of four houses, the other three built to match a couple of hundred years later. It was three storeys high but very narrow. It had a small front garden and a private courtyard at the back. The view from the front was of a narrow walkway and the side wall of the Royal Mail sorting office.

It was a ludicrous choice for a big man as it was cramped with low ceilings, but Watts realized he was punishing himself. When his marriage had broken up, he'd first chosen to live in a horrible bungalow. Now this.

When he let himself in, the landline was ringing. It was his wife, Molly, phoning from Canada, where she'd gone to get a perspective on the things that had happened between them.

Molly was his home. He recognized that now. Recognized too that he had totally fucked it up. Not because of his one-night stand with Sarah Gilchrist. Long before then. When he was busy turning his wife to drink and away from him.

He shook his head. He was trying to process what Molly had told him.

'I'm not coming back.'

She had been staying with her sister in Canada.

'Well, I guessed that,' Watts said. 'I told you it wasn't necessary. The funeral will be pretty low-key.'

'I'm not ever coming back.'

Watts thought for a moment.

'That's coming straight to the point,' he said.

'I've met someone.'

'Oh.' It was all he could manage.

'Actually, I met him years ago. A neighbour of my sister. I've seen him every year for the fortnight I come here. We don't communicate the rest of the year. He was married, I was married. Nothing happened between us.'

'I'm sure,' Watts said, unsure whether he was being sarcastic.

'He's a widower now. We want to try to make a go of it.'

'I thought *we* were going to try to make a go of it.'

She was silent for a moment.

'There's so much I can't forgive you for,' she said. 'Not just screwing that woman. So much else.'

'I'm sorry. It's a wonderful romantic story you're telling

me. A fortnight of romance every year for – how long, did you say? Fifteen years?'

'Fourteen. Yes, it is.'

'Doesn't seem quite so romantic from where I'm sitting, of course. The person you were actually married to all those years. What are you going to say to the kids?'

'They've known about David for months. They fully support my decision.'

Watts bowed his head.

'I didn't realize how distant my children were from me.'

He slumped on the lumpy sofa. He was trying to remember that he had once been a chief constable, used to making major decisions. Now he just felt overwhelmed by his father's illness, his wife's abandonment, the attack on Kate.

'Ah, Jesus,' he whispered, pressing his fists into his eye sockets.

SEVENTEEN

Laker's Milldean plan had been vague at best. It had evolved. He'd had half a dozen coppers in his pocket for years. There was a gap-toothed git, Connelly, from Haywards Heath, who was rotten to the core. He brought a mate on board. Philippa Franks was easy – people with kids always were. Finch couldn't be relied on so he had to go – rolled up in a blanket and chucked off Beachy Head. The other copper whose grass had passed on the information couldn't be relied on either.

Laker had been sitting in the back of the car when his men did Finch. The one Laker had done personally, though, the one he'd enjoyed doing, was the deputy chief constable in his poncy little beach hut in Hove. It was necessary. Guilt was written all over him. Laker had simply strolled in through the open door and the poor sod had virtually handed over his gun and begged to be put out of his misery. Laker had shot him in the temple, stuck the gun in the dead man's hand and got out of the hut just ahead of the stream of blood.

Other people, though, just never learned.

Bob Watts took the train up to Victoria the next morning. He got a taxi from the station to Millbank. The cabbie took him the scenic route but he didn't mind. He gawped like a tourist at Westminster Abbey and the Houses of Parliament.

The taxi deposited him at Tate Britain. He spent half an hour wandering through a handful of the galleries, ten minutes intently examining Richard Dadd's *The Fairy Feller's Master-Stroke*. Dadd, the artist who killed his own father. He painted with such attention to detail.

Then Watts walked round to the City Hotel to beard William Simpson.

'Wait here,' Charlie Laker said as he got out of his car on a quiet Holland Park avenue. His driver, a knucklehead with muscles, looked worried.

'You want to handle this on your own, boss?'

Laker didn't even bother to reply.

A skinny, tight-faced woman answered the door.

'Yes?' she said, no friendliness in her haughty voice.

'You got a poker up your arse?' Laker said.

'I'm sorry—?' she said and then, presumably just realizing what he had said, began to close the door.

Laker stepped forward and pushed the door open.

'You sound like you've got a poker up your arse.' He walked past her into the house, pulling her with him by her arm. 'And who knows – before the end of the morning you might have.'

She tried to pull back, clutching at her necklace. He back-heeled the door closed.

'Who are you?'

Laker released her arm and touched the scar on his lip.

'Oh, I think you know. Willy home, is he? Willy Simpson?'

William Simpson was wearing a well-cut charcoal suit and sitting with a pretty young man at a table in the centre of the upstairs bar. He was running his hand through his hair in an affected manner when Watts walked up beside him.

'William.'

Simpson looked up.

'Bob. Not exactly a pleasure. How did you—?'

'Find you? Circumvent your security? Doesn't matter.'

The truth was, he'd lied to Simpson's secretary who had then told him readily enough where William might be found at lunchtime.

'I'm rather busy at the moment.'

Watts smiled at the young man sitting across from William Simpson.

'Please excuse us.'

The young man looked from Watts to Simpson. Simpson nodded. The young man huffed away. Watts took his seat.

'You're getting less discreet,' Watts said.

'Say a word and you're dead.'

Watts smiled.

'I recognize that as a valid threat, coming from you.'

'What do you want?'

Watts appraised his former friend. He looked for any sign of his father in him.

'We have so much to talk about,' he said. 'So much.'

'Funny. I had exactly the opposite notion.'

'Let's start with your daughter, Kate.'

Simpson waved his hand.

'It's terrible what has happened.'

'Yes, it is. And it's your fault. It means you owe her.'

'Owe her?'

Watts nodded.

'And I'm here to collect.'

'You?' Simpson sneered. 'What business is it of yours? You have no link to her, except maybe the girlish crush she must have on you.'

Watts said nothing.

EIGHTEEN

'I wonder if you're worth fucking?' Laker said to William Simpson's wife. She was sitting on the edge of a sofa, her knees pressed tight together. 'Hard to tell sometimes. You're a bony cunt, aren't you? But the scrawny ones are sometimes the most fun. You got kids?'

'One,' she said, crossing her arms across her breasts.

'Oh, of course – Kate. And I don't know why I ask about the kids really as I was assuming I'd be using the tradesman's entrance. Has that had much use? Aside from the usual function, of course.'

She hugged herself.

'No? Can't say the same for your husband's. I must say, he's egalitarian when it comes to sex with his boys. Sometimes he's up them, sometimes they're up him. Very equal opportunities.'

'How do you know my husband?' she whispered.

'Ah, now that's a long and not particularly edifying story. Suffice it to say that I do. Your daughter too. Well, kind of. Heard she had a lucky escape the other day.'

Laker stood and she shrank back on the sofa, a moan escaping her lips.

'Trust me, darling – you'll have the time of your tight-arsed life. Although you might be – how shall I say this? – changed when I'm done with you. If I'm done with you. Who knows? I might put you to work to pay off Willy's debt. You're getting on, it's true, but some men get a kick out of doing snooty cows like you. At a stretch I could get a year out of you before you need diapers.'

She moaned again.

'What do you want to know?'

'Simple: when is your husband going to deliver the fucking goods?'

'I've no idea what he owes you.'

'That's a shame.'

He held out his hand.

'Let's be civilized and do it upstairs, shall we?'

William Simpson tilted his head.

'What do you want?' he said to Bob Watts. 'I'm a man without power now. The pretend coalition government has done for me. I don't have Peter's clout. I can't sit in a wing-back chair wearing a smoking jacket and a cravat and pitch my memoirs.'

'Scum like you always come up smelling of roses. I'm sure you're consulting somewhere.'

'I still have value, it's true. This government wants to cut. I know how to cut. I've probably missed the free school gravy train but another will come along in due course.'

'What about this thing going on in Brighton?'

'This thing?'

Watts leaned forward.

'For God's sake, William, your daughter has just been beaten almost to death. Don't you have any feelings about that?'

Simpson grimaced.

'My feelings are my own and not to be shared with others – especially with you.'

Watts wanted so badly to hit him. To drag him to the floor and give him a good kicking. This man was his brother? He scowled at Simpson, though actually he was scowling at his father for doing this to him. He scowled at his father for many things.

'What are you caught up in, William? I thought it might be Cuthbert or John Hathaway putting the screws on you but they are both out of the picture. Is it Charlie Laker, sending you a warning.'

'Charlie Laker?'

'Don't play innocent, for God's sake.'

Watts examined Simpson's face. Nothing. Just that cold sheen of complacency.

'You don't have your government support now, William. You can't call on the intelligence services to help you out. You're on your own. In fact, you're fucked.'

'Well, there's fucked and there's fucked, Bob. I'd say you're fucked big time and I'm . . . inconvenienced.'

'William, I admire your resilience. But I loathe your lack of feeling for your daughter.'

Simpson flushed.

'Bob, in a world of change it's good to see that some things don't. You're still a sanctimonious prick. You have no idea what I feel about my daughter and what's happened to her. No idea. But I'll tell you one thing. Those who did it will suffer. Have no doubt about that.'

'You're sounding confident. Who are they? Maybe I can help.'

Simpson laughed and waved the waitress over.

'I'll take another gin martini and get my comedian friend whatever he wants.'

'The same,' Watts said. 'With olives, not lemon.'

'You sound like your father,' Simpson said. 'How is he?'

Simpson was putting on a good front – his lifetime's work – but Watts could see the strain behind his eyes.

'He's in hospital. He's had a stroke.'

'Sorry to hear that. Always liked him – he was a bit of a buccaneer. I never knew my father, of course. The cancer . . .'

'William, I'm not here in any official capacity. I will get you for the Milldean Massacre but that's not for today. A lot of shit has gone down in Brighton. Tell me about you and Charlie Laker.'

The waitress brought their drinks. Simpson watched her walk away.

'There's nothing quite like an arse, is there?'

'You'd know better than me, William.'

Watts was deflated. He'd been dreaming for months of bringing William Simpson down but due to the blood ties he now found himself in some sort of Shakespearean drama.

'You and Charlie Laker?'

'I've met him a few times over the years.'

'What does he want from you?'

Simpson watched him over his martini glass.

'How's your pal, Tingley?' he said.

Watts shrugged.

'Doing your job somewhere in Europe.'

Simpson took a sip of his drink.

'You're not with him?'

'Clearly not. I have family matters to sort out.'

Simpson put his drink down carefully on the table. He smiled without warmth.

'Life, eh?'

'Morning, Willy. How's it hanging? Is it hanging? Probably *only* hanging, the stress you're under.'

Laker was standing in the entrance hall of the Notting Hill house, hands on hips. William Simpson put his briefcase down and looked up the stairs. He tugged on his goatee.

'What the hell are you doing here?'

'Willy, you've got a big debt to settle. I did you a massive favour getting that blackmailing scuzz, Little Stevie, off your back. But you seem reluctant to keep your part of the bargain.'

'I paid you for that,' Simpson said indignantly.

'Willy, the dosh was only part of it – you know that.'

'I never agreed to the other – and stop calling me Willy. My name is William if you must call me anything.'

Laker reached out and almost lazily smacked Simpson open-handed across the face. Simpson staggered, his hand to his cheek.

'Watch your mouth, Willy. You promised to put a cabinet minister in my pocket.'

'We're not in power any more,' Simpson said. 'Or haven't you noticed?'

Laker made to move forward and Simpson stepped back, colliding with a spindly-legged table. The vase of flowers on it toppled over and smashed on the tiled floor. Water and broken glass exploded across Simpson's shoes and trouser legs. Laker hopped back.

'Steady on, Willy. Those flowers look like they cost a quid or two.'

'Where's my wife?' Simpson said. He called up the stairs: 'Lizzy?'

'Never mind about her. Focus on me. I want you to get me

one of the new lot – we know for sure that one half of them can be bought.'

Simpson looked down at his sodden trouser bottoms.

'*I'm* not in power any more,' he muttered. 'My sway was over the other side.'

'I've heard you're still doing stuff for the new lot.'

'That's small beer.'

Laker shrugged.

'Well, you're going to have to come up with something, old son. Do you want me to go after your daughter again?'

Simpson glanced upstairs again.

'What have you done to my wife?'

'She's upstairs. I'm afraid she's a bit of a mess. She'll be right as rain in a few days – just not as toffee-nosed. I was thinking of bringing her into my stable but I don't think she has the stamina.'

Laker could almost see Simpson's brain working angles.

'I'm going to give you a week to arrange a meeting with someone in the cabinet.'

'Why is it so important to you anyway?' Simpson said. 'I thought most of your business interests were in the US?'

'Don't you worry your pretty little head about that.'

Laker pushed past Simpson and opened the front door.

'One week or your daughter's mine.'

PART THREE
Jimmy Tingley

NINETEEN

J immy Tingley drove south in a thunderstorm. Lightning leaped between wooded hills, thunder rumbled along the valleys, rain fell in sheaves across wheat fields and olive groves. He drove slowly for the road was treacherous. Twice his car slithered on steep bends.

He dawdled through the soft Tuscan countryside, then observed it become harsher south-east of Siena. The road through San Quirico passed between crumbling chalky cliffs and on either side of him the rocky ridges that separated the river valleys were without the familiar blanket of trees.

He ate a melancholy lunch in the sullen perfection of Pienza's renaissance square. In the late afternoon he stopped at the village of Montepulcello, high on a promontory. He stood in the rain at the medieval gateway, gazing blankly at the seashells embedded in the yellow stone.

Around six, he came to Orvieto, a beached galleon stranded on a rocky plateau, wreathed in mist. He entered through the west gate and the bleak buildings that lined each narrow street swallowed up the sprawling hills beyond.

Lost in the one-way system, he parked carelessly in a large, deserted square, then sat for a moment, squinting through the fast beat of the windscreen wipers. Old palaces with stained walls and blank windows on every side. The rain drubbing the car roof.

Jimmy Tingley, ex-SAS tough guy, marooned in the rain. So overcome with exhaustion he did not even want to leave the car. Jimmy Tingley, killer, trying to hold himself together.

He knew he was fragmenting. He'd known it was inevitable for years. Years of not allowing himself to show that he cared. Years of the serpent in his belly.

A quote from Thomas Wolfe, the Yank writer, constantly ran through his head. Read years ago in an essay entitled *God's Lonely Man* and memorized.

He whispered it: 'The whole conviction of my life now rests upon the belief that loneliness, far from being a rare and curious phenomenon, peculiar to myself and to a few other solitary men, is the central and inevitable fact of human existence.'

Tingley was a Barnardo's boy. An orphan. No, not correct, he reminded himself. Abandoned. When he was in the intelligence community, he'd easily tracked down his mother. Well, if you can't take advantage of the resources at your disposal for you own purposes, what was the point?

She was dead and she'd been a prostitute, and, understandably, couldn't deal with a little kid. Understandable, but it meant that all he'd ever known was the orphanage and foster homes.

He didn't think about his childhood. Daren't.

The army saved him. He had a sense for righting wrongs. He didn't go so far as to think himself a good man but he had a belief in wrong and right. He watched out for the underdog. In the army it was given a context.

Except that he didn't really like being part of a gang. He'd long been a man who loved solitude, drawn to remote places. Not that he was one of those desert-loving Englishmen like Thesiger or T. E. Lawrence.

He had done his share of desert work but he'd thought it would be the sea for him. However, many oceans crossed had left a lack in him. In his best moments, he thought himself a romantic loner. In his worst, he thought himself something else.

He was thinking about the last time he had seen the Albanian assassin, Drago Kadire. Not so long ago the long-range sniper had been tied to a chair in John Hathaway's Brighton house, bloodied and beaten. Kadire had given Tingley the information he'd needed. Tingley had gone on to kill several of Kadire's associates but he had spared the sniper. He'd handed him over to the police, knowing he wouldn't be in custody long.

There came a night on the Brighton seafront. Hathaway was dead and Tingley was standing beside the gangster's one-time mistress, Barbara, discussing taking revenge on the last king of Brighton's killer.

Tingley liked Barbara. He was sorry for the life of prostitution that had been thrust upon her by others. His mother had been in the same line of work. He mourned her still.

He remembered the distant crack a moment after Barbara's head exploded. Tingley ducking, turning, scanning the near and the distant horizons. A glint of light reflected somewhere high, then gone.

A sniper. It had to be Kadire.

There was no reason for him to kill Barbara. But then Tingley didn't think he intended to. With a damaged eye from the beating he'd sustained, Kadire would not have been at his best. Tingley had been the target. He'd given the man a break and Kadire had repaid the gesture by trying to kill him.

There was only one way to respond to that.

Tingley roused himself, took a small case from the back seat and walked towards an illuminated hotel sign outside one of the larger palaces. The glass door shuddered as it caught in the wind and slammed behind him. He stood in the high, arched entrance hall for a moment. He thought he heard a baby cry; it might have been a cat.

He walked to the foot of a broad, marble staircase. It was unlit. He hesitated, drawn by the shabby grandeur, made cautious by the gloom. A soft voice, so close Tingley could feel the warm breath on his ear.

'There is someone to meet you on the first floor.'

A tall young man, in a black suit and a white shirt, was standing beside him. He could have stepped from the sixties, a period now fashionable again in Italy. His hair was long over his ears and a large black moustache emphasized the paleness of his cheeks. Rather than a member of the Italian Mafia, he looked every inch the romantic hero.

Tingley stifled his surprise. He nodded his thanks and, conscious of his tired legs, started slowly up the steps into the shadows. He entered a spacious reception room and raised an eyebrow when he saw the same young man awaiting him there.

The young man glanced carelessly at the passport and car keys Tingley thrust into his hand.

'Federico di Bocci. You have met my twin brother, Guiseppe, downstairs. My sister Maria will show you to your room.'

A young woman detached herself from the gloom and stepped across to the doorway.

'Please,' she said, in a voice even softer than her brother's. She smiled and inclined her head slightly to indicate that he should follow.

She led him to a tiny lift. She walked gracefully, lightly. There was scarcely room for the two of them in the lift. He was conscious of her physical presence as they made their shaky progress up to the next floor. She was a shapely woman and her black woollen dress emphasized her breasts and hips. Her heavy perfume filled the chamber.

She had her brother's melancholy eyes and thick black hair but her lips were fuller, her face less pale. Tingley found it hard to assess her age. Somewhere between twenty-five and thirty-five perhaps.

When the lift jolted to a halt, she squeezed past him into the blackness. She reached for a switch on the wall and a dim overhead light illuminated about ten yards of a corridor. He followed her as she walked ahead and pressed another switch. As the light ahead came on, the one behind went out. And so they progressed, from darkness into light.

She stopped before a broad, carved door and he heard the rasp of a key in its lock. The room was long, with an ornate four-poster bed at its far end. On the left-hand wall were two long double windows. He went to one of them. It looked down into an interior courtyard strewn with broken marble and fragments of stone. Across the yard, identical windows, shuttered.

'The Di Bocci family lives here long?' Tingley attempted in his feeble Italian. He only knew the present tense, as she only seemed to know the present in English.

'For three centuries. We are the last.' She gazed at him until he turned his face away. 'My father will be here in the morning,' she added.

'Good,' he said.

He slept on top of his bed through the rest of the afternoon then went back into the rain. He found a trattoria and ate and drank hungrily, thinking about the task he had set himself. Thinking about the futility of revenge. Determined to have it anyway.

TWENTY

Tingley had gone first to Varengeville-sur-mer with his friend, Bob Watts. Old friends, old companions in arms. Survivors of many a conflict. They had returned to John Hathaway's grand house in the picturesque village a few miles outside Dieppe a few days after Barbara's murder.

At first sight the two of them together looked like some old comedy double act. Of an age, but Tingley compact and tidy, hair plastered down; Watts towering over him, rougher round the edges, hair wild.

They'd picked up a car in Dieppe and driven through the rain to find a posse of French toughs gathered around the gate of Hathaway's house.

Tingley and Hathaway exchanged glances. Tingley and Watts had got embroiled in a gun-battle here some weeks earlier, fighting alongside Hathaway against the Balkan gangsters. Now they were back, but for different reasons. Tingley was thinking revenge but knew Watts was thinking justice.

'I don't know what I feel about killing people outside the law,' Watts said. 'I was a policeman.'

'And a soldier,' Tingley said. 'You've seen a lot of deaths.'

Tingley sought revenge not just for recent events in Brighton but also for atrocities committed by the same people in the Balkans in the nineties when he was there covertly and Watts was part of the UN peacekeeping force.

The murderers, then as more recently, were led by the sadistic killer, Miladin Radislav, known during the Balkan conflict as Vlad the Impaler. Tingley had intended to track him back to the Balkans and serve justice on him. Battlefield justice. When Barbara was killed, he had added to his list the sniper, Drago Kadire.

Watts and Tingley were taken through to the old library where a middle-aged man and a woman waited. The couple introduced themselves as Patrice and Jeanne Magnon.

'And why you are here?' Watts said.

'The Hathaway family did business with the Magnons for decades,' Patrice said. 'And whilst we liked John very much, business is business. He is gone, he will be missed, but the waters close over.'

Hathaway's last moments had been spent in agony, impaled on a stake on the cliff just a few hundred yards from this house.

'He left a will disposing of his property,' Tingley said.

'And we have heard that the woman who inherited is also dead. Barbara? Nature abhors a vacuum, does it not?'

'I was standing next to her when she was killed,' Tingley said quietly.

'I'm sorry to hear that.' Patrice Magnan shrugged. 'It is the modern world.'

'In our family, Sean Reilly will be missed even more than John,' Jeanne Magnon said. She had the gravelled voice of a heavy smoker. Of Jeanne Moreau, whom she vaguely resembled. *Jolie laide.*

Sean Reilly had been the right-hand man first of gangster Dennis Hathaway, then his son John. He had retired to this house and blown up himself and the Bosnian Serbs who had come to get him. That had been the start of the bloodbath.

'Did you betray Hathaway?' Tingley kept his voice low.

'It is complicated,' Jeanne said. 'Charlie Laker visited us. You know him? A very bad man. He told our father, Marcel, that Hathaway had killed his own father, Dennis Hathaway. Marcel had wondered for forty years what had become of his old friend, Dennis. Now he felt the son had betrayed him. He wanted revenge. Then, we had warned John Hathaway we could not get involved in rough stuff.'

Watts indicated the two men hovering by the door.

'Looks like you have your own tough guys.'

'These?' Jeanne said. 'These are local boys. No match for the men from the Balkans.' She shuddered. 'That man Radislav . . .'

Patrice put an arm round her shoulders for a moment but looked at the two Englishmen.

'We betrayed him in that – like your Admiral Nelson – we turned a blind eye.' Jeanne rubbed her face wearily. 'But we had no choice.'

'Charlie Laker knew our businesses, knew our weaknesses,' Patrice said.

'Where are Laker and Radislav now?' Tingley said.

'Long gone,' Patrice said. 'Laker back in England. In the north, I think. Radislav back to Bosnia.'

'And Kadire?'

'Drago Kadire? Was he even here?'

'He shot the woman, Barbara, in Brighton a few days after Hathaway was killed here,' Tingley said. 'His face showed the signs of a bad beating. He could not have left England by plane. He would have been recognized too easily.'

Patrice Magnon tugged at his ear.

'He probably went via Calais. Albanian gangs control the port. They smuggle girls and drugs and who knows what else into Britain every day. Then he would make his way south overland.'

'Back to Bosnia,' Tingley observed flatly.

Patrice and Jeanne exchanged a glance.

'Actually, he is based in Italy,' Jeanne said. 'In Chiusi, north of Rome. He does work for the Mafia from time to time. Killing work. But he is involved in the smuggling of ancient artefacts and is also a kind of liaison between the Italian and the Balkan mafias.'

'There is a man in Orvieto you should see,' Patrice said. 'Crespo di Bocci. He bears Kadire a grudge. Crespo is a smuggler of antiques, mostly. Not the worst in the hierarchy of crime. But he has killed, when necessary.'

'And smuggled artefacts are one way the Mafia launders the money it makes from the traffic in despair,' Watts said. 'Drugs and people.'

Magnan nodded.

'Sadly that is so.'

Tingley stood.

'I want access to Hathaway's armoury.'

'And a car, I would imagine,' Patrice said.

'You can provide that?' Tingley said.

'Of course. And a passport?'

'Why would you do that?'

'We did like John Hathaway. Our small betrayal we did with a heavy heart.'

'But now you take over his house – and French businesses?'

Patrice shrugged again.

'That is the nature of our trade. It is not personal.'

Tingley nodded.

'Show me the armoury.'

Patrice looked at Bob Watts.

'You too?'

Watts shook his head.

'I have other plans. But there is something I need from you. Papers. Old papers to do with an unsolved murder from 1934.'

Watts was interested in the identity of the Brighton Trunk Murderer, the never-identified man who had so callously left a naked woman's torso at Brighton railway station, her legs and feet in a suitcase at King's Cross.

John Hathaway had mentioned before his death that his gangster father, Dennis, had acquired from a bent copper in 1964 most of the police files on the Brighton Trunk Murder. They were thought destroyed that year by then Chief Constable Philip Simpson, a close friend of Watts's father. Dennis Hathaway had used the contents of the files to blackmail the corrupt Chief Constable Simpson.

John Hathaway had left them in the safe keeping of Sean Reilly in Varengeville-sur-mer.

Watts didn't for one moment think his father had been the Brighton Trunk Murderer but there were other things hinted at in his father's diary. Rape. Corruption. Betrayal. He wanted to see what the files said about those things.

'I need some papers,' he told the Magnons. 'Old papers of no interest or value to you. They were in Sean Reilly's keeping but I don't exactly know where in the house they are.'

Patrice Magnon had gestured round the library.

'I would imagine papers would be somewhere here. Papers you can have. Old papers, that is. Feel free to look.'

A half-hour later Tingley came back into the room. Watts was putting his mobile phone away.

'I've got to go back,' he said.

'I know,' Tingley said.

'On the next ferry.'

Tingley waited.

'My father's housekeeper has just telephoned. My father has had a stroke.'

Tingley reached out and squeezed his friend's arm.

'I'm sorry, Bob.'

Watts nodded.

'You got the papers you needed?' Tingley said.

Watts indicated boxes of files beside a long table.

They went to a bar on the waterfront. Windows fogged, rain sluicing the streets.

'Your dad is a fine man,' Tingley said.

'I don't know what my father is,' Watts said.

They parted at the ferry terminal in Dieppe. A clap of thunder sounded like artillery fire.

'You going to be OK?' Watts said.

'I'm loaded for bear,' Tingley said, patting the boot of the car.

'You're loaded for World War Three,' Watts said. 'God knows what Hathaway intended to do with rocket launchers.' He put his hand on Tingley's shoulder. 'God knows what you're going to do with them.'

'Radislav is long overdue.'

'But first Kadire?' Watts said.

'But first Kadire.' Tingley held out his hand. 'Once everything is sorted about your dad, you're going after Charlie Laker?'

'Him and others.'

They shook hands, then Watts turned and walked to where

his own car was parked. He looked back and Tingley was watching him go. Thunder rolled. Neither man waved.

TWENTY-ONE

Crespo di Bocci had pale, papery skin and black eyes that glittered in the gloom of his drawing room. He was sitting behind a broad desk in an ornate chair when Tingley was ushered in by Guiseppe di Bocci. Federico was already stationed inside the door.

The old Di Bocci was thin within his suit, narrow-shouldered. He watched Tingley walk over to take the chair in front of the desk and saw Tingley's eyes flicker to the large tapestry hanging on the wall behind him.

'My ancestors were merchant explorers. That is a scene of their ships departing from Genoa – or returning. I have never been sure.'

Tingley sat and fingered the pendant at his neck. St George slaying the dragon, represented as a winged serpent. When Tingley was young, he believed you only had to slay the dragon once.

How wrong he was. He soon learned that the dragon's teeth, falling to the earth, seeded it with evil yet again.

Over the years, he had killed the serpent many times. He saw that it would never die but he also recognized something else. Somewhere in the struggle he had ingested the serpent. Now it writhed within him.

He looked back at Di Bocci.

'*Mi scusi,*' he said. 'I believe we have an enemy in common. Drago Kadire. I wondered if we might make common cause.'

Di Bocci's English was good.

'Kadire betrayed a trust some years ago,' he said. 'He lied to me. His lie had consequences.' He spread his small hands. 'It is in the nature of our work that we are not always able to respond to provocation as we might wish.'

'I could respond to that provocation for you and only he would know it was repayment for your slight.'

Di Bocci looked at Tingley for a long moment. Tingley looked beyond him to the tapestry. He saw how the colours had faded. He looked back at Di Bocci, who had an intense expression on his face. Tingley tilted his head.

'You should visit my cousin in Chiusi,' Di Bocci said. 'It is only twenty, twenty-five miles away. He will have something for you.'

'What will he have for me?' Tingley said.

'Kadire is away, in Ravenna, but in a few days he will be in Chiusi. Go to my cousin. We must not be seen to be implicated but he will help.'

Tingley took his time on the short drive to Chiusi. The road was dusty, narrow and empty. He was thinking about Kadire and a long, long day when John Hathaway's men were beating the bejesus out of the sniper to get him to give up his colleagues. Hathaway stretched out on a recliner on the balcony of his mansion in Brighton, nursing a rum and pep in honour of Tingley, who drank nothing but. Clearly hating the drink but saying:

'Not bad. Not bad at all. Maybe we can do something with it at cocktail hour in my bar.' He grimaced. 'My former bar.'

The bar in the Marina that had been blown to smithereens by Kadire's comrades.

'You know, Jimmy, I look out over my kingdom – damn near forty years I've been ruling Brighton – and all I can taste in my mouth is ash. It's all I've tasted for years. Every decade I've moved into legit stuff. And every decade I've got drawn back in to keep others off me. And I've been bad.'

Tingley grudgingly liked Hathaway, even though he knew he had done terrible things. But then Tingley had done terrible things. The difference was that Tingley had done them for good reasons. He hoped.

'Do you ever wonder what might have been?' he said.

Hathaway put his drink down.

'What might have been was what was. I don't think in any other terms. I don't know how to think in any other terms. But the thing I've wondered about over the years is whether I genuinely care about all the shit that has happened in my life. The shit that happened to other people in my life.'

'And what do you conclude?' Tingley said.

'That I don't. Which begs the bigger question – when did I stop caring? Sean Reilly asked me once, straight out: "Whose death from the early days do you regret most?" I guessed he was wondering about my girlfriend, Elaine, or my father or anyone from that early roster. What he didn't know was the truly terrible thing I did when I was a kid – a thing I can't explain even to myself.'

'The only true account is the thing itself,' Tingley said. Hathaway looked across at him. Tingley shrugged. 'Words to live by.'

Hathaway picked up his drink again, took a sip. He couldn't quite conceal his distaste, but whether for the drink or the sentiment Tingley couldn't be sure.

Tingley was jolted from his thoughts. Something long and thin was stretched across the curving road. By the time he realized it was a snake, sunning itself, he had already driven over it. Glancing in the mirror he saw the snake thrashing, frenzied, trying to bite its own tail. He lost sight of it as he rounded the next bend. He smiled grimly. Was this some kind of sign? He felt the stirring in his belly.

He settled back into his drive.

Hathaway had been in a gabby mood that night. Maybe it was the rum and pep.

'I was a right tearaway when I was a teenager and I liked the idea of setting fire to one of the Lewes bonfires, up the road from here, before Guy Fawkes Night. Just for the crack.' He saw Tingley's look. 'Bonfire night was big in Lewes. Still is big – burning the Pope in effigy remains the town's idea of a good time.

'I'd gone up on the train doing a recce a few times. I'd settled on a bonfire erected by a bunch of Teddy boys calling themselves the Bonfire Boys. I hated Teds.

'So I go up there with petrol in a little bottle. Two Teds are standing beside this huge pile of wood, shielding cigarettes in their cupped hands. Both wore jeans with big cuffs and fake leather jackets. Very James Dean. I remember they were hunched against the wind off the Downs. It was biting.

'I hid between two garages, watching them. After ten minutes or so they went down the street to a café. When they went inside, I walked over to the bonfire.'

Hathaway tilted his head back and stared up at the sky.

'It was about ten feet high, a conical pile of tree branches, planks and one railway sleeper with smaller lumps of wood and crates hanging precariously halfway up. An unbroken privet of tree branches around the base. I poured the petrol over the driest-looking piece of kindling and crouched down to light a match. The wind gusted the match out. And the second. I bent closer and put the matchbox and the next match into the wood. I struck the match.

'The kindling went up with a whoosh. It surprised me. I staggered back, shaking my hand and twisting my head. Within seconds the flames were leaping high about the bonfire and racing round the perimeter, igniting all the kindling. I felt the prickly stumps of hair where my eyebrows had been. I looked down at my burned hand, already bright red with the skin puckering. I looked at the bonfire. It was burning well. I looked down the street towards the café. I turned and left.'

Tingley waited, sensing there was more.

'Did I know the kid was in the den inside the bonfire when I lit the match? That's the bit I can't remember. I can see him peering at me through the piles of wood when I was crouching down but did I really see that? Do I just imagine it?' Hathaway rubbed his eyes. 'I really don't know.'

Tingley couldn't think of a single thing to say. Hathaway sat up.

'You reap what you sow, Jimmy boy. You reap what you sow.'

TWENTY-TWO

The countryside was lusher near Chiusi. Tingley saw the town perched on its tufa hill when he was still some way off. The land sloped gently away to a small lake. The road wound round the hill, threading between a series of steep, cultivated step terraces. He entered the town with the cathedral on his left and the Etruscan Museum on his right. He parked on a side street nearby.

The sun was bright. It was quiet. Siesta time in a backwater. He looked across the countryside. Then he turned towards the Villa di Bocci to get on with the job.

Crespo di Bocci's cousin, Renaldo, was twenty years younger and as unlike him as it was possible to be. Plump, a cruel curl to his lips. A hint of the actor Peter Ustinov at his most lascivious.

He offered Tingley wine on a terrace looking out across the countryside. Renaldo waved his arm expansively.

'All this is a vast necropolis. As Camars, this town was one of the twelve cities of the Etruscan Federation. The Etruscans lived among their dead. With every rainfall, new treasures rise to the surface. There is a thirst for such treasures around the world.' He pointed to the west. 'That tufa hill there. It is the Poggio Gaiella. It has three storeys of passages and galleries, a labyrinth of them. It is regarded by some as the likeliest site for the mausoleum of Porsena, the great Etruscan emperor. You have heard of him?'

'Horatio defended the gate of Rome against him, didn't he?'

Renaldo bowed his head in assent.

'There is a labyrinth of catacombs beneath the town, of course. Beneath this very house. Porsena was buried in the middle of a labyrinth with all his wealth about him. Now that would be a treasure worth finding.'

'You smuggle artefacts, do you not?'

Renaldo ignored him.

'Our family owned these fields and hills for generations. Then my grandfather took the wrong side.'

'In World War Two?'

'Before then. He became a fascist in the thirties. After the war our fortunes declined.'

Tingley nodded, wondering why he was being told this but thinking: only connect.

'Your cousin said you would help me.'

'My cousin does not speak for me.' Renaldo di Bocci touched his fleshy lips with a forefinger. 'Which is not to say that I won't help you.'

'You know who I want?'

'Of course. But you must wait. You are welcome to stay here. In fact, I insist. Are you a reader?'

'Not particularly.'

'Nor I, but it is a pity. We have a fine library here with many rare books. For a bookish man it would be a profitable place to pass a couple of days.'

'As you say – a pity.'

'A woman perhaps? A man?'

'I'll be fine as I am,' Tingley said.

Tingley was not a religious man. He did enjoy the calm of churches, however. Their susurrating silence. He was sitting in the cathedral beside the palazzo watching a choir assemble when his solitude was disturbed by a hunched old woman in black who sat down beside him.

He stepped to the back of the church and phoned his friend, Bob Watts.

'How's it going?' Watts said. 'What's that noise in the background?'

'Evensong,' Tingley said. 'I figured the church might be the safest place from which to phone.'

'How far along are you?'

'Pretty far. These Mafiosi are being unusually helpful with Kadire. Suspiciously so.'

'You think they're setting you up?'

'I'm not sure. Maybe just to do their dirty work for them.

The old guy has a grudge against Kadire for some friend he offed. But his children seem strictly business. I don't think they'd help if there weren't a business advantage.'

'And you are a business advantage,' Watts said. 'You're not connected. Whatever you do can't come back and hurt them.'

'I know that will be how they see it. But they're keeping me on ice at the moment.'

'Watch out for yourself, Jimmy.'

A sudden spasm in his stomach made Tingley double over. He forced himself erect.

'How are things your end?' he said through gritted teeth,

'My father has died.'

'Bob, I'm really sorry.'

'I have mixed feelings myself, as you know, Jimmy. I'm sorting out the funeral and so on. I'm staying at his place.'

'I don't think I'll be back in time.'

'Don't worry. Where next? And when?'

'I'm already here – place called Chiusi. Crespo's cousin is putting me up – a dodgy piece of work called Renaldo. I think this is where it's going to go down.'

'Don't know the place.'

'Old Etruscan hill town, north of Rome.'

'You OK?' Watts said.

'I'm fine. Locked and loaded. Gotta go, amigo. Raise a glass for your father from me.'

Tingley closed the connection. He looked up at the ceiling, letting the music wash over him.

TWENTY-THREE

Tingley and Renaldo dined alone that evening in the villa's gloomy dining room. Two men in black were stationed by the door.

Tingley didn't like Renaldo. He knew better than to deal in stereotypes but he could sense something depraved in the man.

The obvious thought was paedophilia, the twenty-first century disease.

Renaldo's mood had changed.

'Any word of Kadire?' Tingley said.

'If we deliver Kadire – what do we get in return?'

Tingley hesitated with his reply. He no longer had any clout with the British secret services for whom he'd so often been contracted. In recent months, he'd first used up his favours then burned his boats.

'I'm sure there are deals to be done,' he said. 'As I understand it, this is returning a favour to the late John Hathaway.'

'Hathaway. Dennis Hathaway I knew many years ago. We met in Spain. His son, John, I am aware of. Favours, however, I do not know about. And you say John too is dead? This is a favour for a dead man, then?'

Tingley put his knife and fork down and stood.

'I don't wish to waste your time.'

Renaldo looked surprised.

'What are you doing?'

'I understood you could help me. If you cannot . . .'

Tingley turned and walked to the door. Renaldo di Bocci's two men moved to block his way. Tingley wagged a warning finger at them.

'Signor Tingley, please,' Di Bocci called after him. 'Please sit down.'

Tingley kept walking. He was sure he had been sent into a trap. The two men looked beyond him for a signal from Di Bocci. The serpent writhed. Tingley ruptured the knee of the man to his left with a heel kick. He brought his elbow down hard on the collar of the one to his right and felt the bone snap.

He pulled open the doors and strode down the long corridor to the exit. He wasn't armed but his car – and its arsenal – was nearby. He heard footsteps behind him but he ignored them. He pulled open the outer door, rabbit-punched the man standing outside it as he started to turn, ran down half a dozen steps and continued running for his car.

He had lifted the lid on the boot when he heard the clatter of a dozen men following him down the street. When he turned, he was cradling the Gatling gun. Cartoon-like, the men facing him stopped abruptly, cannoning into each other or slipping on the cobbles.

Tingley wasn't worried about these men. He was most worried about someone in a tower a mile away with a high-powered rifle trained on him. Not now, though, not here. Here the streets were narrow, the buildings high. Here it would be at close quarters from an upstairs window.

He walked back down the street. The men made a ragged line. Two in the middle parted and Renaldo di Bocci stepped from behind them. Tingley halted ten yards away.

Di Bocci was flushed and angry.

'You insult my hospitality,' he said.

'Oh, please,' Tingley said. 'Spare me all that "my house is your house" rubbish. You would have no compunction about drowning me in the bath if that's what was required.'

Di Bocci frowned as he struggled to comprehend. The man next to Di Bocci whispered in his ear. Di Bocci scowled at Tingley.

'You are not what I expected,' he said.

'Whereas you are exactly what I expected.'

Di Bocci looked from Tingley's face to the Gatling gun.

'Kadire will be at Sant'Antimo at eleven in the morning, the day after tomorrow. He has a meeting with some colleagues of mine.'

'How many colleagues?'

'Sant'Antimo,' Di Bocci said, turning away and signalling his men to follow.

Tingley watched them go, wondering where Sant'Antimo was and, more importantly, where it would be safe to sleep tonight.

TWENTY-FOUR

Tingley drove out of Chiusi on winding roads, watching for any sign of a follower. The abbey church of Sant' Antimo was in Montalcino, a French Romanesque building plonked down in the middle of Italy. He had been online getting images of its location and its layout. He intended to be there twelve hours before the meeting was due to happen.

He had spent several hours with Google Maps and other online resources getting the lay of the land around Sant'Antimo. He was confident he could avoid any kind of ambush going in. Coming out was something else again.

It took two further hours to reach Sant'Antimo. For most of his journey, Tingley was caught in a convoy of lorries grinding slowly through the hilly landscape. He saw the church from the road in a valley; it was set among low wooded hills a couple of miles below the little village of Castelnuovo dell' Abate. A tall cypress stood alone beside the square tower, equalling its height.

He pulled over to the side of the road and took out his binoculars. The way he figured, if it was a set-up, Kadire would be somewhere up here or in the church tower. Either way, he would be waiting to shoot him as he approached. He watched the tower for any sign, anything at all.

After half an hour he got back in the car and drove slowly down towards the church. He parked lengthways against the church wall, passenger side out, the church between him and any vantage point on the hill.

He came out of the car between driver's door and church wall and made the five yards to the entrance in a crouching run. Once inside, he ducked into a corner angle and swept the interior.

There were a dozen or so people scattered around the church. Nearest were a fashionably dressed young Italian couple who were scratching their names with a penknife on to one of the twelfth-century capitals. Aside from that vandalism, nothing untoward that he could see.

The high walls were undecorated, honey-coloured brick but, with the light coming through the plain windows, they seemed luminous. Beams of sunlight fell through those windows like solid slabs, their edges sharply defined.

He knew the layout of the church from the research he'd done online. He moved down the south aisle towards the altar. He looked into a doorway that led through to the sacristy and then up a spiral staircase that he knew from the floor plan led to the matroneum. He passed the altar, ducking his head to look down into the tiny crypt beneath it. He'd read it had formed part of a ninth-century church, supposedly founded by Charlemagne on this site. He walked behind the altar into the north aisle, stopped at the entrance to the bell tower.

He glanced up at the windows to the matroneum in the blank wall opposite. He could see a figure standing in the window recess, although he couldn't make out the face. He had the impression that the person was studying him. Tingley stared back.

'Tingley, nice to see you again,' a voice beside him said. Kadire, his face still a bruised mess, was standing by his shoulder, leaning on a walking stick. Tingley turned.

'You're early.'

Kadire smiled – it looked grotesque given his facial injuries – but said nothing. He pointed with his stick across the church to the spiral staircase.

'Shall we get out of everybody's way?'

Tingley glanced back at the window. The figure had gone.

Kadire led the way slowly up the spiral staircase, pausing once to catch his breath. At the top of the stairs he stood aside to let Tingley enter the room first. Tingley went by him warily but the room was empty.

'Did the exterior of the church look familiar, Tingley? Andrei Tarkovsky filmed it for use in his film *Nostalgia*, you know.'

'I didn't know,' Tingley said, looking around the matroneum. It had been divided into two rooms, both hung with wall paintings and furnished with chairs and wooden sofas. Tingley walked past the enormous fifteenth-century fireplace to look into the next room, then went across to the window recess. He could see the length of the nave below him. He couldn't see any of the people who had been in the church when he arrived. There was no sign of anyone resembling the figure he had seen in the window.

'Is Radislav here?' he said.

Kadire touched his face.

'That doesn't really matter,' he said.

'It matters to me.'

'I tried to kill you.'

'You killed someone I cared about instead. You have to pay for that.'

Kadire looked him up and down.

'I don't think your situation is of the best.'

Tingley looked down into the nave. The grey-faced Radislav and two other men were walking along it.

'You were expecting me?' Tingley said.

'The Di Bocci situation is . . . difficult. A rock and a hard place.'

'You know you killed the wrong people in Brighton, don't you? Hathaway wasn't involved in the shootings.'

'Not my people. I am Albanian. Radislav's people. The pregnant woman in Milldean shot in her bed during the massacre was his sister.'

Tingley had come here to kill Kadire but this was too cold-blooded, the man too defenceless. Kadire seemed to read his thoughts. He released his stick, spreading his arms wide in a gesture of surrender as it clattered to the floor.

Tingley could do it with one blow. He should do it, he knew. He could be out of the room before Kadire realized he was dead. He glanced at the stairs – he could hear Radislav coming up them – and back at Kadire.

Kadire watched him.

Tingley backed into the next room. He turned and ran for the door in the far wall. He thought at first it was locked but after a few moments hurried tugging it came open. He pelted down a flight of narrow stairs, almost colliding with a door at the bottom. It opened on to the gravel car park. A moment

later he made a dash round the perimeter of the church to
his car.

As he stabbed his key into the ignition, he looked around
to see if Radislav and Kadire had any other men with them.
No one visible. In a squeal of tyres and a flurry of dust,
he sent the car hurtling two hundred yards down the dirt
road alongside the church to the main road. Gunning the
engine, he dashed towards the vantage point he'd spied
earlier.

TWENTY-FIVE

Tingley lost track of time, lying in the hide, sighting
down the sniper's rifle at the church and the car parked
beside it. He wasn't a crack shot like Kadire, but with
the magnification on this scope he didn't need to be.

His mind wandered, but all the time he had half an ear on
his immediate surroundings, alert to anyone creeping up on
him. Cicadas rasped. There was an ants' nest somewhere
nearby and tiny red ants swirled over his hands, biting
furiously.

Radislav, here in Italy. And an easy target. Tingley had
expected to be blasting his way into some remote hilltop
compound with some of the weaponry weighing down the
boot of his car.

When the minute hand of his watch ticked on to the third
hour, he put the rifle down and rubbed at the eye that had
been glued to the scope. He realized he was drenched in sweat,
though the day was cool.

Tingley pictured that staircase down into the crypt underneath the altar. Realized there must be a secret tunnel by which
to leave the church. He wondered where Kadire and Radislav
now were. Running from him? Or towards him?

Jimmy Tingley edged the car through the medieval gateway
into the small, walled town of Gubbio. He parked and walked

up the steep, cobbled streets to stop for a beer at a small bar on a terrace below the gnarled ninth-century church.

There was a service at 7.30, a celebration of a local saint's day. The saint was actually an Etruscan god who had survived down the centuries by disguising himself as a Christian.

He joined a short line of people dipping their fingers in the water in the font at the back of the church to bless themselves. When it was his turn, he had barely touched the surface of the water before he withdrew his finger sharply. The water was scalding.

He moved on and glanced back. The woman behind him dipped and made the sign of the cross with her finger on her forehead. He looked down at his burning hand. It was an engorged purple-red.

He raised an eyebrow. Ant-bites from the hide, not God's judgement.

As he was sitting in a pew, the snake bit, doubling him over. Bile rose in his throat but he held it down, his jaw clenched tight. Maybe this was God having his say.

The two musicians were elderly peasants dressed up in their Sunday suits. The church was lit entirely by candles. Shadows pressed down on him. The service lasted an hour. Tingley wept at the beauty of it. He bowed his head when Renaldo di Bocci stepped from the front pew and walked down the aisle past him.

Di Bocci was without bodyguards. Tingley fell in step behind him, and as the church exit filled with people and progress slowed to a shuffle, he put his hands on Di Bocci's arms and guided him a few yards off to one side. Di Bocci didn't resist at first, though he tried to turn his head to see who was pushing him.

A couple of yards away from the rest of the congregation, Tingley stepped beside him and thrust his pistol into his side. Di Bocci half-turned his head and his eyes widened.

'I need to know where Kadire and Radislav are,' Tingley hissed.

'I told you,' Di Bocci said quietly. 'Kadire will be in Sant'Antimo tomorrow. Radislav – I do not know.'

'You told me that when you were lying to me. Now you will tell me the truth.'

As Tingley said this, he gripped Di Bocci tightly by the elbow, pinching the nerves, and moved him to the door behind the font. He released his grip, opened the door and pushed Di Bocci through. Di Bocci stumbled on to the marble steps at the other side of the door and fell to his knees, gasping as his shins banged against the lip of the marble.

Tingley closed and bolted the door behind him.

'My men are waiting for me outside,' Di Bocci said.

Tingley shook his head.

'No one is waiting for you. Except your mistress. And she was not expecting you for another half an hour. And now she is not expecting you at all.'

Di Bocci turned awkwardly, rubbing his shin.

'How—?'

'—do I know all this? In betraying me, you have betrayed your cousin in Orvieto. He is not pleased.'

When Tingley had left Sant'Antimo, he had found a quiet place to pull over and telephoned Crespo's family in Orvieto. He had told them what had happened. He had also told them he guessed that Charlie Laker had given them permission to help him and, having done so, would not be pleased that things had gone awry.

'How do you know he did not change his mind?' Crespo had said quietly.

Tingley had thought for a moment.

'Not likely. But had I realized you had no control over your cousin, I would have done things differently.'

Crespo had been silent for a moment.

'Let me call you back.'

Tingley had stayed in the car, the windows wound down, feeling the snake shift, listening to the birdsong and the cicadas, until his phone had rung again.

'Go to Gubbio.' It was Maria's voice. 'Renaldo has a mistress there. He thinks nobody knows.'

She gave him the details.

'You would betray family? In Italy?'

She paused before replying.

'That side of our family . . . our cousin we do not regard as family.'

Now Tingley said: 'I want to know where both Kadire and Radislav are staying and where they will be over the next couple of days.'

Di Bocci looked up at him, his dead eyes only lightly tinged with alarm.

'You think I will tell you?'

Tingley felt the stirring. He could only nod.

PART FOUR
Victor Tempest

TWENTY-SIX

OBITUARIES
VICTOR TEMPEST, THRILLER WRITER
1913–2011. AGE 98.

Best-selling thriller writer Victor Tempest once claimed that he and Ian Fleming played baccarat for the right to author the James Bond novels. In a 1985 interview, to coincide with the publication of his bestseller, *Licensed To Die*, in which an unnamed secret agent commits deeds of 007-like derring-do, he stated that at a house party in the New Forest in 1946 he and Fleming came up with the idea of James Bond. Tempest claimed to have come up with the 007 code-name and 'licence to kill' tag, and to have invented Spectre. The Ian Fleming estate has never publicly commented.

Tempest's own characters, including Alex Pope, have not had the longevity of Fleming's globally recognized creation. Although popular in the 1960s, 1970s and early 1980s, Tempest's novels are now largely forgotten.

Victor Tempest was born Donald Robert Watts in Blackburn, Lancashire, on 27 November 1913. His father, Robert Watts, was a weaver, his mother, Jennie Scott, a qualified teacher who was the daughter of a mill-owner. They had two older children, Derek and Angela.

Robert Watts was killed at the Battle of Mons at the start of the Great War and some months later Jennie moved the family to Haywards Heath, Sussex. There she worked as a teacher. She taught all her own children. She never remarried.

Donald Watts left school at 16 in 1929, just as the Great Crash led to mass unemployment. A keen sportsman – he boxed and played regularly in Sussex amateur cricket and football leagues – his fitness probably helped him pass the physical for Brighton constabulary, which he joined in 1931.

His police career was undistinguished, although he claimed that in 1934 he was one of the two police constables to discover the victim of the first Brighton Trunk Murder. They had been summoned to the railway station's left luggage office because of a foul smell and had opened a trunk containing the naked torso of a murdered woman. Her body was never identified, her killer never found.

Watts left the force in 1936 still a constable. He was vague about how he made his living in the years between 1936 and the outbreak of war. He joined the Sussex Rifles in 1939 and was at Dunkirk, spending six hours in the water under heavy fire until a small boat rescued him.

In 1941 he joined the commandos. He saw action behind enemy lines in Greece, Italy and Yugoslavia. He was an excellent linguist. Captured in 1944, he was tortured by the Gestapo but escaped and made his way on foot back across Europe to England. This remarkable adventure formed the basis of his first best-seller, *One Hour to Midnight* (1957).

Back in England, he joined military intelligence, where he worked briefly with Ian Fleming. He remained in uniform until 1947 and may have reverted to his commando role in Burma (records are unclear). He certainly re-enlisted for service in the Korean War in 1950, eventually leaving the armed services with the rank of major.

He took a job as manager of a civil engineering firm in Hove but had already begun writing thrillers in his spare time. Following the success of *One Hour To Midnight,* he turned to writing full time. He had a string of best-sellers: *Fly High Tonight, Tomorrow At Noon, The Devil's Alliance, Spy Shroud.*

His trio of spy novels featuring Alex Pope – *Pope's Prayer, Pope's War, Pope's Benediction* – are perhaps his best-known works. In the late 1960s, Cubby Broccoli optioned them for movies that were set to star David Hemmings (the Jude Law of his day), but for reasons that are unclear negotiations broke down.

Tempest was a prolific writer and he continued to produce a string of best-sellers through the 1970s and into the early 1980s. *The Berlin Inheritance, The Belgrade Intervention, The Moscow Ultimatum* and *The Saragossa Testament* were all very popular, but the fashion for such straight-ahead thrillers slowly dwindled.

His personal life was the subject of much speculation. His name was linked to a number of women – including Vivien Leigh – before his marriage in 1965, at the age of 52, to Elizabeth James, an artist twenty-five years his junior. They had a son, Robert, in 1970. He went on to a distinguished army and police career that recently came to an abrupt end when, as Chief Constable of Southern Counties Constabulary, he resigned over the notorious Milldean Massacre.

Donald and Elizabeth divorced in 1990. His name had continued to be linked to a number of women during his marriage. After he divorced, he moved to Barnes, where, at the age of 77, he is rumoured to have had an affair with a world-renowned ballet dancer many years his junior. His former wife, Elizabeth, forged a successful career as an artist. She died of cancer in 1998.

Always a vigorous man, Donald Watts was running marathons until his early nineties. And, if rumours are true, his fiction will soon get a new lease of life: Quentin Tarantino is said to be in pre-production on a film of *Pope's Prayer*.

Although Tempest stopped writing novels early in the new millennium, he is believed to have completed an autobiography before his death in which he reveals the true identity of the Brighton Trunk murderer. He is survived by two sons and a daughter.

Where the hell did the obits get that story about the identity of the Brighton Trunk murderer? Bob Watts put his newspaper aside. He looked out across the Thames to the mudflats on the other side, focusing on a crew trying to get a boat into the water down a concrete ramp. They were choosing a bad time. The tide was turning and any minute the tide coming in and the tide going out were going to create a stasis on the water that it would be hard to work through.

His father had always liked this high-ceilinged Victorian pub with its ornate balcony hanging over the river. It was just a couple of hundred yards from his river-front Georgian house by Barnes Bridge. Watts was having a drink in his dad's memory as a break from sorting through the piles of papers in his father's musty study.

A tourist boat went by from Ham, heading up to Westminster. As it went under Barnes Bridge, its sluggish wash hit the base of the pub and the oarsmen at the same time. The pub weathered the surge of water. The rowers did less well.

Watching them, Watts phoned his father's agent, Oliver Daubney, an old-style publishing man approaching retirement.

'Bob, terribly sorry to hear about Don's death – but not a bad innings, eh?' Daubney had a mellifluous drawl.

'This stuff in the obits about dad knowing the identity of the Brighton Trunk Murderer? Did that come from you?'

'It's what Don told me – and if it helps to sell the autobiography . . .'

The rowers, soaked, were clambering over the side of their boat, lugging their long oars with them.

'He once told me he didn't have a clue,' Watts said.

'You should always take what fiction writers tell you with a pinch of salt.'

Watts sipped his drink.

'Is there an autobiography?'

'So he told me,' Daubney said. 'And I had no reason to doubt him.'

'You don't have it, then?'

'I'm waiting for you to find it among his papers. Have you thought any more about your own autobiography?'

Daubney had been keen to take advantage of Watts' notoriety post-Milldean to rush out an autobiography of some sort. Watts had decided he should wait another couple of decades.

'I haven't begun my career yet, Oliver,' he joked. 'I told you that.'

Daubney chuckled.

'I'll tell my son to get back to you after I'm gone.' He paused. 'How are you getting on with the papers?'

'Badly. I haven't even found a will – but it is early days.'

'Not in his bureau? Your dad was an orderly man.'

'Nothing there.'

'You know there are always a couple of hidden drawers or compartments in those old bureaux?'

Watts laughed.

'I didn't – but that's typical of my dad to hide things away. Him and his bloody secrets.'

TWENTY-SEVEN

Bob Watts ran his hands over his father's mahogany bureau, pushing randomly at extrusions. A concealed drawer sprang out from one side.

He took out a large brown envelope marked for his attention. In the envelope were smaller envelopes marked 'Will', 'House Deeds', 'Insurance Policies', 'Passport', 'Birth Certificate' and 'Bank Details'. He skimmed the will. There were no surprises. Everything split three ways, with small bequests for grandchildren. He shuffled the other envelopes and saw a second one also addressed to him.

He took it over to the wingback chair in the bay window. Slit the envelope with his father's ivory-handled letter-knife. There was a single sheet of paper inside. A letter, dated only a few weeks earlier, addressed 'Dear Robert'. He thought for a moment. He was pretty sure the date was the last time he'd seen his father, in a pub beside Kew railway station. He laid the letter on the chair-arm and got a whisky from his father's old-fashioned drinks cabinet.

Settled again, he picked up the letter.

Dear Robert,

I know I don't make things easy for you. Never have. I don't really know why. Perhaps because I had you so late in life I didn't know how to be a father. Perhaps it's just my temperament.

Anyway, I've always loved you, in my way. For what that's worth. I was sorry to see you come a cropper and proud of the determination you have shown to get through it.

I've been keeping a few things from you. I got caught up in things when I was young and stupid, and mistakes made early on have a habit of clinging to you down the years. Not that I didn't make mistakes late in life too.

I've tried to be open in some jottings I've been writing for a while now. Not quite a diary, perhaps. Notes for an autobiography, if you will. Flakes of my life, to be published after my death, if anyone is interested. The notes aren't complete – just different things that came into my mind.

You'll find them on the top shelf in the study, piled up with all the manuscripts of my novels. A couple of Yank universities have been asking for those manuscripts, by the way. There will be a big cheque.

I don't believe in regrets but I do regret the way I treated Elizabeth, your mother. She was a fine woman. I like to think that next time round I'd treat her better. But I fear that I'd treat her just the same.

Good luck, son,

Your father.

Watts dropped the letter into his lap and sipped his drink, looking down at the rushing Thames. The wind whipped a tree branch against the long window. The rain started again, sluicing down the glass. He put music on. Arvo Part's

Lamentate. Melodic for him, but suitably melancholic. He let the tears prick his eyes.

TWENTY-EIGHT

George Watts, Bob's brother, came from Australia for the funeral. George was an accountant. Quite successful. The two brothers didn't have much in common – didn't even look alike – but Watts took him down to their father's local to talk about this and that, looking over the river Thames, then went back to the house and talked some more until both made their excuses and went to bed.

Watts put his brother in his father's room at the front of the house. Whilst staying at Barnes Bridge, he hadn't been able to sleep in his father's double bed in the large front bedroom. The room in which, if the obits were to be believed, his father had bedded the world-famous ballet dancer.

Instead, he slept in the poky box-bedroom at the back of the house, overlooking his father's pleasant courtyard garden. It had been used by the live-in Polish housekeeper, but Watts had given her a month's paid leave whilst he decided what to do with the house. She had gone home to see her family in Kielce.

There were only three mourners at the graveside. George decided it was because his father had outlived everybody. Watts wasn't so sure – and was stupidly disappointed that the enigmatic woman had not turned up and solved her mystery for him. Watts's sister, Alicia, could have come over from Canada but had refused. She had sided with her mother after the divorce and had refused to have anything to do with her father. According to Molly, Alicia took a dim view of her brother's 'shenanigans' too.

The funeral was a dank affair in the chapel in Mortlake cemetery, then the three men went over to stand around the tree planted in Kew Gardens in memory of Donald Watts. They stood in the driving rain, Daubney and George sheltering under Daubney's incongruously gaudy golf umbrella. Watts's black umbrella turned inside out so he abandoned it and stood, rain-bedraggled, contemplating the sapling shaking in the wind, feeling stupid.

After, they had a desultory lunch in a small restaurant beside Kew station. Daubney, a trencherman all his life, attempted to liven things up by telling stories of the celebrated fellow residents of The Albany, his home off Piccadilly for the past fifty years. George remained taciturn.

'So who was the ballet dancer?' Watts said after a solemn toast to Donald Watts aka Victor Tempest.

'Bob, I hardly think that's appropriate at such a time,' George said, his Aussie accent grating on Watts. 'We're remembering our mother too.'

Daubney winked at Watts.

'You know, of course, how he came to adopt the name Victor Tempest?'

Watts and his brother shook their heads.

'It was suggested to him by a crime writer he met in the early thirties. Peter Cheyney. Heard of him? No? Well, Cheyney was a best-seller in England, though he never did very well in the United States, where he set most of his books. Perhaps because his fervid attempts at American slang came out as cockney. He was a supporter of Oswald Mosley's National Party – its secretary, in fact, though I don't think he was in its successor, the British Union of Fascists, for very long.'

Daubney paused to take a sip of his wine.

'Don – your father – was a serving policeman at the time so had to join the Blackshirts under another name. He'd told Cheyney that he intended to be a writer and Cheyney thought Victor Tempest sounded good, both as *nom de guerre* and *nom de plume*.'

'Whoah – back up there, Oliver,' Watts said, putting down his own wine glass. 'You're saying Dad was a fascist?'

George shook his head wearily.

'Our father was an anti-Semite too? That's the last bloody nail in the coffin.'

Watts and Daubney looked at each other. Daubney cleared his throat.

'Apt words on such a day as this,' he said.

George looked from Daubney to Watts, then all three men burst out laughing.

'But it's not funny,' George said. 'I don't have time for prejudice of any sort.'

Daubney nodded.

'Your father was one of Mosley's biff-boys for a while. But when Don joined, it was a youthful passion and there was no hint of anti-Semitism. Mosley was regarded as more of a radical than a fascist. The moment the Nazi anti-Semitism came in, Don went out.'

George raised his glass and the others followed suit.

'To Dad, then – the complicated old bastard.'

They chinked glasses.

Watts turned to Daubney.

'There was this beautiful woman once, came to the house – George doesn't remember . . .'

'Here we go again,' George said with a sigh and a smile. 'He tried this on me last night.'

Daubney leaned over and squeezed Watts's arm.

'Families *are* secrets, Bob. And some never get revealed. Others just lead to yet more secrets. You can't know everything. So many things you wished you'd asked at the time. So many things you just have to let go.' He picked up his glass again. 'Some things never will make sense – you just have to accept that.'

After lunch Watts walked his brother and Daubney into the foyer of the tube station. George had his overnight bag with him. He was staying with his wife up in central London – she had declined the invitation to come to the funeral – before they set off for a tour of Scotland. Daubney was going back to The Albany.

Watts dawdled until they'd gone, then wandered into the pub next to the platform, relieved to be alone. The last time he'd been with his father was in this pub. Nursing his drink, he stared blankly at the trains arriving and departing.

TWENTY-NINE

B ob Watts had piled his father's exercise books beside the wingback chair in front of the window looking over the Thames. A bottle of his father's whisky was set on the table beside the chair with a jug of water and a shot glass. It was raining again, pocking the waters of the river. He picked up the first book.

Notes on Brighton and the Trunk Murders
by
Victor Tempest

Exercise book one

A lot has been written about these two 1934 murders. The one of a prostitute by her pimp, the other of an unidentified woman by person or persons unknown.

At the time the public confused the two – thought one man had done both. And, at first, that's what the police thought. But here's how it was.

On either 10th or 11th May, a small-time crook and pimp called Tony Mancini – I recall he went by other names too – killed Violette Kay, his prostitute mistress a decade older than him, in their basement lodgings on Park Crescent, off the Upper Lewes Road in north Brighton. He crammed her, fully clothed, into a trunk and moved digs to Kemp Street, up near the station.

He took the trunk with him and kept it by his bed. Some say he ate his meals off it. He told Violette Kay's sister that Violette had gone off to the Continent for a good job – she had been a music hall performer until the drink and the morphine got to her.

Nearly a month later, on Derby Day, Wednesday 6th June, between 6 and 7 p.m. in the evening, someone else left a trunk at Brighton railway station's left luggage office.

The next day, incidentally, Oswald Mosley and his Blackshirt biff-boys tore into hecklers at his Olympia rally with coshes and razor-blades. A party of Blackshirts had gone up from Brighton on the morning train.

On 10th June, in the evening sun, a boy and a girl taking a walk on the beach at Black Rock found a head half-wrapped in newspaper in a rock pool. The boy persuaded the girl to leave it there, on the idiotic grounds it was the remains of a suicide the police had finished with.

On Sunday 17th June 1934 – a hot, close day – the attendants at the left luggage office at Brighton station were being overpowered by a foul smell coming from somewhere in their store. They narrowed it down to the trunk that had been deposited on Derby Day. After a bit of to-ing and fro-ing, I went up there with a colleague and we opened the trunk. It fair stank. It wasn't Violette Kay inside – she was still in a different trunk at the end of Tony Mancini's bed. It was the naked torso of a woman wrapped in brown paper.

Once this hit the newspapers, it was bedlam in Brighton. We were overwhelmed with information – no computers back then. It was big news every day. When the big news should have been Adolf getting into position to try to take over Europe. I remember that at the end of June Hitler ordered the massacre of almost a hundred of his former supporters whom he now saw as opponents. They were calling it the Night of the Long Knives. But that didn't even make it on to the front page because there was some daft new clue found in Brighton.

The press went even more insane when Violette Kay's body was found on 15th July. Her friends had reported her missing and thought she might be in the trunk found at the station. Mancini was called in and acted suspiciously enough for the police to call round at his house the next day to question him again. He'd scarpered. A decorator reported a foul smell in the basement.

Strangely, neither Mancini's landlord nor landlady had a sense of smell. They had noticed nothing.

The two Trunk Murders were front-page news; didn't matter what else was going on in the world. Well, except for about a week later when the front pages were taken with the story of how on 22nd July, in Chicago, John Dillinger – America's Public

Enemy No. 1 – had been shot to death by FBI agents as he came out of the Biograph Cinema. One policeman apparently shook hands with the corpse. A mob gathered to dip their hankies in his blood. Later, at the autopsy, someone stole his brain.

Needless to say, every copper in Brighton went to see the film he'd been watching when it came out over here, probably hoping the glamour of police work Chicago-style would somehow rub off. It was *Manhattan Melodrama*, with William Powell as a public prosecutor sending up his best friend, Clark Gable, for murder.

Dollfuss, the Chancellor of Austria, was murdered on 25th July but that was buried somewhere on page three. A bloke in Ohio who had slipped on a banana skin and died made the bottom of page one.

Anyway, to cut a familiar story short, Mancini was eliminated as a suspect in the Brighton station trunk murder (it was being called No. 1) but put on trial for murdering Violette Kay (No. 2). His barrister, name of Norman Birkett, got him off, claiming that Kay had been murdered by one of her clients and that Mancini had come home and found the body and panicked that he would be blamed so he'd packed her in the trunk.

By mid-September, with 12,000 letters, cards and telegrams on file – plus notes of phone calls – the police were no nearer finding either the identity of the first trunk murder victim or her murderer. Nor ever were. No policeman ever had a clue. Except one. Me.

THIRTY

Victor Tempest exercise book one cont.

Now I need to go back a couple of years to just after I joined the force. I came under the influence of Charlie Ridge, who rose through the ranks and eventually became chief constable in the late fifties before being brought up on corruption charges. He ran crime in Brighton by the fifties but even in the early thirties he had his arrangements.

I don't mean I became crooked. This was something else. He'd been in the force in 1926 and got stuck in against strikers in Brighton during the General Strike. He'd been befriended by a bunch of toffs who'd provided a mounted auxiliary volunteer support for the police just so they could break a few working-class heads. They regarded strikers as communists who should be treated like dogs.

Quite a few were members of the British Fascists and Charlie joined them. He persuaded me and my friend, Philip Simpson, to join Sir Oswald Mosley's new party, the British Union of Fascists.

Simpson wasn't slow to put the boots in dealing with what he called 'oiks'. He was a bit of a bastard, actually. He had a vicious streak although he didn't have the muscles for it – he was a long streak of piss. So he was always ready with his baton. He would disable with blows to elbow and neck, and once they were down he started kicking.

I heard about one occasion he almost went too far. He'd started to get into it with this bloke. The bloke had been around. He could see the way this could go.

'Don't knock me about,' he said. 'If I'm doing any wrong, take me down to the station and charge me.'

But Simpson kept pushing and shoving him, trying to make the man retaliate so he could book him for assault. The man wouldn't, though, so Simpson used his baton to knock him down, then gave him a good kicking.

Charlie Ridge came along. The future chief constable was a sergeant then. He didn't stop the fight. He ordered the bloke to get up and fight like a man. The bloke wouldn't (he had more sense) so Simpson kept kicking him between his legs. Eventually, Ridge told Simpson the bloke had had enough and the two bobbies left him passed out in the street.

The man later complained officially. The kicking had ruptured his urethra. He was in hospital for three months being operated on, then a month convalescing. Simpson and Ridge denied anything had happened and, of course, they were policemen so they were believed.

You could always count on the magistrate to side with the bobby when it came to giving evidence. They were pretty uncritical, however unlikely your story was.

Simpson hated costermongers, I don't know why. He was always moving them on – at least until he worked out a system of getting them to pay him to look the other way. God help them if they didn't pay up.

I didn't go for any of his kind of behaviour. Bobbies had to be tough, of course. Generally, they were pretty rough – their batons weren't just for show. I didn't use mine much. You had to be careful. A mate of mine walloped somebody over the head and killed him.

My way was fists and boots. But they'd know what I was doing. I wasn't like Simpson. I'd take my tunic off, fold it and put in on the floor, put my helmet and belt on top of it. Nobody would ever touch my uniform during the ensuing fight.

It was a fair fight, except I always aimed to get my retaliation in first. We were taught only to use sufficient force but we'd also been blooded – well blooded – in the boxing ring. We boxed all the time. And, of course, they taught us a few things about self-defence when we signed up.

But speed and the first good blow would usually do the trick. You had to be fit then – not like coppers today who couldn't chase a thief down a street if they wanted to, which most of them don't.

I did try to play fair. I didn't always come out on top, but if I did come unstuck, I'd never complain of assault, unless they started it. If I started it, then the most they had to fear was a charge of obstructing an officer in the execution of his duty.

I would explain away the injuries by saying I'd fallen or walked into a wall because other bobbies saw it as weakness to be beaten, whatever the odds. Having said that, most policemen in Brighton got hurt sooner or later. It was just part of the job.

Some districts of Brighton were particularly hostile to policemen. Policemen who were a bit uppity were given these roughest areas as punishment beats. One street was known as

Kill Copper Row. Generally, it made more sense to give someone a leathering for something small instead of nicking him. Problem was, in these no-go areas, kindness was taken as weakness.

And come closing time every pub in Brighton was a potential trouble spot. Gangs fighting when the pubs had closed on a Friday and Saturday night would turn on any bobby daft enough to try to break it up.

I liked night duty, even in the bad weather, because you could give it to them hotter then. The real hooligans, I mean, not some poor bloke who'd just had a couple of drinks too many.

For me it was the razor gangs. Nobody carrying a cut-throat razor, a switchblade knife or a knuckleduster is a man in my eyes. If I came up against anyone like that, then my truncheon did come out – and I didn't much care how I used it.

THIRTY-ONE

Victor Tempest exercise book one cont.

So there we were, Ridge, Simpson and me: fascists together. Oswald Mosley intrigued me. He'd started out Tory, then gone to Labour, then struck out on his own with his New Party when Ramsay Macdonald headed the new National Government in 1931. And the secretary of the New Party was a crime writer I liked called Peter Cheyney.

The New Party had been trounced in the 1931 general elections. On 1st October 1932 Mosley had launched the British Union of Fascists with a flag-waving ceremony in the old New Party offices at 1 Great George Street up in Westminster.

These days, fascism has terrible connotations and we associate it with the far right. But at the time it had a perfectly proper place on the political spectrum. It was just a radical movement. My leanings were actually to the left, except that I didn't like unions.

Mussolini – who created the name fascism in Italy – was much admired, even after his ruthless attack on Abyssinia. He was admired by the upper classes for bringing firm government that held back the perceived threat of the Red Menace that the Russian Revolution had conjured up. He was admired by the young and the progressive for looking to the future, not to the past. In Italy, the trains ran on time.

Mosley took on his mantle in Britain. Although from a wealthy background, he presented the British Union of Fascists as a classless organization in which merit was the only qualification for advancement.

He presented the BUF as a youth movement against the 'old gangs' of British politics. He wanted to cure unemployment and prevent Britain's economic and political decline.

I was an energetic young man, eager to get on. The police force was incredibly hierarchical – it took Charlie Ridge thirty years to rise from constable to chief constable. The BUF was for me, especially as Stanley Baldwin from the old establishment called Mosley 'a cad and a wrong 'un'. That was almost all the recommendation I needed.

The big newspaper proprietor Lord Rothermere was a fan of Mussolini and he backed the BUF in the *Daily Mail*. That's where I read about them and that's why I joined, alongside Philip Simpson.

Neither of us fancied the uniform – we had enough of uniforms in the day – or the processions or the flag-waving but we could tolerate them.

When we joined, Mosley wasn't interested in all that Protocols of Zion nonsense. The BUF stood for religious toleration, not anti-Semitism. Mussolini was the same, actually – it was the National Socialists in Germany who added that to the mix. In fact, other British fascist groups – and there were many factions – called the BUF kosher fascists.

It probably sounds now like I'm protesting too much. I probably am. Anyway, anybody could join and the first thing I realized was that anyone did. Philip, Charlie Ridge and me usually went up to London for our meetings, but there was a Brighton branch that we went to a couple of times that was full of eccentrics.

The Brighton meetings were something and nothing – someone

would give a talk, then we'd go to the pub for a drink. There was a bloke called Tony Frederick who was a music hall performer. A dancer. He and his wife – well, he said she was his wife – performed as Kaye and Kaye. He just seemed to be down on everything, a man full of envy. His wife would join us for a drink afterwards. Her dress was a bit gaudy and she was past her best, but she was nice enough. She had a big thirst.

There was quite a lot of those types in the party – people who'd failed in life and were now trying to get in through the back door. I got friendly with a young chap called Martin Charteris who was at both meetings. He worked as an attendant in the public lavatories at the Brighton railway station – that's what I mean about the BUF being open to everybody.

He was a sharp bloke, a couple of years older than me, with a quick sense of humour. He said he split his time between Brighton and London. He couldn't wait to get his uniform. Mosley had designed a black shirt based on a fencing jacket – he fenced épée for Britain even though he had a gammy leg. Mosley thought the shirt reflected 'the outward and visible sign of an inward and spiritual grace'. Charteris just fancied prancing around in his shirt and his jackboots.

The first meeting I attended, in London, Peter Cheyney gave a talk. I fancied myself as a writer – I was always scribbling on whatever piece of paper came to hand, even if it was only my diary – so I got chatting to him. He wrote crime novels. Not those Agatha Christie country house ones, though. These were what were later called hard-boiled. American pulp. Lots of violence.

Anyway, Charlie, Philip and I didn't want to join under our real names because we were bobbies. When I told him I wanted to be a writer, Cheyney suggested I join under the name Victor Tempest, which had a good sound for a crime writer. So that's what I did and the name stuck.

I actually went to a dance hall with Charteris in Brighton one evening. Shelleys. We both met girls and went our separate ways, and I didn't see him again for a good few months. I took the girl to a show at the end of the pier and Kaye and Kaye were on down the bottom of the bill. They didn't set the stage alight.

I spent most of my time off in Brighton on the seafront or

I'd nip up to London. The line got electrified in 1933 and a third-class return fare was only 12s 10d. I liked the seafront best, though. The smells – all the seafood stalls and the fish-and-chip shops. The bustle – locals going about their business and visitors in big, screeching gangs.

I remember fortune tellers' booths decorated with pictures of Tallulah Bankhead; waxwork dummies in amusement booths; cafés with signs saying 'Thermos flasks filled with pleasure'; and my favourite – the booth promising 'Ear piercing while you wait'. As if, at other booths, you had to leave your ears and come back when they were done.

I used to hang out in the Skylark, a café that was rough but attracted a lot of girls. Around September 1933, I got chatty with a regular in there called Jack Notyre. Only about five feet seven and he had a stutter, but the girls seemed to like him. In fact, he had to fight them off.

I was a bit younger than him – he was in his early twenties – but we were both single and enjoyed a joke and liked a game of cards for pennies. Then one day it turned out he wasn't exactly single. An older woman turned up, a bit the worse for wear, and sat with him. He seemed a bit embarrassed, she being so much older. He introduced her as Mrs Saunders. They lived together.

I recognized her, though she didn't recognize me. She'd been Tony Frederick's dancing partner and 'wife'.

THIRTY-TWO

Victor Tempest exercise book one cont.

I was a bit wary of the Blackshirt organization by now. Mosley had made a big thing about not being anti-Semitic. That suited me as I'd no time for such stupidity. But I'd heard him give a speech about a month after I joined at which he'd responded to hecklers by calling them 'three warriors of class war, all from Jerusalem'.

I mentioned that to Charlie Ridge but he shrugged it off.

'Do you know who Mosley has hired to teach self-defence to the stewards? Former welterweight champion of the world, Ted Kid Lewis.'

'What's that got to do with anything?'

'Ted's real name is Gershom Mendeloff. He's a Jew from Whitechapel.'

But I was hearing other things that were both disturbing and funny. The Brixton branch was organized as a brothel. The secretary of one of the Newcastle branches had been convicted of housebreaking. The first national leader of the women's section had been caught with her hand in the till and kicked out.

Then there was the violence. The minute Mosley organized his defence force on military lines and put his men in jackboots, he was making it clear he was out for trouble. In the cities Blackshirts were driven to meetings in armour-plated vans.

When he set up the New Party in 1931, Mosley said he would defend his meetings with 'the good clean English fist'. He was a good boxer himself, with a straight left that had knocked hecklers out cold a couple of times, so the stories went. I was fine with that – as I've said, I was used to getting stuck in whilst on duty, especially when the pubs called time.

However, party members didn't just rely on their fists. I read in the papers that Blackshirts in Liverpool had clashed with rival fascists – the Social Credit Greenshirts – and used knuckledusters and leaded hosepipes.

I wasn't sure about the classless thing either. Although I never knew him, my dad had been a weaver in Blackburn. He died in the Great War. My mum was a teacher. So I suppose I was a working-class/lower-middle-class mix. The BUF magazine – *Action!* – had quite a lot of posh society stuff alongside the uplifting political sentiment. It was edited by A. K. Chesterton, the cousin of G. K. Chesterton, the author of the Father Brown stories. There was a regular gardening column by Vita Sackville-West.

I read an article once saying that Mosley's wife, Cimmie, wanted to turn Sousa's *Stars and Stripes* into a fascist anthem with words by Osbert Sitwell. William Walton was asked to write the music. This all sounded a bit highfalutin to me.

As a read, I much preferred *Wide World*, the magazine I
got second-hand for sixpence on Brighton market. It was full
of stories of adventure from all over the world. I liked the
monthly column at the back of the magazine written by 'The
Captain' called 'Man and His Needs – a monthly causerie of
matters masculine'.

In March 1934 Martin Charteris turned up again. He was vague
about where he'd been. Turned out he knew Jack Notyre and
the three of us hung about a bit. Charteris wasn't working but
he always seemed to have money on him. He was definitely
a chancer. He was staying with Notyre and Mrs Saunders.

I didn't tell them I was a copper but someone saw me in
the white helmet and word got back. They got stand-offish.
We still played cards in the Skylark and I saw them down the
dance halls, but they pushed me out a bit. I'd always been a
bit of an outsider with them anyway as they'd known each
other in London.

Then a funny thing happened at the end of the month. I
was off-duty and went into the Bath Arms in the middle of
the Laines for a pint. I could hardly see for the fug in there.
Pipe and cigarette smoke hung in a solid grey mass below the
ceiling and billowed down over people's heads. It was as if a
heavy sea fret had come through the door.

It was noisy too. Quite a few street girls came in here and
they were hogging the bar now, screeching and laughing about
their clients. I forced my way through to the counter and
ordered a pint of mild.

I made a space for myself at the bar and took a sip of the
beer. I could see Charteris over in the corner.

He was with a man in his early forties. Clipped moustache,
hair plastered back, check sports jacket, striped tie. They were
sitting at a table, so I couldn't see his legs, but I guessed
cavalry twill. Ex-army officer. And I guessed white socks. He
was one of the brown-ring boys, I could tell.

There were a lot in Brighton. Brighton Pier gave its name
to them in rhyming slang: Brighton Pier = queer.

I watched Charteris. He didn't notice, although he kept
flicking his eyes round the pub. He and the captain kept a

certain distance between them. All very respectable. Two men talking in a pub. But I knew.

One of my first jobs when I joined the police was going to a crime scene in Hove. A queer suicide pact. I didn't know what it was about Brighton that attracted all the back-room boys, then another bobby told me it was all the bloody thespians down here.

'They prefer backstage to front-of-house,' he said. 'Half of them are fairies and half of them pretend to be, putting it on.'

When I was younger I just wanted to punch them in the face, and if they approached me I did. But now I wasn't so definite. My pal Philip Simpson told me once, after a bit of a pub crawl, that he liked boys as much as girls.

'Why limit your options?' he said.

'Live and let live, Phil,' I told him, 'but keep your hands off my trouser buttons.'

So my views mellowed a bit, especially as I saw how quick Simpson was to get stuck in when it was required. And even when it wasn't.

Anyway, we broke down the door of this flat in Hove. Big living room, nice furniture. There was a man lying by the fire. He was wearing a blooming cravat. His head was near the gas fire. There was a terrible smell of gas.

We cranked the window open. The hot air didn't really gush in, it just hung there, but the gas eventually cleared away.

It was too late for the man in the bedroom. He was my first dead body. His tongue looked horrible, like a fat slug, hanging down from one side of his mouth. There were blankets tucked up round his neck.

It was a strange scene. Everything so tidy – it looked like a film set, especially as they were so well dressed. That cravat.

I felt sorry for the one who survived – the bloke lying by the gas fire. He got done and put away in prison, which seemed bloody harsh. Though you know what they say about queers in prison.

The next time I saw Charteris, he was in SS Brighton, the big new swimming pool on the seafront, ogling the girls draped around the pool. Same reason I was there.

I came up behind him quiet – though a stampede wouldn't have made any difference as the noise bounced around so much in there – and flicked his back with my towel.

'Oy!' he said, turning so fast he almost slipped on the wet floor. 'Don, you almost copped for that. 'Ere, that's almost a whatchamacallit.'

'A pun,' I said.

'That's the one.'

'But not a very good one.'

'You going in?' he said.

'Bit nippy for me. All very well having a seawater pool but they should warm it up before it gets here.'

'At least they take the fishes out,' he said, flashing a grin.

He had a quick sense of humour did Charteris. He was a good-looking boy with black wavy hair and a little Ronald Colman moustache.

I smiled and said to him: 'How's the Galloping Major?'

He looked shifty for a moment.

'Who?'

'You know. The Bath Arms the other night?'

'Oh him. Just a party member, Don. A fellow Blackshirt.'

'Come off it, Charteris, and we'll get along much better. I know your game.'

'You do?'

'You're a cut-rate gigolo.'

'No need to be insulting, Don.'

'Which bit?'

He grinned again.

'Cut-rate.'

'So what's your game? He just pays for your company or you get into a bit of blackmail with him after?'

Charteris looked around.

'Nothing he can't afford.'

I shook my head.

'Is Jack Notyre in the same line of work?'

Charteris looked sly.

'He's a step up. Managerial.'

I frowned.

'Meaning?'

'He's living with a tart. And off her.'

I digested that.

'Charteris – what are you both?'

He gave me the wide-eyes.

'Just men trying to make a living.' He leaned in. 'He's taking me to Eastbourne for a fortnight. In a caravan.'

'Notyre?'

'The Galloping Major.'

'Definitely not cut-rate,' I said sarcastically. He looked a bit miffed at that.

'What's it to you anyway?' he said.

'It's illegal,' I said.

'So are a lot of things you turn a blind eye to.'

He stepped back as I stepped forward.

'I'm just saying, Don. Is it a cut you want?'

'I want information, Martin Charteris. Always. Good stuff. Keep your ears open when you're up to your shenanigans. Keep me informed and we'll continue to get along fine.'

In May 1934 quite a few things happened. For one thing, Jack Notyre started work at the Skylark as a waiter. I think it was because there was a waitress there he was doing things with and there was a room out the back they'd disappear to from time to time.

Then Oswald Mosley came to Brighton on a visit.

THIRTY-THREE

Victor Tempest exercise book two

There was a big meeting on in Olympia in June and Oswald Mosley was rallying the troops up and down the country. He brought a few of his bigwigs down. He stayed at the Grand, of course. The local branch hired the Music Room in the Royal Pavilion for the meeting. Very ornate. We were all sitting there waiting when the back doors opened and he came in with about a dozen men. We jumped to our feet and I felt a fool half-heartedly shouting: 'Hail Mosley!'

He was a big man – around six feet four – and held himself very erect. His walk was an odd stride. I'd been told he'd broken his ankle twice. Once in 1914 at Sandhurst, jumping out of a window to escape some other cadets who were out to get him. He fell thirty-five feet. Then, when he'd finished his training to be a flier in the First World War, he broke it again when he crashed his plane at Shoreham, showing off in front of his mum and her friends.

Before his ankle had healed he'd gone off to fight in the trenches. His leg rotted. He was invalided out and ended up with one leg an inch and a half shorter than the other. Hence the limp. Even so, after a twenty-year lay-off he came back into fencing in 1932 and was a runner-up in the British épée championship.

You had to admire someone with that determination. But at the same time you could see why I wondered whether the other cadets would have thrown him out of the window if he hadn't done it himself.

He was arrogant and vain. He stood behind the top table and thirty or so of us sat waiting. There were four men sitting with him. The rest were his bodyguard, stationed at the doors now. Strapping blokes, all my sort of height.

He introduced his companions – his Top Table, he called them. William Joyce – another tall man. I'd heard him speak when I first joined up. Bloody clever bloke. A real orator. He'd started off quoting Greek. He said it was Greek – it was double Dutch to me. When he wanted to make a point, he put his right foot forward and shook his fist, his jaw thrust out. He had a bad scar running from his ear to his mouth – he'd been slashed with a cut-throat razor in a street fight with the Reds. He became notorious later, of course, as Lord Haw-Haw. I knew his hangman, but I'll get on to that in due course.

He sat now, leaning forward on the table, his chin resting on his fist, scanning the room with keen eyes. I was sitting in the front with Philip and Charlie. We'd changed into our Blackshirt uniforms in the toilets downstairs. It was the first time we'd worn the jackboots. Bloody hell. It took us about ten minutes to get them on, three of us tugging at the same boot, weak with laughter. You had to get your foot as if you were standing on tiptoe in order to get it in. We'd decided we wouldn't get them off again this side of Christmas.

William Joyce kept glancing at me. I thought I was imagining it until he leaned over to the man next to him and whispered something, pointing my way. The man next to him gave me a cold, appraising look, then nodded. Maybe Joyce was thinking what I was thinking: that this man, though slighter than me, looked like me twenty years on. Then again, I am a type. Aryan poster boy. Tall, thick shock of blond hair, blue eyes, long face.

The man was introduced as Eric Knowles, who had fought alongside Mosley in the trenches and was now one of his most important aides. His duties weren't specified.

I only remember the name of one of the men on the other side of Mosley. Captain Ralph Morrison, the BUF's quarter-master. I knew him better as the Galloping Major.

I glanced back to where Charteris was sitting. He caught my eye but sat there as if butter wouldn't melt in his mouth. Then gave a quick wink.

Mosley launched into a long speech about the parliamentary system having failed us. Mosley wasn't a natural orator – I'd heard he practised in front of the mirror and had taken lessons in voice production. His voice was shrill. He yelled at us as if he was at a mass rally of thousands instead of in a small room with forty people. It was exhausting.

At the end there were cups of tea, but somebody – Joyce, I think – produced a couple of bottles of whisky so we all toasted Mosley and the party out of chipped cups. Mosley went round speaking to each of us in turn. Joyce and Knowles came over to me.

'Are you in work?' Knowles said.

I nodded.

'You're a big lad,' Joyce said. 'Can you look after yourself?'

'So far,' I said.

Knowles gestured to a couple of the big men at the door.

'We're always looking for fit fellows to join our leader's praetorian guard. Are you interested?'

'In theory,' I said. 'But I like to work my brain too.'

Both men looked at me but I held their look.

'Do you?' Joyce finally said. 'Do you indeed?'

'What's your name?' Knowles said, taking out a small pad with a pencil sticking out of one end.

'Victor Tempest.'

'OK. Well, we'd definitely like you to attend the Olympia meeting on the seventh of June. We'll be in touch.'

Just then Oswald Mosley joined us. I didn't know what the form was so I stood to attention. He appraised me for a moment.

'Do you box?'

'Yes, sir.'

He suddenly feinted a left jab at my head. I swayed out of the way and automatically got my fists up and shifted my feet. He smiled and opened his fist to give me a pat on the arm.

'Quick reflexes.'

'He says he's got a brain too, sir,' Joyce said drily. 'Name is Victor Tempest.'

'Mind and body – that's good. That's what we should all aim for. Where are you from, Tempest?'

'I was born and bred in Haywards Heath, sir, but the family is from Blackburn.'

'A fellow northerner,' Mosley said in his upper-class drawl. 'My family is from Manchester – Rolleston's our home. Got to protect our cotton.'

'Yes, sir.'

'What did you father do?'

'He was a weaver, sir, but he died in the war. I never knew him.'

I was aware that during this conversation both Joyce and Knowles were staring at me intently, weighing me up.

'A lot of good men died far too young.' He looked from Knowles to Joyce then back at me. 'We could do with a good man in the north-west. A man with a brain.'

'He's in work,' Knowles said.

'Quick advancement for the right people in the BUF,' Mosley said, his eyes still fixed on me. 'I promote on merit. What's your job?'

I lowered my voice. Unless Charteris had blabbed, nobody in the branch knew Simpson, Ridge and I were policemen.

'I'm a bobby, sir. A constable.'

Mosley tilted his head to one side.

'Are you? Are you? Good man – I already know then that you stand for law and order – as do we.'

He exchanged glances with Joyce and Knowles again.

'Stay where you are for now but let's talk again after Olympia. That rally will be the making of us. Eric, make a note.'

'Already done, sir.'

And that was it. I left that meeting thinking this day could mark the start of a new life in uncharted territories for me – 10th May 1934. The same day the first Brighton Trunk Murder was committed, though nobody knew it then.

THIRTY-FOUR

Victor Tempest exercise book two cont.

Over the next few weeks I talked with Charlie and Philip about what I should do. I had a nice little number in Brighton. Did I want to chuck it in for the uncertainties of the northern wilderness? I was keen to get on, but Charlie pointed out that in the police that didn't have to mean promotion. Getting on financially, being able to afford the good things in life, was more important.

I thought I saw Eric Knowles in Brighton once, going into the Grand. I wondered about having a talk with him but I wasn't sure it was him, I didn't know what to say and I was a bit discombobulated after an unexpected sexual encounter underneath the West Pier.

The thing was, I enjoyed my time in Brighton. The girls were easy, for one thing. I decided to put a career with the BUF out of my mind until the Olympia rally.

The days before, the newspapers were full of it, especially the *Daily Mail*. On 6th June, though nobody knew this at the time either, the trunk containing the torso of the second murder victim was deposited at Brighton station left luggage office. The next day Philip Simpson and I took an early train up to London. Charlie Ridge couldn't make it – he'd suddenly been given a double shift. We were in our civvies, our Blackshirt uniforms in bags. We intended to change at Olympia. A couple of dozen from Brighton were going up on a later train.

That Olympia meeting is now famous. This vast conference hall with about 12,000 people in the audience. A lot of society people and nobs. About 2,000 of us had been bussed in from all over the country. There were also around a thousand people out to disrupt the meeting.

Blackshirts around the auditorium were chanting: 'Two, four, six, eight, who do we appreciate? M-o-s-l-e-y . . . MOSLEY!' It was several years before the opposition came up with a counter chant: 'Hitler and Mosley, what are they for? Thuggery, buggery, hunger and war!'

When Mosley came on, there was an enormous roar and a discernible amount of booing. He yelled his speech without notes, head thrust forward, fists on hips. I didn't really catch a word of it. Reading about it in the *Mail* the next day, he said once in power he would pass a bill to enable the prime minister and a small cabinet of five to bypass parliament to make laws. He would also abolish other political parties.

Whilst he was saying all this, hecklers were being ejected. The stewards were forceful. I was stationed with Simpson at one of the upper exits on to the foyer. I helped drag some of the interrupters out but I'd been clearly instructed not to leave my post.

However, I didn't like what I was seeing once the interrupters were outside the auditorium. Some were hurled down the stairs. Others had their heads banged repeatedly against the stone floor. Stewards were ramming fingers up their nostrils so they couldn't easily move or breathe.

All the stewards were armed with something – rubber piping, coshes, daggers, knuckledusters. I saw something I hadn't seen before. Razors set in potatoes. The other thing I'd never seen before was that the stewards used razors to cut the braces or belts of the interrupters so they couldn't fight back because they were trying to hold their trousers up.

I was disgusted. I intervened a good few times to pull my comrades off the ones receiving the worst beatings. The stairs grew slick with blood. Broken bodies lay huddled everywhere. And all the time, on stage, Mosley postured and grimaced, stepped forward pugnaciously and then back, fists on hips, head tilted back, bellowing his message.

Going back on the train, the stewards took their uniforms off because they were frightened of being set on. I'd lost Simpson in the crowd in Olympia so I travelled back alone. I took mine off because I was ashamed.

After that, decent folk ran a mile from the BUF, whilst the violence attracted all these other supporters looking for trouble.

I didn't know what to do. It wasn't that I hadn't seen violence before. I'd turned a blind eye many a time to bobbies putting the boot in. But what kind of organization was I in?

I went down to the Skylark to see if Charteris had anything to report but he wasn't around. I hadn't seen him in Brighton for a while.

Then the trunk was discovered at Brighton station's left luggage office and bedlam broke out. On 19th June I spotted Charteris hurrying along the prom. He didn't have time to talk – couldn't wait to get away in fact.

'What does the Galloping Major have to say about Olympia?' I said.

Charteris was darting looks left and right.

'Look, it's doing my reputation no good being seen with a bobby in public.'

'What does he say?' I insisted.

'I haven't seen him for ages. That was just, you know . . .'

'What do you think?'

'I wasn't there. Sounds like some Reds got what was coming to them.'

'Are you down here for long?'

'Two or three weeks,' he said. 'I'm staying with Jack Notyre.'

The next couple of weeks were hectic as we dealt with the avalanche of information coming our way. The next time I saw Charteris, he was at least a witness and possibly an accomplice in the second Brighton Trunk Murder.

The one thing he hadn't told me was that Jack Notyre's other name was Tony Mancini and for six weeks he'd been carting around in a trunk the corpse of Violette Kay. Violette Kay, the woman I'd once seen dancing as one half of Kaye and Kaye on the Palace Pier and again as Mrs Saunders in the Skylark.

THIRTY-FIVE

Victor Tempest exercise book three

There had been a lot going on I didn't know about – or maybe didn't want to know about. For instance, whenever I'd seen Charteris in Brighton he'd been living with Notyre/Mancini and Violette Kay. The last time, after he'd killed Violette, Notyre had moved another woman in for a bit – the waitress from the Skylark. On that occasion, Charteris stayed with Notyre nearly a month with the poor dead woman in an increasingly smelly trunk at the bottom of the bed.

Charteris and Notyre had met in prison in July 1931. Charteris was in for a month for stealing. Notyre was in for three months for loitering with intent in Birmingham. They palled up in London on and off over the next couple of years.

The police questioned Notyre about Violette Kay on Friday 13th July in connection with the murder victim found in the left-luggage office at the station. At the time he said she'd gone away and because she was not in the age range specified by the pathologist who'd examined the torso we'd let him go. But somebody must have been suspicious – or Notyre thought they were – because on that Sunday 15th July he did a runner.

First, he and Charteris went dancing until the early hours, then on to an all-night restaurant. They went back to the flat for a couple of hours until at 4.30 they returned to the all-night restaurant. Charteris walked with Notyre to Preston Park – they thought the police would be watching Brighton central station – and put him on the first train to London.

'You were in Brighton on the tenth of May,' I said to Charteris, in his formal interview in the Royal Pavilion. 'Where were you staying then?'

He looked shifty.

'I was staying with Jack – but not that night.'

'Just as well or you'd have been sharing a bed with a corpse. Where were you?'

'I was at the Grand with the Galloping Major. When I got back the next day, Jack had this big black trunk and said he was packed and ready to move. Said that Violette had buggered off with a bookie. I went and hired a trolley for a couple of pence and helped him wheel it up to his new place. The trunk weighed a bloody ton. He said he had crockery and stuff in it and I had no reason to disbelieve him. I didn't know I was carting Violette around.'

Charteris had always been a plausible liar so I didn't know how much he knew about the murder. Certainly he had a good alibi for the murder itself – he would have had to be a pretty cool customer if he'd helped earlier in the day, then gone to the Blackshirt meeting at the Pavilion in the evening.

Early in 1935 I left the police. A combination of things. My bosses didn't like the relationship I'd had with the press. And word had got back I'd been with the Blackshirts at Olympia. They didn't seem to know about Philip Simpson and I didn't say. It was ironic that I'd been thinking of quitting the BUF yet my membership had lost me my job.

I'd been hesitating because I'd been impressed that Mosley had set up a youth movement that was a bit like the Boy Scouts – Baden-Powell was a fascist sympathizer, of course. There was a lot of paraphernalia – uniforms, badges, saluting, flags – but the idea was a good one.

I went up to Chelsea for a meeting with Joyce and Knowles.

'I'm ready to move up. Is there anything for me?'

Knowles picked up a sheet of paper.

'You're from Lancashire, yes?'

'My family is.'

'You still have family there?'

'Not who speak to me.'

I think my mother's father was still alive but we didn't have anything to do with him.

'We've got a problem up there. Last week a group of our members in Colne overheard a bunch of men talking in a foreign language. Someone told our members these foreigners were learning about cotton so they could go back home and set up in competition. Defending cotton is one of our main aims. Our members attacked the foreigners. Beat them perhaps too enthusiastically. And then we discovered the foreigners were a bunch of Esperantists from Burnley and Bacup, in Colne to celebrate the opening of their new premises.'

I burst out laughing. Joyce and Knowles both gave me fierce looks.

'You have to admit—' I started to say, then stopped when Joyce gave me a warning look. 'That wouldn't happen under my command,' I said more soberly. 'I've been a policeman. I know how to assess situations.'

'The BUF official policy is against chain stores and in favour of local shopkeepers. A number of chain stores are moving into those northern towns. That and cotton must be our focus.'

Joyce leaned forward, his hands clasped.

'Are you up to it? Will you help us revolt against the united muttons of the old gangs of British politics?'

Two weeks later I was back in the town of my ancestors. My district stretched across through Accrington and Burnley to Nelson and Colne. I found the BUF were popular in the north-west because of that history of individualism that came out of Methodism decades before. The Tories usually got a lot of working-class votes and even the unions were conservative. The cotton manufacturers were major contributors.

But the set-up was a bit of a joke in my area. My second-in-command was the head of the woman's unit, Nellie Driver. First thing she said to me was: 'A God-fearing non-boozer can thread ten needles whilst the boozer is still trying to pick the needle up.'

She complained all the time that nobody saluted her with a 'Hail Nellie' when they saw her. Nellie moaned that in Nelson they had to share premises with a spiritualist group doing shell and photograph seances. The spiritualists kept putting their notices over the Blackshirt ones on the joint noticeboard – and wouldn't let them use the sink.

The Blackshirts were the biggest load of misfits you could imagine. Crooks, faddists, Mormons, pacifists, Christadelphians, antivivisectionists. None of them would go out on the street selling our newspaper because they didn't want anyone to know they were members and they were frightened of getting beaten up by the Reds.

One bloke who worked on a lathe in a factory offered to knock off some knuckledusters from odd scraps of brass or some other hard metal. The north-west was tough in those days. My uncle had been kicked to death in a drunken brawl with some Irish navvies outside a pub in Burnley back in 1922. An argument, the newspapers called it. Some bloody argument. The papers blamed the number of pubs in Burnley for the violence – there were fifty-six licensed houses within three hundred yards of the market hall.

There were fights every night. Fists, feet and broken glasses. If you went down, it was all over. Weavers, colliery workers and navvies all fought in their clogs. They had wooden soles, shod with iron. If you were on the dole and had no money, you shod your clogs with bits of old car tyres cut to shape.

I couldn't stay in this job. I realized I'd made a mistake when a few weeks later, in March 1935, the word came about a change of emphasis in our message. We were told to give more prominence to the question of the Big Jew and the Little Jew. Jews had always been prominent among those disrupting Blackshirt meetings. The memorandum insisted it was not about race, it was about nationality. Some Jews were acting against the British national interest through their role in international finance. They were in fact an 'alien menace'.

I have my faults but anti-Semitism isn't one of them. And it was clear Mosley had taken this decision to appeal to the worst kind of bigots, although anti-Semitism was rife in his class as a matter of course. I didn't think it would wash in the north-west. Not so much because the folk were particularly tolerant, just that there were hardly any Jews around, except in Manchester.

Was picking on people really 'the steel creed of the iron age'?

I went down to London to give my notice in person. I wasn't sure what exactly I was going to do with my life but I couldn't in all conscience do this.

Just before I left, I had a strange encounter in a butcher's shop in Clayton, over Bradford way. The butchers were called Pierrepoint and the open secret was that three of them had another job. Hangmen. Henry and then his brother Tom were both Official Executioners as a sideline. Henry had not long ago been fired for turning up drunk in Chelmsford and fighting with his assistant. Tom had taken over.

Then Henry's son, Albert, had applied. They were all non-descript but Albert was a very quiet one. He was an assistant first, in 1931, and told me he was looking forward to being in charge. He said this while wearing a bloodstained white coat with cuts of meat in trays before him, skinned pigs and legs of lamb hanging on steel hooks behind him.

People remain a mystery to me.

I got in to see William Joyce back in London. His office was bedecked with BUF flags. He looked up from behind a long polished desk and didn't ask me to sit down. He listened but shook his head throughout my little speech.

'As you wish,' was all he said at the end, returning to his work.

As I was standing on the pavement outside, wondering where to go next, Martin Charteris came down the steps behind me in his civvies with Tony Frederick, the former music hall performer.

'What are you doing here?' I said to Frederick.

He pointed at the camera slung round his neck.

'I live here now. I'm the official photographer for the BUF.'

He excused himself and strutted off down the street. I watched him go, then turned to Charteris.

'You here to see the Galloping Major, then?' I said.

'Nah, I work here too. I'm head office now. You got time for a drink?'

'I've got nothing but time. How's your friend Tony Mancini?'

Mancini/Notyre had got off his murder charge thanks to his cunning barrister, Norman Birkett.

Charteris laughed at that.

'You'll see.'

We walked across St James's Park. Charteris stopped me at one point and indicated the bushes beside the lake.

'I've spent a lot of time in those bushes with guards from the barracks across the road in St James's Palace. Do you fancy a quick one?'

I looked at the big grin on his face.

'Not my thing, Charteris. You know that.'

He laughed again and led the way across to Piccadilly, then over into Soho.

'You can tell me now, Charteris,' I said at one point. 'Did you help stuff her in the trunk?'

He didn't say anything, just winked.

He took me along Wardour Street. We turned into a gloomy hallway with a cramped set of stairs ahead of us. On the right was a solid-looking door. He swung it open and ushered me in.

THIRTY-SIX

Victor Tempest exercise book four

The club was as rough as they come. The floor was sticky from years of spilled beer and worse. The room smelled of stale booze, disinfectant, tobacco and sweat.

The pugnacious-looking men playing billiards at the two beaten-up tables paused to watch our progress to the bar. Other men sat around bar tables littered with cards and dominoes, their heads haloed with smoke from the cigarettes clamped between their teeth.

A tough customer at the bar turned at our approach. About five feet ten, broad-shouldered, hard eyes.

'Martin – always a pleasure.' He glanced at me. 'You're bringing the law here?'

'Ex-law,' I said.

'He's one of us, Baby, one of us,' Charteris said, his smile nervous. He turned to me. 'Don, I'd like you to meet Tony Mancini.'

The man nodded. I looked at Charteris.

'What are you playing at? I've met Tony Mancini and this isn't him.'

The man at the bar grimaced.

'You met Cecil England. Also known as Jack Notyre. He nicked my fucking name and my reputation.' He stuck his chest out. 'Trust me – I am the one and the only Tony Mancini. "Baby" to my friends.' He put a grotesque expression on his face. 'On account of I look so angelic.'

He stuck out his hand. I took it and he tried to crush mine. Then he looked over my shoulder. I glanced back to the door. Eric Knowles was loitering there. He nodded and disappeared up the stairs.

Mancini let go of my hand.

'Excuse me,' he said. 'Duty calls.' He looked over at the barman. 'Get these gents whatever they want.'

He followed Knowles up the stairs and I looked at Charteris.

'What's going on? Did you see who just turned up?'

'Business in common. The Big Jew and the Little Jew. Baby is having trouble with the Little Jew – kike gangsters who run half of Soho. Except the BUF is going to come to some arrangement.'

I looked around.

'With Italian hoodlums.'

'Don't be such a snob, Don. We all want the same thing in the end. Self-betterment.'

I took a sip of my drink.

'What's the story on Baby?'

'Ha – well, there's a weird thing about him and the Trunk Murder—'

But I didn't hear what it was. What I heard instead was the hurried, heavy tread of half a dozen policemen who burst into the room a moment later.

'Police raid!'

The barman was already out of a door behind the bar and Charteris and I were right behind him. Charteris went left, I went right and that's the last I ever saw of him.

I went back to Wardour Street in 1942 with some mates on leave. The bar was still there but Baby Mancini wasn't. In October 1941 he'd gone to the gallows for the murder of a Jewish gangster in a brawl in the club upstairs.

THIRTY-SEVEN

Victor Tempest exercise book four cont.

At the outbreak of the war I'd immediately volunteered. I'd enlisted as Victor Tempest. I'm not quite sure why – perhaps because the name sounded heroic. I felt prepared, but the violence I'd witnessed in the police and in the Blackshirts had not prepared me for the dreadful reality. I was taught how to kill in commando training but it still seemed like a game at which I could excel. Detached, I did well in training, keeping a cool head in the most heated of simulated situations. With secret masculine pride, I thought I would make an efficient killer. Until I tried to kill for the first time.

I was with a group of partisans in Greece. We decided to wait in ambush by the side of a narrow road between the German barracks and the nearby village where the soldiers drank. It was night. Six German infantrymen approached. They were armed but they had been drinking all evening and were off their guard. They had no idea there were partisans in the area.

We couldn't afford to attract the attention of the rest of the garrison so we had knives and garrottes. We waited in bushes as the infantrymen, talking loudly, drew nearer. Two of the soldiers were trailing behind the others. These were the targets for me and a scraggy teenager called Mikos.

The other soldiers went by. It was a bright moonlit night and I could see them clearly. Young, open-faced men. One of them was chuckling as he told a story about his sister's wedding day. (I was by that stage of my life proficient in German.)

Another was wearing steel-rimmed spectacles. My senses quivered. I could smell the alcohol on their breath as they passed by. I felt I could hear their hearts beating.

Cicadas rasped in the long grass. I waited for the two who were trailing to draw level. Slender young men with cropped blond hair. They were discussing poetry. When they were within five yards of my hiding place, one of them looked up at the stars and quoted a poem by Rilke that I knew well.

The moment they passed, Mikos ran out, wrapped his hand round the mouth of the nearest one and drew his knife across his throat. The soldier who had quoted Rilke stood stock still, open-mouthed in surprise. The partisans jumped out at the other soldiers. For a moment I was unable to move, then I too dashed on to the road. I reached the young soldier, whipping the wire garrotte up and round his neck.

Almost in slow motion, the soldier raised his arm to ward me off. I stepped behind him to tighten the garrotte as I'd done many times in training. I twisted the wooden ends. His hand was caught between the wire and his neck. I was bigger and stronger. I twisted harder, felt the wire cut deep into the hand. A terrible gurgling noise came from the soldier's throat.

I looked down into my victim's twisted face. For a long moment our eyes met. I could see the pleading and the terror. I couldn't look away as I tightened the garrotte another turn. I held him off balance, cradling his head.

The soldier was scrabbling desperately at my leg with his free hand. Blood was running in huge gouts down his trapped hand. I noticed the long fingers and wondered absurdly if the young man was a pianist as well as a lover of poetry. I was thinking that this wasn't going to work. I would never get through the hand so that the wire could do its job on the neck.

Mikos came up in front of us. He moved close and thrust his knife up beneath the ribs of the soldier. I saw the terror go from his eyes and then watched them slide back to look again at the stars – athough I knew the man was already dead, had felt his dying exhalation softly brush my cheek.

Later, I casually mentioned that I had heard the German Mikos had killed quoting poetry. Mikos, who was desperate to grow a moustache but was not yet old enough to produce more than straggly whiskers, stroked his top lip. He was illiterate but he wasn't stupid.

'Would it have been easier if he had been a peasant like me?'

And the answer was, yes, it would have been. But that was before I learned people could weep at the beauty of Beethoven's music in the evening after a day shovelling fellow human beings into ovens.

In London, on a brief leave three months later, I fell into conversation with a fellow commando in our club bar. We didn't swap names but he was an Irish fellow from south of the border. A literary man. We spent an intense couple of hours trying to get at it until he said:

'The only true account is the thing itself.'

And that was it, right there.

We were both readers and we exchanged the novels we had on us. I gave him Geoffrey Household's *Rogue Male* about an assassin stalking Hitler. He gave me James Joyce's *Ulysses*. He was big on it. He'd gone over to Paris before the war to buy a copy and smuggle it back into Ireland, where it was banned. He told me he'd packed it into a woman's sanitary towel box, guessing correctly that customs wouldn't want to search it. Claimed he learned the trick from the IRA.

His name is in the book but I don't remember it and, you know, the minute he'd gone out the door I'd forgotten what he looked like. We could have passed each other in the street many times after, or sat down opposite each other, and I wouldn't have recognized him. One of those things about the extraordinary circumstances of war.

Bob Watts put the exercise book down on the floor and walked over to his father's bookshelves. He scoured the fiction ranged in alphabetical order by author. *Ulysses* was there, though he missed it the first time. The spine was so cracked the title and author's name was almost obliterated. He took it down and opened it to the flyleaf. Underneath the flyleaf, in a clear hand, was the name of its original owner.

Watts weighed the book in his hand, smiling as he looked

at the neat signature of Sean Reilly, the ex-commando who
had been Dennis's then John Hathaway's *aide de combat*.

He resumed his seat, observing he was halfway down the
bottle of whisky. He resumed his reading.

THIRTY-EIGHT

Victor Tempest exercise book four cont.

I went into Tuscany by parachute in November 1943 to help
wreak havoc behind Kesselring's wavering line. I first made
contact with a small band of partisans near Perugia. They
were led by a middle-aged man called Franco. He had worked
in the wool mills until the dust and fibre from the machines
had ruined his lungs and forced him back to the hill village
of his birth. He was a communist whose hatred for fascism
stemmed from the time the local squads had brutally destroyed
the workers' organization at his mill.

He was a brave man but he was not a natural guerrilla
fighter. Most of his men were local teenagers who had taken
to the hills to avoid fascist call-up. If caught, they were likely
to face the firing squad. I was with them about two months,
trying to train them, going out on sorties, before disaster struck.

We had been using a barn as a refuge. One morning we
were attacked there by a well-armed squad of fascist militiamen. The partisans had little in the way of up-to-date weapons.
Their one machine gun, an updated World War One weapon,
jammed. The barn became a death trap.

Behind the barn the ground sloped up some three hundred
yards to the crest of a hill. I tried to persuade the others to
take a chance but only one of them, an intense, bony young
man called Fabbio Cortone, agreed to come with me. The two
of us made a zigzag run for it up the hill and got away. The
forty who stayed behind were all killed.

Killing had got no easier for me, but I got the job done.
And under fire, as at the barn, I found I could think and act

coolly. This was not because I felt myself in some way invulnerable, rather that I was able to disassociate myself from what was happening to me. As a survival mechanism, this took its toll. I forgot how to feel. Eventually, I even forgot about the young soldier quoting Rilke to the night sky.

Cortone, a former schoolteacher who had been in exile in the south, came from Chiusi. He told me it was the old Etruscan capital, built on a hill with a labyrinth of tunnels beneath it. He was heading that way. He guided me over the hills in that direction because it was en route to Rome. He was a communist and very cynical about Allied support for the partisans. I could say little in response because I knew from my own orders that what Cortone said was true.

I had been left in no doubt by London that the partisans were there to be exploited and ultimately sacrificed. Churchill, an admirer of Mussolini, had never forgiven him for choosing the wrong side in the war. When Italy wanted peace, Churchill wanted to make the country pay for its 'disloyalty', to earn a 'return ticket to the company of civilized nations'.

His hard line was supported by Eden at the Foreign Office. Eden loathed the Italians for their perfidy. Early on in the Allied occupation of southern Italy, the monetary exchange had been set at 400 lire to pound. This devastating devaluation ensured that the Italian economy would not recover. But then a revival would have threatened the British economy. Italian textiles would have competed with cotton from Lancashire. I felt that somehow even if Mosley hadn't triumphed his economic policies had.

The BUF had declared itself neutral during the war but many Blackshirts had chosen to fight. The first two RAF pilots to be killed in the war had been Blackshirts. The rest, including Mosley, had been interned. William Joyce, who had been kicked out of the BUF a couple of years before the war, had gone to Germany to broadcast sneering anti-British propaganda as Lord Haw-Haw.

Cortone left me to rejoin his original partisan group near Chiusi and I made my way to Rome. I stayed there doing what I could until the Allies liberated it in June. Reporting to Allied command, I was ordered to attach myself to the Sixth

South African Armoured Division right bloody sharp for a
special mission.

The Sixth was the most powerful individual formation in
Italy because rolled into it were the Guards Brigade Group
plus British, Indian, American, Polish and even Brazilian
divisions.

I was briefed on my mission by a Major Rampling. Rampling
was tough, gnarled. He sat bolt upright behind his makeshift
desk although I doubted he'd been to sleep for twenty hours.

My destination was Chiusi. My mission was not assassination, as I had assumed, but protection.

'Chiusi is currently in German hands but we are expecting
a withdrawal any day,' Rampling said in his upper-class drawl.
'Your job is to protect a fascist count – Alfonso di Bocci –
and his family from partisan reprisals when the town is liberated. He's been the mayor of the town both before and during
the German occupation. The partisans have him marked down
as a fascist and a collaborator – both of which are undoubtedly true – but we're instructed that he is needed for the first
Italian post-war government. Winnie, as you may know,
doesn't care whether he is fascist, just so long as he isn't a
Red.'

Two things occurred to me. The first, that once again
Mosley's views were widely shared amongst Britain's governing
elite. The second, that I was undoubtedly going to come into
conflict with my travelling companion, Fabbio Cortone.

Three weeks later I was with the 12th Motorized heading
for Chiusi. I'd joined the massive convoy a week earlier in
Orvieto. The rest of Di Bocci's family lived there. In heavy
rain the convoy headed north, winding its way across hills
covered with thick forest. Along a road reduced to a muddy
track we came upon the remote village of Allerona, high above
the tree line.

It seemed impossible that war should have reached so high,
yet the village was in ruins, its inhabitants already sorting
rubble for good bricks and stones for rebuilding.

We occupied Chiusi railway station below the town and
found about twenty civilians hiding in the cellars. Captain
Miller from 'A' Company went up the road past a large *albergo*

to reconnoitre the town and returned with half a dozen prisoners.

I was sitting under an olive tree smoking a roll-up when Miller came over to me and squinted down. He was a chubby man with a handlebar moustache that suggested he had joined the wrong service by mistake.

'Sorry to bother you, sir, but could you help us with some prisoners we've taken. We can't understand what they're saying.'

The other officers were wary of me but they knew what a useful linguist I'd turned out to be. I'd started the war proficient in German but by now I could get by in Russian, Polish and Czech. I towered over Miller when I put out the roll-up and got to my feet. I looked at him and he looked away. I knew why. He, like everyone else, thought I was an assassin.

The prisoners were cowed but well fed. Two, neither of them older than eighteen, were wearing snipers' camouflage jackets and the blue armbands of the Herman Göring Division. The other four were Czech deserters from the 362 Infantry Division. I spoke with them quietly for ten minutes, then went with Miller to see the commander, Major Ian Moore.

'Their officer deserted the snipers yesterday,' I reported. 'They say there are two companies of the Hermann Göring Division in the area. The Czech deserters say they saw thirty Mark IV Panzer tanks north of the town yesterday. Looks like Chiusi is more strongly defended than HQ realizes.'

Chiusi was an irritation to Moore, who was eager to be in on the main push to dislodge the German army from central and northern Italy. He shook his head vigorously.

'Tanks in such force? No, no. They aren't going to hang around to defend Chiusi. They'll be heading north to support Kesselring's Gothic Line. My intelligence has it there is only a parachute division in the town itself. I intend to have taken Chiusi and be advancing north within forty-eight hours.'

THIRTY-NINE

Victor Tempest exercise book four cont.

At five that evening 'B' Company arrived to support our advance on Chiusi. Moore frowned and tutted when I repeated to its commanding officer, Major Arlington, what the deserters had told me about the strength of opposition in the town. Moore gave his own view. Forcefully.

Arlington frowned at me.

'I tend to agree with Major Moore,' he said. 'Chiusi has no strategic value. There is nothing there to warrant defence in depth. We will proceed as planned. I understand, Captain Tempest, that you are in something of a hurry to get there. Do you wish to join us this evening?'

It was a fresh night. As 'B' Company moved cautiously up the road, I felt alert and vigorous. I could smell honeysuckle and wet earth, feel the cold wind on my face. I walked lightly, carrying a machine pistol I'd taken from one of the Czech prisoners.

When the Company was within five hundred metres of the town, Arlington sent three patrols ahead to reconnoitre. One got to within ten yards of an Etruscan arch at the entrance to the town before it was challenged by a sentry and quickly withdrew. The other two walked into German posts and came under heavy rifle and machine-gun fire. One man was killed, others wounded.

It was two in the morning. Arlington had the company dig in and rest for a couple of hours. Near dawn he invited me to lead a six-man patrol to observe enemy movements.

The mist lay heavy on the road. I sent two men ahead to act as a listening post. When the mist dissolved with the coming of the dawn, I saw the two men were completely overlooked from a church tower to the right and the tower of an old fort to the left. A couple of minutes later the Germans spotted the exposed soldiers and began rapidly firing down on them. The four of us laid down covering fire as the two men made a dash back down the slope, bullets slashing the air around them.

We withdrew. At six in the morning, I commandeered a bench in the station waiting room. I don't know how long I slept – possibly only minutes – before I was woken by the deafening roar of the Allied artillery opening up on the town. Ten minutes later there was an ear-splitting explosion and I was thrown off my rudimentary bed. The Germans were responding with concentrated Nebelwerfer and mortar fire on the station.

Nebelwerfers were always alarming. The name suggested they fired smoke mortars but the Germans often used them to fire chemical weapons. These seemed to be delivering smoke and low-grade explosives. For the moment.

I gave up any idea of sleep. I withdrew with other soldiers to the shore of Lake Chiusi and waited there, exhausted but awake, whilst the heavy brigade rolled up: the 11th South African Armoured. The tanks of the Natal Mounted Rifles clanked up the road, but within half an hour were bogged down. They were being pounded by heavy artillery, mortars and anti-tank fire – thickened by Nebelwerfers, of course. Individual tanks on reconnaissance stumbled on to well-protected anti-tank posts or were ambushed by heavily armed roving tank-hunting parties. By noon, with a hard rain falling, the South Africans had retreated.

Around eight in the evening, the Allies began pounding the town again. The heavy battery was softening it up for rifle companies from the Cape Town Highlanders. When they arrived, I was sheltering gloomily in the station waiting room. I watched through the open door as they struggled forward on foot over the soggy ground, their progress impeded by shellfire, ditches and canals.

As darkness fell, I saw them, silhouetted by the flash of shells and mortar bombs, scrambling towards the town up the steep slopes broken into terraces and dotted with twisted olive trees. My ears were ringing with the constant bombardment, my body shaking as each explosion set the earth juddering.

At one in the morning of 23rd June, so tired I was beyond

tiredness, I set off once again with 'A' company in loose formation up the winding road between the terraces. Moore had been mistaken, the deserters accurate. There were estimated to be 300 enemy infantry in town and a battalion of the Hermann Göring Division supported by artillery and tanks.

We reached the Etruscan arch without being challenged. Then the familiar pop of flares sounded and we were caught in their ghastly light. Grenades pattered in the mud. The instant the flares died, we broke for the terraces, scrambling, slipping and sliding into the rude cover of the olive trees.

For a further twenty minutes we were pinned down by the impatient stuttering of machine guns. Two soldiers coated in mud slid down in front of me and lay still. As another flare went off, they looked at me and I looked at them. The same thought occurred in the three of us. My heart leaped and I swung my machine pistol round just as the flare died away. When the next flare went off, the two Germans had gone.

As the firing eased, we lifted each other over on to the next terrace. Someone found a ladder and we swarmed up it on to the terrace above that. From here I could make out the town as a dark mass against the sky. The German fire was now going over our heads. Then it ceased.

We entered a well-tended garden. We crossed into another one, then another. Keeping low, we made our way along cobblestone paths until we were almost in the town. It was eerily quiet. There had been no flares or gunfire for fifteen minutes.

Five minutes later we reached a road that led into a small square. We gathered beside what a sign told us was a winery. Across the square was the Teatro Communale. In front of it I could make out a bulky shape, black in the blackness. Men crept to within fifteen yards of the massive machine and began to roll grenades underneath it.

They scurried back, identifying the tank as a Panzer. The grenades exploded with a dull rattle, doing no damage. Nevertheless, with a low roar, the Panzer's engine started up and it rumbled out of the square.

We took up positions around the theatre. The rest of 'A' Company joined us. We put men into two adjoining houses and the winery. A platoon headed towards the *rocca*. A group of us went into the theatre via a staircase at the rear. It brought us directly into the dress circle.

It was a solidly built theatre, with little in the way of fenestration. We could only watch the square through a couple of windows in the corridor behind the dress circle and from the ground-floor offices and foyer. I positioned myself by an upstairs window. I had a lot of ammunition for my machine pistol and half a dozen grenades on my belt. It was three a.m.

At four a.m. I heard the heavy clang of gears and the screech of metal treads in the square. The Panzer was back, milling around in front of the theatre.

A cold, misty dawn broke thirty minutes later. If everything had gone to plan, 'B' and 'C' Companies would now be in position in town.

I could see ghostly German soldiers moving through the mist in the square around the tank. I was stiff, cold and tired to the bone. The soldiers on the ground floor of the theatre and in the buildings to either side opened fire. I saw a dozen or so Germans go down. The tank's motors ground, its turret cranked round and I was looking down the muzzle of its main gun. I thought blankly that I was about to die. I tensed, shut down my emotions, focused on the black maw.

The Panzer fired a 75mm shell point-blank at the theatre.

I fell back a good five yards as part of the front wall gave way in a great billow of dust and smoke. When I scrambled to my feet again, coughing and deafened, I looked into the foyer and saw that at least six men were down. There was another roar, a deafening concussion and more of the wall fell in. The landing on which I was standing lurched away from the wall.

I scrambled off it and halfway down the stairs to the foyer. Another dozen men lay wounded or dead in the rubble and the billowing dust and smoke. Choking, I pulled my neckerchief up round my mouth.

From the foyer I could see the square fill with more tanks: Mark III, Mark IV and Mark IV Special Panzers. They opened fire and the building juddered as shell after shell punched it. The concussion deafened me.

I was scarcely able to breathe because of all the dust and

smoke billowing around me. I fired on a German paratrooper who had climbed on to the turret of a tank as it tried to batter down the theatre walls. I couldn't hear my own gun firing. When Spandau and rifle fire ripped around me, I realized that the wall I had been sheltering behind no longer existed.

I ducked back and returned fire.

At nine in the morning the theatre had somehow withstood the bombardment but there were only a handful of us left alive. We were in the Dress Circle, surrounded by rubble. I was coated in dust and dirt that filled my mouth, my nostrils, my eyes, my every pore.

Then the Germans blew a huge hole in the side wall of the stalls. Soldiers swarmed through it and up the stairs towards us. Not one of them reached the Dress Circle.

They didn't try that again but the bombardment was relentless. At ten, the roof came down on us. I watched aghast as bricks, slate, plaster and beams crashed on to our heads.

Buried but still alive, I lay blinded as well as deaf. I could smell fire. With a massive effort, I struggled free of the wreckage. I couldn't see anyone else near me. I had two grenades left in my belt. I stumbled across to the jagged hole in the wall and hurled the grenades through. I followed and fell into a side street.

I tried to suck in air but my nostrils and throat were clogged. I looked down the street. A tank blocked it. I looked the other way. A dozen infantrymen were pointing their rifles at me. I lowered my weapon to the dust.

I was hurried through the streets to a villa near the *rocca*. I stumbled often. I coughed and spat up the filth I had swallowed in the theatre. At the side entrance of the villa my identity disc was taken and I was handed a pitcher of water. I glugged it eagerly, spitting and snuffling to unclog my throat and nose. My ears rang but at least I could hear again.

I was taken into the villa and down a dimly lit corridor that led into a flagged kitchen. The only light came from a broad-shaded lamp hanging very low over a long table. It obscured the three people who were sitting on its far side. They all stood, but one of them stepped to the side. It was a beautiful, raven-haired woman.

'I am the Contessa di Bocci, Captain Tempest. Allow me to introduce my husband, Count Alfonso di Bocci.'

I nodded to the count – a ruddy-faced, stout man of middle height and middle years – and he to me. She indicated the third person.

'And this is—'

The middle-aged man standing erect on the other side of the table thrust out his hand.

'I'm—'

He still looked how I might look in twenty years' time.

'We've met, actually,' I said to Eric Knowles.

FORTY

W atts was reeling and not just from the whisky he'd consumed. Years ago he'd read his father's first book, based on his heroic journey across Europe to get back to England after escaping from a Nazi concentration camp. But he'd never heard his father talk about his wartime experiences and didn't think he'd written about them. He felt an unexpected gush of pride about a man he in many ways despised.

But more astonishing than that was the mention of Chiusi. What kind of coincidence was it that Jimmy Tingley had been in this very same town to have dealings with the same family his father had been sent to protect?

Everything is connected, he murmured to himself, dialling Tingley's mobile. It went straight to voicemail.

'Jimmy, call me when you get this or when you can. Stay safe.'

He put his phone down on the table beside the whisky bottle, now two-thirds empty, and reached for the next exercise book.

Victor Tempest exercise book five

After the introductions I was taken to a room in a cellar where I fell on the cot and slept until evening. When I woke, I drank from a pitcher of water and coughed and spat for ten minutes.

Then I stripped off my clothes and washed as best I could in a bowl of freezing water.

I ached in every bone and I was covered in cuts and welts and bruises. A suit, a clean shirt and a pair of tennis shoes had been set on a chair whilst I slept. I put them on. They weren't a bad fit, although I felt slightly ridiculous in the plimsolls. But then I felt I had gone through the looking glass. This wasn't the usual way captured enemy were treated.

Someone must have been watching me, because no sooner was I dressed than the door opened and an Italian militiaman escorted me back to the kitchen. The three were sitting at the table as if they had never moved. As if, indeed, they only came alive when I came into the room.

'My suit fits you well enough,' Knowles said. 'I thought it might be tight on you.'

They ushered me to a seat on the other side of the table and food and a glass of wine were placed before me.

'Perhaps I should explain that the count arranged that any prisoners be brought to him first. He is on good terms with the Germans and the German commander is clear-sighted enough to see that the count will have to come to an accommodation with the Allies when the occupying force withdraws, as it will inevitably do. But then to stumble upon you, Captain Tempest, the very man sent to protect him. Well . . .'

'You knew I was coming?' I said, inhaling greedily the strong smell of the food set before me.

'But, of course,' Knowles said. 'I have been negotiating for the arrival of someone like you for some time.'

'Let Captain Tempest eat,' the contessa said, laying a hand on that of Knowles for a moment.

I thanked her and picked up my fork. I was ravenously hungry. I ate quickly, washing the meal down with the rough red wine that soon had my cheeks burning and my senses swimming. The contessa had a small smile on her face as she watched me stuff my face. Her husband looked pained.

Knowles did most of the talking. He answered many of the questions I wanted to ask him. The first thing he impressed upon me was that he wasn't a collaborator.

'I'm no Lord Haw-Haw,' he said. 'I was sent to Italy before the war as the BUF's ambassador to Rome. Mussolini greeted me warmly and the state provided accommodation for me near the Spanish Steps. But I had a change of heart and became a wanderer.'

'A wanderer?' I said between mouthfuls. 'What kind of wanderer?'

'I was researching the surviving pulpits of Cimabello. You know his work?'

I shook my head. The count, obviously bored, looked at the ceiling, taking deep swallows of his drink.

'No matter. Then I came down to Chiusi to research the wall paintings in the funeral barrows scattered around the town and was trapped here when war broke out. I have been a kind of prisoner of war, under very pleasant house arrest. First of the Italians, then of the Germans, but always in the safe keeping of the count and contessa.'

I pushed my empty plate away.

'Thank you – and I apologize that I ate like a pig.'

The count grunted.

'I expect the vigorous defence of the town came as an unpleasant surprise to you,' Knowles said.

'The Germans handled their defences well,' I said evenly.

'The reason the town was defended so strenuously is Hitler's belief that there is a great tomb beneath the city. Hitler himself ordered the field commander to retain the town at whatever cost until it is located. As you possibly know, Herr Hitler is keen to acquire some of the world's most sacred relics from every corner of his everlasting Reich.'

'I'm aware he loots treasures from occupied countries for Germany.'

'Sometimes it is a little more than that. If the object is said to have magical powers . . .'

I'd read about Hitler's determination to get a Christian relic, the spear of Longinus, for its supposed magical properties. The man really was as mad as a March hare but much more dangerous.

I mentioned the Longinus spear. Knowles nodded.

'Ah yes, the Roman centurion who attended Jesus on the

cross and the spear he is said to have thrust into Christ's side. Such nonsense.'

'And you've been helping the Germans loot relics?'

Knowles looked almost comically aghast.

'I don't pilfer.'

I took another glug of wine.

'Is the tomb beneath Chiusi also nonsense?'

Knowles glanced at the count and the contessa.

'Well, that remains to be seen.'

The count broke in.

'It is the mausoleum of Porsena. You have heard of him?'

'Vaguely.'

'Porsena was Etruria's greatest king. He was buried in a golden chariot pulled by six golden horses, his weapons and his fabulous treasure piled all around him. The tomb was concealed in the centre of a labyrinth. Whoever finds his tomb will have found one of the wonders of the world. Tutankhamen's tomb would pale by comparison.'

'I wouldn't have thought, as an Italian patriot, you would want such a find to be looted by the Nazis,' I said to the count.

He glanced at Knowles, who looked down at the table, then looked back at me for a long moment.

'They must find it first.' He gestured at me. 'And time is running out.'

I nodded vaguely. A moment before, exhaustion had washed over me like a wave. The wine and fatigue had made me bleary.

'I think the major needs to rest,' the contessa said.

'My dear fellow, of course you must,' the count said. 'I'm sorry you are in a cellar but we all are until we are sure the Allied bombardment has ended. When it is over, you will, of course, have a room upstairs.'

Over the next two days I continued to feel that I had gone through the looking glass. I could see from the windows of the villa that the Allied bombardment had done severe damage to the town. Buildings were reduced to rubble, the Etruscan arch had collapsed, streets were blocked by fallen masonry. But the weather had cleared, the sun shone brightly and the shelling had stopped. The townspeople, who had been hiding in the catacombs for the duration of the attack, had returned to take up their lives as best they could. I scarcely saw a German soldier, and never in the villa, which was guarded by Italian militiamen.

I found myself a participant in a bizarre house party, hosted by the count and contessa. As prisoners of war, Knowles and I were restricted on our honour to the villa, but were free to go wherever we wanted within it. I wanted to talk to Knowles about things from before the war but I never found him on his own. On the third morning I did find the count, morosely gazing out of a window overlooking the church, a jug of wine before him. It was ten a.m.

He invited me to join him and I didn't refuse. What the hell – it was wartime. You grabbed at life wherever you could find it.

'You will protect me from the partisans when the Germans leave.' The count said it as a statement as he handed me a beaker of red wine.

'I will be here to see there is justice done, yes.'

The count looked anxiously at me. He had been a good-looking man but in his middle years he had thickened, become jowly. His eyes were red-rimmed, broken veins clustered on his cheeks and the bridge of his nose.

'Justice,' he sneered. 'Those communist bastards just want to share in what others have worked for years to build up. Nobody in this town supports them. And anyone will tell you I haven't done anything wrong. The Germans have treated us decently. More than decently.'

Franca, the contessa, entered the room. She glanced at the flask of wine but didn't acknowledge it.

'Captain Tempest. You look much better this morning.' She sat on the sofa. 'Doesn't he look better, Alfonso?'

The count's eyes flickered between his wife and me.

'He does indeed, my dear.'

I recognized jealousy in his look. The contessa was a shapely woman and her black woollen dress emphasized her breasts and hips. She had dark, melancholy eyes and thick black hair. Her lips were full, her complexion olive. I could smell her perfume but I could also feel her sexual heat, as, I imagine, did any man who came across her.

The count indicated a tapestry behind him. It showed ships at sea, merchants standing in harbour.

'My ancestor Guiseppe – the one wearing the hat – was a great adventurer. A man of vision. But there was none to follow him, He marks our family's greatest expansion. After him, we contracted, slowly at first, then at a greater pace. During the Risorgimento we alone in Chiusi sided with the Pope. We lost much of our fortune and earned the enmity of others. Thereafter, for a hundred years, we converted investments into cash.

'I tried to expand. With the fascist revolution, anything seemed possible for a man of vigour and courage.' The count scowled. 'But then the war came. And suddenly honest labour had no reward.' He looked at me, measuring me.

'In the last century my grandfather and my father both made a little money selling antiquities they uncovered on our land. You may know we live in an area rich in Etruscan remains. I did a little of it myself before the war, selling to private collectors what I was able to discover in the tunnels that run beneath this villa. For pocket money, really.' He stopped abruptly. 'You will protect us from the partisans when they come down from the mountains.'

FORTY-ONE

Victor Tempest exercise book five cont.

The Allies bypassed Chiusi, whilst keeping it hemmed in, so the bombardment stopped. Our unreal existence continued. Mostly the count loitered, seething with unfocused jealousy. Listening in doorways, whispering in quiet corners with his fascist cronies.

I'd been moved to a bedroom on the first floor. One afternoon I lay on the bed wondering if I was behaving improperly in the villa. Was I collaborating in some way? I couldn't see how. Although I might find the activities of the Italian fascists towards internal opposition before and during the war distasteful, I had been clearly instructed to safeguard the count against any post-war settling of scores.

I didn't realize I'd fallen asleep until the music woke me. I opened my eyes and thought for a moment I was out in the country. Stars in a turquoise sky shone above my head on the bed's painted canopy. After splashing my face at the sink, I went out into the corridor to locate the others. I took a wrong turn and found myself in an unfamiliar part of the house. I could not hear the music here and I was about to retrace my steps when a sliver of light shot out from beneath a door a few yards to my left.

I made my way cautiously to the door. I knew what I'd find even before I pushed it open. The soft candlelight. The black woollen dress discarded on the floor beside the man's dark trousers and jacket. The contessa, coiled on the bed with Knowles, asleep in his arms.

As I turned away from the tableau, I saw Knowles smile. He opened his eyes and looked at me, still smiling. I pulled the door closed.

The next day I found Knowles in the library. He was examining some ancient book. He looked up.

'I didn't know you were such an academic,' I said, sitting down opposite him.

'Why would you?'

'You don't remember me, do you?'

Knowles put the book down.

'Should I?'

'I briefly ran the north-west branch of the BUF in 1935.'

He narrowed his eyes.

'That's ringing a bell. A Blackburn lad?'

'Born but not bred.'

'A bobby in Brighton?'

'I am that man.'

'Well, well. Yes, I do vaguely remember. Last time I saw you was when we gave you the north-west job.'

'Last time I saw you was in a members' billiards club in Wardour Street. Meeting the manager – an Italian gangster who was later hanged for murdering a Jewish one.'

He looked sharply at me.

'I vaguely recall that club. We were trying to get the kike gangsters out of London – the small Jews. It was a Sabini brothers club. Those gangsters and the BUF had the same goals in that instance.'

'The manager had the same name as one of the Brighton Trunk Murderers. Tony Mancini.'

Knowles frowned.

'And was it him?'

'No – seemed Mancini the Brighton man had stolen his name. You know the cases?'

'Doesn't everyone of our generation?'

I sat down opposite him.

'Tell me about you and the contessa.'

'It means nothing.'

'Does Alfonso know?'

'Are you mad? He would kill anyone he thought was her lover. He has always said that and I have no reason to doubt him.'

'Why does she tolerate him?'

'She is from a poor family. He has a position and money. He gave her a life of ease. Parlaying sex for a life of ease is not unknown . . .'

'So why does she jeopardize her position by taking a lover?'

Knowles laughed ruefully.

'Alfonso's mother encourages it. Alfonso is the last of the line but he is infertile. They cannot have a child. His mother advises her to take a lover from outside the family but to tell no one.' Knowles shrugged. 'She told me.'

'Does he know he is infertile?' I said.

Knowles looked up at the ceiling.

'To the count, manliness – virility – is everything. It is the core of Italian fascism. That is why he despises me because I do not exhibit manly qualities.' He paused for a moment. 'I do not get drunk and belch in other men's faces. I do not wrestle with them after dinner. I do not go into the hills to shoot boar and birds. I am thoughtful, so I must be homosexual.'

'The perfect cover. And you are going to give the contessa a child?'

Knowles just looked at me.

That evening, after dinner, the count took me aside.

'The German commander has been ordered to pull out tonight. Kesselring has finally persuaded the High Command that redeploying the weaponry from here after an orderly retreat makes more sense than leaving it exposed whilst this futile search for a tomb goes on. They will leave the town in your hands.'

'He will disobey Hitler's direct command?'

'Hitler is already doubtless obsessed with some new nonsense his astrologers have brought to his attention, even as his thousand-year Reich crumbles around him.'

When the Germans left, Knowles left too. The count's fascist friends melted away. The count and contessa packed in preparation for their move to Rome.

'Under your escort, Major Tempest,' the count said, an ingratiating smile on his face. 'I think it advisable until feelings here have died down a little.'

I did not hide my distaste for the count. I had been in radio contact with the Allies as soon as the Germans had left. I had asked if my orders to protect the count still stood. The answer had been in the affirmative. On no account should I allow the count to be subjected to any unfavourable word or act. Investigation of his wartime activities was to be discouraged.

In the hospital I found Allied prisoners of war, captured during our failed attack on the town. They had been well looked after. I armed those who had recovered from their injuries and went to the cathedral square to announce that the Allies had formally liberated the town. Then I returned to the villa with them to await the arrival of the partisans.

Six came out of the hills the next day. Fabbio Cortone led them. When they came to the villa to arrest the count, I showed them the safe-conduct passes for the count and contessa. I insisted that they were under Allied protection. I stood firm when Cortone declared that the count had committed atrocities against the partisans during the war.

All the partisans were armed and angry. I showed no emotion even when Cortone showed me the injuries the fascists, at the count's behest, had done to two of his men. As I closed the door on them, I saw the disgust in Cortone's face. It scarcely compared with the disgust I felt for myself.

FORTY-TWO

Victor Tempest's final exercise book

I never saw Knowles again, but in 1945 I attended the Nuremberg trials. I was trying to make sense of what had happened in the war. Not the people I had killed, but the millions murdered. Nuremberg had been chosen as the venue for the trials for symbolic reasons. It was there Hitler had held his grandiose rallies; there he had passed a law stripping Jews of their German citizenship. For the same symbolic reason the RAF had pretty much demolished the medieval quarters in bombing raids. Nuremberg was war-wrecked, its citizens gaunt and exhausted.

Lord Birkett was the British black-capped judge pronouncing the death sentence on Nazi war criminals in the Palace of Justice. The last time I'd seen him, he'd been plain Norman Birkett, barrister, successfully defending Tony Mancini, aka Jack Notyre, at Lewes Crown Court against the charge of murdering his mistress, Violette Kay.

The man hanging the criminals Birkett sentenced to death was Albert Pierrepoint, the butcher from Clayton I'd met in 1935. It had taken him until 1941 to move from assistant to official executioner. He told me that when I bumped into him in a *bierkeller*. I reminded him of our last meeting, almost ten years earlier.

'I remember,' he said. 'You still a Blackshirt?'

'That was a mistake,' I said. 'We stood for order but we caused disorder.'

'Some mistakes you can recover from. I deal with people whose mistakes have consequences they can't evade.'

'When were you first in charge of the whole thing?' I asked. 'The hangings.'

'1941. Seventeenth of October. Pentonville Prison. Happy enough fellow. Last thing he said before he went through the hatch was "Cheerio".'

Pierrepoint and I sipped our beer. It was rubbish but then we'd bombed the breweries to buggery.

'I did tell him he should have had a word with my dad,' he said.

I frowned.

'You've lost me.'

'Well, I was hanging him for knifing somebody in a brawl but he also told me that, years before, he'd chopped up some lass and he'd had a bugger of a time doing it. Didn't know anything about jointing meat, you see. My dad, now, he could have jointed an elephant without breaking sweat.'

My mind reeled from more than the drink.

'What was this man's name?'

Pierrepoint thought for a moment.

'Antonio Mancini. "Baby" to his friends. Soho gangster. Knifed a thug from a rival gang. A Jewish gang. It could have gone either way – who lived, who died, I mean. It would have made no difference to me – one of them would have dangled from the end of my rope.'

'Baby Mancini.'

'Daft name for a grown man, I know.'

I nodded slowly.

'I met him once,' I said. 'Just for five minutes.'

Pierrepoint was an unnervingly placid man. He remained still, watching me, waiting for more.

'This lass,' I said. 'He killed her?'

He shook his head.

'I don't think so. Helping out his brother-in-law after the fact, apparently.' He shrugged, though he seemed to make heavy work of the gesture. 'Strange favours some folk do.'

'Who was his brother-in-law?' I said. 'It wasn't a bloke called Martin Charteris, was it?'

Pierrepoint frowned.

'No idea.'

And that should have been it with regard to the Brighton Trunk Murders and the hangings of Albert Pierrepoint and the two Tony Mancinis. But, of course, nothing ever finishes. No story is ever really done.

A year later I was back in London working for military intelligence. I bumped into Pierrepoint again. I was on my way to meet Ian Fleming – he had some girls lined up. But this bloke and his feelings for his chilly occupation fascinated me. Since I'd last seen him, he'd executed at least two hundred Nazi war criminals. Now he was back at Pentonville, hanging home-grown traitors.

Over a pint he said: 'Good job you got out of the Blackshirts when you did. I hanged two of your former comrades yesterday. Lord Haw-Haw and another bloke who'd been high up. Mosley's unofficial ambassador to Italy. Picked up in Germany.'

'Eric Knowles?' I said.

'You knew him too?'

I was remembering the time Charteris had taken me to Tony Mancini's club. As we were standing at the bar, Eric Knowles had come in and gone upstairs.

I laughed. A bleak laugh.

'Albert, as I get older I'm not sure I know anybody.'

PART FIVE
The Thing Itself

FORTY-THREE

K ate Simpson was dressed and sitting on the edge of her bed when Sarah Gilchrist walked in. She gave the police-woman a lopsided grin. The bruising round her eyes had turned yellow and the swelling on her lip had subsided a little.

'Ready?' Gilchrist said.

'You're sure about this?'

'Sure I'm sure. You did the same for me.'

'Only for a few days, though.'

Gilchrist picked up Kate's backpack from a chair.

'Stay as long as you like.'

Kate's legs trembled as she got out of bed. Although physically she was making a rapid recovery, emotionally and psychologically she was still fragile from the shock and viciousness of the attack.

What she'd actually done to defend herself was something of a blur. She remembered the man hitting her, his weight crushing her, his hand jammed between her legs. She remembered scrabbling under the pillow and grabbing the volt gun. Pressing it to his temple and pushing the button.

She couldn't face the thought of going back to her flat. Her mother had originally suggested she go up to London and stay at the family home but she had made it sound like an inconvenience. Anyway, Kate didn't want to be in the same house as her father. Plus, her mother had not bothered to get in touch since the initial offer.

Her father hadn't visited. He'd phoned, pleading pressure of work. She'd asked him what was behind the attack and he'd been evasive.

'Some business complications, that's all.'

'That's not all. That man made it very personal.'

'It will all be taken care of, darling,' he said.

She cringed at the word 'darling' coming from a man she despised.

Her father had at least taken care of her bail. She found it hard to take in the fact she had killed someone and might go to jail for it.

Gilchrist had offered the sofa bed in her new flat. This was by way of thanks for Kate putting Gilchrist up when the policewoman's flat had been torched to discourage her from investigating the Milldean Massacre. Since Kate had a crush on her, it was a no-brainer, as Simon at Southern Shores Radio was fond of saying. Kate was on sick leave from her job there and looked forward to a week or two of rest and recuperation.

Gilchrist's phone rang as they stood on the steps of the hospital.

'DI Gilchrist. Hello? Yes, ma'am. Immediately, ma'am.' She put her phone away and turned to Kate's inquiring look. 'The chief constable wants a word.'

Kate panicked.

'Are we in it?'

'Not we,' Gilchrist said. 'Me. And I've a horrible feeling I know what she wants a word about.'

Tingley slept late. After a quick breakfast he headed for the trolley car that went to the top of the nearby mountain. He walked down the Via Garibaldi, the sky a deep blue and the sun glaring on thick white walls. He was sweating again. He bought a newspaper from a kiosk and stuffed it in his jacket pocket.

The road widened as it neared the southern entrance gate and the signs to the *funivia*. He turned left immediately outside the gate and walked a couple of hundred yards uphill towards the ticket office.

When he saw the procession of slight green baskets making their way up the mountain face on a narrow black thread, he shook his head. He'd been expecting a proper cable car, with room for sixteen or so in each cage.

He bought a ticket and went to join a small queue. He watched the baskets come down. They were like birdcages with standing room for maybe three adults. Protective wiring came up to waist height. They were spaced at twenty-yard intervals on a cable loop that never stopped moving. Passengers jumped on as the cage swung round in a slow arc at ground level, the mechanic slammed the gate closed and they were on their way.

The cages looked fragile and the top of the mountain a long way away. Tingley thought he could see the cages wavering in the wind. He tidied things away in his pockets, felt the pistol fastened at the small of his back.

He clambered aboard the next cage and with a jerk it began a smooth ascent towards the mountain. Within moments Tingley was looking down at a rough scree of broken white rocks some hundred feet below.

He looked back at Gubbio falling away behind him. The plain beyond was vast, the foothills beyond that tiny. His cage brushed the tops of a clump of pine trees. Tingley smiled a hello at a couple with a little girl coming down about ten yards across from him.

He overbalanced as the cage reached the first of a series of tall metal pylons through which the cable was threaded. He grabbed for the guard rail as his cage tilted and juddered by. The sun was high in the sky, wisps of cloud hanging motionless. Tingley closed his eyes.

There was a flat concrete platform at the top, about twenty yards long. A man grabbed his cage and pushed away the safety bar so that he could drop out on to the concrete. The platform was beside a terrace café.

Tingley got a beer from the bar. He threaded his way through noisy youngsters playing table tennis, table football and video-games. He found a table with a view over a gorge and back across the Gubbio plain. Below him Gubbio seemed tiny, its red shingled roofs bright against the light green of the fertile plain.

To the side of him the mountain opened up into a series of valleys, their slopes clad in dark green firs and pines. In the cool under the umbrella Tingley looked for the glint of a scope attached to a sniper's rifle.

Three girls at the next table were discussing a boy. An old David Bowie song, *The Man Who Sold The World*, was playing on the radio. Tingley sipped his beer. It was warm. He looked over as the cages bobbed up and on to the landing stage.

He went cold inside his shirt; his mind and his heart both raced. He watched Drago Kadire drop off the cage and walk into the café.

FORTY-FOUR

'DI Gilchrist, come in.'

Sarah Gilchrist noted the formality as she stepped into the chief constable's office. Karen Hewitt usually addressed her as 'Sarah'.

'Ma'am.'

Hewitt looked at her over her glasses.

'We have a problem.'

Gilchrist said nothing.

'The weapon Miss Simpson used to defend herself is illegal in this country.'

'Yes, ma'am.'

'And I gather you have admitted that the weapon is yours.'

'I have, ma'am.'

Hewitt shook her head, her long blonde hair swaying as she did so. Her skin was pale and tired.

'You understand that when you lost your right to carry arms after the Milldean incident, those arms included the taser legally issued to British police officers.'

Gilchrist shuffled her legs.

'I do.'

'So the fact that a serving police officer in such a situation has an illegal volt gun, illegally imported . . .' Hewitt shook her head. 'For God's sake, Sarah – what were you thinking?'

Gilchrist bit back what she wanted to say. That at the time she was thinking someone had just burned down her flat and she felt her life to be in danger.

'I'm sorry, ma'am.'

'So am I, Sarah, so am I.' Hewitt looked weary. 'I think this might cost you your job.'

'It was used in self-defence—'

'I know that,' Hewitt said fiercely. Her sour breath wafted across Gilchrist. Last night's garlic and too much coffee today. 'But I need to distinguish between that fact and the fact that you, not Miss Simpson, had illegally imported this weapon.'

Gilchrist bowed her head.

'You are under immediate suspension—'

'But, ma'am, DI Williamson and I—'

'—pending a tribunal to consider your dismissal.'

Gilchrist left the office red-faced. She considered going back to tell Williamson but decided simply to go home.

Back at her flat, Kate was fast asleep on top of her bed. Gilchrist stood by the balcony looking over the square, her mobile phone in her hand. She got through to Reg Williamson on the first ring. She told him what had happened.

'I'm sorry to hear that, Sarah. Damned sorry. But, listen, we can turn this to our advantage.'

'I don't see how.'

'Take a holiday. Take a friend with you. I'd go myself but I wouldn't get the leave now you're not in the office.'

'Reg—'

'I hear Homps is very nice at this time of year.'

Tingley reached mechanically for his beer. Kadire emerged from the café carrying a coffee cup, looked around for somewhere to sit. Tingley turned his head away and watched out of the corner of his eye. Kadire found an empty table between Tingley and the cable railway and sat down, facing the platform. Tingley noted he had dispensed with his cane.

Renaldo di Bocci had told Tingley where Kadire was going to be just before he died. Tingley didn't kill Di Bocci – well, unless the shock he'd given him hustling him into the stairwell had brought upon the old criminal's heart attack.

Tingley put his glass back heavily on the table. Just do it and get out, he advised himself. Just walk over and put the silenced gun in his ear, pull the trigger and walk away. Except that there was nowhere to walk. There was no way off this mountain except by the cable car.

Then leave. Tingley got to his feet. His chair scraped loudly on the concrete floor. Kadire was sitting quite still about fifteen yards away.

Tingley didn't hurry, choosing a route as much out of

Kadire's line of vision as possible. He itched to look back but resisted the temptation. He felt sure he could feel cold eyes boring into his back.

In the café he made a pretence of looking at postcards whilst watching Kadire. He was sitting as before, except that now he was reading a newspaper, ankles crossed. According to Di Bocci, he was waiting to meet an important drug dealer.

Tingley went out of the side door of the café, skirted the edge of the terrace and watched the queue of people waiting to take the cable car back down the mountain. A basket arrived every forty-five seconds so a queue of six groups cleared in about six minutes. A fuck of a long time to be standing on the top of a mountain with a dead man slumped at a table twenty yards away.

Tingley was hidden from Kadire, but even if he abandoned his assassination of the sniper, once he stepped forward on to the platform he would be directly in front of his intended victim. Kadire had only to glance up to see him. Then all hell would break loose.

Fuck it.

Tingley had always moved deceptively fast. Liquid. Probably nobody at the tables he slid between even noticed him as he came alongside Kadire.

Kadire noticed. Tingley doubted the sniper knew who it was but he saw him jerk to see who was suddenly beside him.

Tingley had been thinking about a pay-off line but hadn't come up with anything. So he leaned down, stuffed the silenced gun in Kadire's left ear, clapped the folded newspaper to the other ear and pulled the trigger.

FORTY-FIVE

Watts was huddled over a mug of black coffee in his father's wingback when his phone rang. He recognized the number.

'Hello, Sarah.'

'I'm sorry to disturb you but I wondered how easy it would be for you to go back to France.'

'Varengeville-sur-mer?'

'No. Carcassonne.'

'Cathar country.'

'You know it?'

'I know the history books. The Templars—'

'Don't. My mind freezes when I hear that word. I used to go out with a SOCO who kept trying to force-feed me thrillers that involved the Templars.' Simpson realized she was blathering from nerves. 'I never read any, on principle . . .'

She trailed off.

'You don't like being force-fed?'

'That would be me, Bob.' She cleared her throat. 'We've located Bernie Grimes in a place near Carcassonne.'

'Bernie Grimes?' Watts thought for a moment. 'The armed robber supposed to be holed up in Milldean?'

'Maybe he can give us a way in to the Milldean Massacre. A way in to Charlie Laker and William Simpson.'

'You want me to go and see him?'

Gilchrist swallowed.

'With me.'

Watts frowned.

'I don't quite understand. Officially? How would that work for Karen Hewitt?'

Gilchrist explained her status.

'I'm sorry to hear that,' Watts said. He pondered a moment. 'What do you think we can achieve unofficially? Why would he even talk to us?'

'I haven't thought that far ahead,' Gilchrist said. 'We might need to overstep the mark.'

Watts considered. Quite aside from anything else, how would it feel to be alone with Sarah for such a length of time? Their brief passion had long faded. Hadn't it?

'What about Kate?' he said. 'Do you think we can leave her on her own?'

'She's safe enough, if that's what you mean,' Gilchrist said. 'What do you think, Bob?'

'I was thinking of Kate's emotional state rather than any immediate physical danger.'

'We could always take her with us,' Gilchrist said.

Watts thought for a few more moments.

'OK. You're on.'

In the movies, brains and blood always splatter everywhere with a head shot. But a bullet from a small calibre gun funnelled through a silencer just rattles around the brain then lodges there.

Tingley cradled Kadire's head for a moment before straightening him in his chair. He put the newspaper down on the table.

'Ciao,' he said, for anybody who might be listening, patting Kadire's shoulder for anyone who might be watching.

He walked over to join the small queue of people waiting to go back down the mountain. He shuffled forward as a couple and their two children went out on to the platform. Tingley could see Kadire now, slumped in his seat. Blood was coming out of his ear.

A fat curly-haired man in drooping jeans and a short-sleeved yellow shirt was regulating the *funivia*. Sweat glistened on his face and had begun to stain the back of his shirt.

Tingley was next but one.

He willed himself not to look back at Kadire. The man was dead and Tingley was the Invisible Man. He always had been. Nobody had seen him kill Kadire.

Another couple went on to the platform, leaving Tingley exposed at the gate. The fat man led him to a point where he was standing directly opposite Kadire. He kept his eyes lowered and for what seemed an age willed himself invisible, always expecting someone to cry out and point the finger at him.

A cage appeared over the rim of the platform. The three young girls inside were laughing. The man on the other side reached forward and unhooked the door. The cage bobbed as he slowed it down slightly with his right arm. The first girl – tall and elegant in shorts, tights and flat pumps – dropped out. The man was walking alongside to help the second girl. She jumped and stumbled slightly, but he steadied her with his right arm whilst keeping hold of the cage with his left.

The cage was between Tingley and Kadire's slumped body when the third girl jumped out. The cage jerked and continued round. The first two girls joined the third and the man on that side cracked a joke with them. They laughed, forming a group with him between Tingley and Kadire.

Within a second the cage was in front of Tingley. Gripping the iron rim, he swung himself in. The gate clanged closed behind him and with a lurch he swung towards the edge of the platform. Just before he dropped over the line, Tingley looked back. Kadire was slumped exactly as before. A waiter was ambling towards him.

Gubbio approached slowly. As the cage made its steady progression, Tingley was strung tight.

The couple in front were larking about. The man shifted his weight to frighten the girl as their cage wobbled. She gave a little scream of pleasure and fright.

The cages coming up were empty. Tingley reached the first pylon and the cage jerked. There were speakers on the pylon and a metallic voice had begun to comment on a football match. Tingley heard the sullen roar of the crowd. The girl in the cage in front shrieked again.

A large insect landed on Tingley's neck. He lightly wafted it away. Two brightly coloured birds chased each other between the pine trees below him. Tingley was acutely aware of bird songs, the faint thrum of traffic, a car changing gear. He looked across at the nearest tree, tempted to reach out and brush the branches with his open palm.

His nerves were screaming. In the bright sunlight the trees were etched sharply against the deep blue sky. He had an intense sensation of now-ness. He was pondering this when he saw Miladin Radislav coming up in a cage thirty or forty yards below him.

FORTY-SIX

Kate Simpson was sitting on Sarah Gilchrist's balcony waiting for her coffee to cool. The sun had come out between the showers but she still felt shivery. Frankly, she was terrified at the thought of going to prison for what she'd done to the man who had attacked her. And mortified that her actions had got Sarah suspended. And furious with her father for visiting this upon her. Otherwise, she was fine.

She gave a small smile and reached for her coffee. Her phone rang. Bob Watts.

'How are you coping?' he said.

'I'm trying to stay calm,' she said. She was surprised to hear the shakiness in her voice and to feel herself welling up.

'Kate, Sarah and I are going to follow up a lead in France about the Milldean Massacre. We've located Bernie Grimes. Wondered if you wanted to come along.'

'France?' Kate was surprised. 'I – I don't know. Following up leads isn't really my thing.'

'We're just a bit concerned about leaving you alone.'

Kate felt tears coming.

'I'll be fine,' she said, a little breathy. 'I'll use a kitchen knife next time.'

Watts laughed but still sounded anxious when he said: 'Are you sure?'

'I'm sure,' she said, her voice stronger, the tearful moment gone. 'But thanks for worrying about me.'

'We shouldn't be more than a couple of days,' Watts said. 'You know, having a focus might be a good idea. When are you back at Southern Shores Radio?'

'I'm not sure that provides any kind of focus.'

Watts was silent for a moment, then: 'Listen. I've got a load more files on the Brighton Trunk Murders. The files that were supposed to be destroyed in the sixties?'

Kate had done all the research into the Trunk Murder papers that had turned up some months earlier in the Royal Pavilion. She had made a radio documentary about it.

'How come?' she said.

'Long story, to do with John Hathaway's father. They've been sitting in the boot of my car. Plus I've got some more stuff of my dad's. You interested?'

'Sure. Can you get them to me?'

'I can come to Brighton tomorrow.'

Kate was conscious of her ragged breath.

'Will you do me a favour?' he continued. 'Check out particularly three people: Martin Charteris, Eric Knowles and Tony Mancini.'

'Tony Mancini is the other trunk murder – the two aren't connected.'

'I know but there's something going on between him and Charteris – and, in fact, there's another Mancini, an Antonio "Baby" Mancini, who's a real Soho gangster. He worked for the Sabini brothers.'

'I think there's stuff about him in the Brighton Tony Mancini file. The two got muddled. Who are the other two?'

'Charteris is a petty crook but maybe more. Knowles – I'm not sure what he is. But I definitely want to find out.'

Radislav was wearing dark glasses and a lime-green suit that made his skin tone even more ghastly. Even from a distance, Tingley could see that he was grinning. The gap between the cages narrowed. Radislav was standing feet apart, both hands resting lightly on the bar in front of him, and he was looking straight at Tingley. Tingley half-expected him to wave.

Before, Tingley had never felt fear. But now, this thing in his belly . . .

He tried to take a deep breath. Half made it. Radislav is not a monster, he said to himself; he is just a man.

He looked down. He was nearing the part of the descent where the cages were only about twenty feet above a rocky scree. He was approaching another pylon. Tingley noted the small platform at the top and the steel ladder going up its spine. He looked across at Radislav's grey face.

The two cages drew closer.

Radislav was almost level and staring directly at him, still smiling his skull's-head smile. Tingley heard bird song, the girl's shrieks, the dislocated voice of the radio commentator coming from above and below him. Radislav was near enough for Tingley to see the grey at his temples, the gold screw in the hinge of his sunglasses, his right hand moving inside his jacket.

Radislav was reaching for a gun.

Tingley reached behind him to take his own gun from its holster. He gauged the distance between the two cages and kept his eyes on Radislav's jacket.

His cage was swaying. Radislav was fumbling, getting a grip on something. Then the hand withdrew. First, the cuff of his cream shirt with the glitter of its cufflink in the sunshine. The thin, pale wrist. The hand.

Tingley couldn't seem to release his gun from its holster. He was totally off balance, the cage swaying alarmingly. His eyes saw a drunken kaleidoscope of rock, trees, shingle roof and blue sky. He fell to the floor of his cage.

He lay curled there for what seemed an age but was only a few moments. He couldn't quite believe he'd been shot but the massive punch in his chest, the blood he could feel soaking him . . .

No second shot came. Tingley straightened and looked over his shoulder. Radislav's cage was about five yards above him and moving away. Radislav had his back to Tingley, facing up the mountain. His left elbow was raised. Tingley saw a plume of smoke and smelled the acrid smell of freshly burning tobacco.

Then a siren sounded and the long necklace of cages jerked to a halt.

FORTY-SEVEN

Kate Simpson immediately went on line to look up the Soho gangster Tony Mancini. In *The Times* archive she found some background on him in the reports of his trial and ultimate execution.

On 1st May 1941 he had killed Harry 'Little Hubby' Distleman at a Wardour Street club and wounded Edward Fletcher. There had been a disturbance, then the police had found Distleman dead in the club's doorway with a wound five inches deep in his left shoulder. Fletcher had a stab wound to his wrist.

There were two clubs on the premises. Mancini was manager of one members' club and a member of the other, on the floor above. After a fight on 20th April in the members' club, Distleman had been barred. He had threatened Mancini and the owner. Mancini claimed he had bought a double-edged seven-inch blade for self-protection.

At three a.m. on 1st May there was a disturbance in the first-floor club. When it was over, Mancini went up to survey the damage. On the stairs he heard a voice behind him saying: 'Here's Baby, let's knife him.'

Mancini ran upstairs. Distleman followed and there was a 'general fight' using chairs, billiard balls and cues. Mancini claimed Distleman attacked him from behind with a chair and a penknife and he responded by striking out wildly with the knife in his pocket, not knowing who he'd hit. He didn't recall wounding Fletcher.

Distleman was a thug too, Kate had no doubt. He had been convicted of assault six times. He had a billiard ball in his pocket and attacked Mancini from behind.

She went to Wikipedia for the other Tony Mancini, the Trunk Murderer who'd got off murdering his mistress. According to his entry, he'd moved down to Brighton after being brutally attacked whilst in a Soho gang. He had a reputation for brutality – once forcing someone's hand into a meat grinder – and had been attacked by razor-wielding rival gangsters on Brighton prom.

She sat back. That didn't square with anything she'd come across about the Brighton Tony Mancini. But the meat grinder thing sounded like just the thing a real Soho gangster like Baby Mancini might do.

In the National Archives she found Baby Mancini born in Holborn in 1902. He had a sister, Maria. Kate yawned.

The siren and the stalled cages could mean only one thing: Kadire's body had been discovered. Tingley didn't hesitate. He shot Radislav in the back of the head. Radislav slumped forward and Tingley spread four more shots across his back. He didn't remember the make of the bullets he was using but he knew they expanded on impact. If the first bullet didn't kill Radislav – and Tingley couldn't see how it could fail to do so – then the body shots would destroy pretty much all his internal organs.

Hugging his own wound, he climbed out of his cage, dangled below it for a moment, then dropped down on to the scree. He let out a cry when he landed and tumbled down head over heels. He fetched up, scratched and bleeding, at the base of a tree.

He hobbled off at a diagonal, sliding down the scree, keeping an eye on the buildings at the base of the *funivia*. He assumed the police had been called and only once they had arrived would the cages move again.

Within five minutes he was round the side of the mountain and out of sight of the *funivia* buildings. He had glanced back only once to see Radislav's corpse, half-hanging over the front of his cage.

He buried his gun behind some bushes and continued down towards a dirt road. He started to shake some twenty yards from the bottom. He gulped down air.

He jumped down on to the dirt road, rubbery-legged. His knees caved in. He straightened and hurried along the road, trailing blood, ignoring someone from a house opposite who called something after him.

As he hurried into town, face burning, he was sure all eyes were on him. He could hear the police sirens as he located his car and drove out of Gubbio.

Reg Williamson gazed blankly at the files scattered over Sarah Gilchrist's desk. His thoughts were on Angela, his wife. Married thirty years. He'd never so much as looked at another woman. As it should be, but in the police that was quite something.

She'd been in decline ever since their son had killed himself. Williamson still loved her to bits but got precious little back.

He sighed and picked up a file at random. He wanted to nail Charlie Laker. He hoped Bernie Grimes would provide the testimony that would make it possible. But whilst Sarah and Bob Watts were going after Grimes, Williamson intended to trawl through the files relating to the Milldean Massacre to see if anything popped up that they'd missed before.

This file had his report about the murder of Finch, the policeman involved in the raid who had been thrown off Beachy Head in a roll of carpet by 'Persons Unknown'. Next in the file was Gilchrist's report of the interview with Lesley White, the posh woman who lived in the converted lighthouse on the clifftop where Finch had been heaved over into the sea.

She'd known nothing about the killing of Finch but she'd banged on about her cat going missing. Bizarrely, this had turned out to be significant when its remains were found in a burned-out car on Ditchling Beacon. Typical of police work: most of the time you had no bloody idea what was important and what wasn't.

Williamson mouthed her name. Lesley White. White in name, white in nature. He remembered her looking at him with distaste as he sweated on her white sofa. She checked her white carpet for his footmarks.

He hadn't taken to her either. Snooty. One of the 'I'm Better Than You But I Want Your Protection' brigade.

That wasn't pricking at him. He rubbed his chin. But something was.

He rolled his chair a yard or so to his computer and pecked the keys.

Why did her name sound odd, despite her white carpeting and furniture?

He brought up Sarah's account of a more recent interview with the same woman. This was about Elaine Trumpler, a girl murdered in the sixties whose skeletal remains had been found under the West Pier. She'd been a girlfriend of the gangster John Hathaway. Laker was in the frame for that too. White had been interviewed because Trumpler had been her flatmate at university.

Williamson cleared his throat. There it was. In the very first line: 'Interview with Claire Mellon, The Lighthouse, Beachy Head.' Suddenly Lesley White had changed into Claire Mellon.

FORTY-EIGHT

Sarah Gilchrist and Bob Watts walked along the towpath of the Canal du Midi past barges bigger than any Gilchrist had ever seen in Britain. She'd once been persuaded to go on a barging weekend with a boyfriend and it had been one of the longest two days of her life. Her idea of hell – a tall woman trapped on a narrow boat going at five miles an hour with someone she realizes she doesn't like very much.

She looked across the width of the canal and down its length, straight to the horizon. The rows of tall plane trees on each bank narrowed to a point on the horizon like an art class exercise in perspective.

'What's the plan?' she said as she kept pace with Watts's long stride.

'Lunch, I'd say. This place on the right is supposed to be good.'

They'd flown from Gatwick to Toulouse the previous afternoon and hired a car to drive over to Homps. She felt awkward and had done so since they'd met at the airport to take the budget flight. This would be the longest time they had spent together and, given their history, it wasn't the easiest situation. Especially as a part of her felt rejected that he had been trying to get back with his wife.

Not that she wanted him, she told herself repeatedly; it was simply a pride thing.

Both tall, they had been scrunched up on the plane, their knees tucked under their chins. It hadn't been much better in the car they had rented, the smallest in the rental agency's fleet but the largest they had available at short notice.

Gilchrist had driven the thirty kilometres to the inn they'd booked just outside Homps. Conversation had been desultory.

'Jancis Robinson is supposed to have a place round here,' Watts said.

'Jancis—?'

'The wine writer?' he said.

Gilchrist liked wine but didn't know anything about it.

'How do you want to play this?' she said.

'I want you to take the lead,' Watts said.

'He's going to be armed, you know,' Gilchrist said.

'Depends where we find him,' Watts said. 'We find his house but we don't necessarily go there.'

'Wait for the cocktail hour, you mean?' Gilchrist said.

'Or the morning trip to the *boulangerie*,' Watts said.

'My French isn't great,' Gilchrist said. 'The where?'

'To pick up his French stick,' Watts said.

They'd scouted around, then Watts had insisted he go off alone to 'do a bit of business'. Gilchrist had bridled at this, which is perhaps why they'd slept in separate bedrooms. Any other notion hadn't seemed to come up. Gilchrist had been cross but she was curious about Watts's reasons for not bringing it up.

The restaurant on the right was set back about twenty yards from the canal bank. A brightly lacquered barge was moored on the water directly in front of it. Gilchrist saw Watts pause as they passed it and give it the once-over.

There were wooden tables and chairs laid out in a courtyard, then a rustic-looking two-storey restaurant with a wall of glass facing out on to the canal.

The entrance was at the side and when they walked in they saw that it was in fact only one storey, with a very high, oak-raftered roof. The restaurant was half full. They were seated at a table by the large window. They could see both the restaurant and the courtyard.

Gilchrist sensed Watts's awkwardness. He ordered a carafe of wine.

'We've got to be alert,' she said.

Watts looked at her intently.

'You're thinking he might come in here?'

'Aren't you?'

'Well,' he said, looking at the white tablecloths and the silver cutlery on each table. 'This might be a bit posh for him. There's a pizza place in town that'll be more his style. We can relax and enjoy the Languedoc. Do you know about the Cathars?'

Gilchrist punched his arm.

'Don't start.'

He rubbed his arm.

'You pack a punch.'

'That'll teach you to go off on secretive missions leaving me to tend hearth and home.'

'They also serve who only stand and wait.'

He put his hands up quickly in a pacifying gesture.

'You'll see why I went off alone.'

He smiled at her, almost shyly, and they looked at each other, then both looked down. She found herself thinking that Watts's voice when it was low was immensely seductive, as she vaguely recalled from their drunken first night.

Bernie Grimes walked in as they were sharing a cassoulet and Gilchrist was feeling flushed from the wine. She flicked a glance, then looked back at Watts and reached out to take his hand as Grimes scanned the room.

Watts, surprised, started to withdraw his hand but she squeezed tightly whilst giving him her best approximation of a lingering look.

He got the message. He leaned towards her.

'Alone?' he murmured.

She gave him a brilliant smile and nodded slightly.

'OK, then,' he said.

She laughed as if he'd said something hilarious. Grimes was being seated at the table for two directly behind Watts.

Gilchrist had been expecting bling. But Grimes was wearing a conservative suit with a crisp white shirt open at the neck. Admittedly, three buttons were open to show off his tanned chest but there was no gold chain round his neck. He was trim and would have looked like a lawyer or accountant on holiday except for his face.

Not his face per se. His face was fine – regular features, neat haircut. His eyes and the mouth were the giveaway. Gilchrist could only flick quick glances because Grimes's eyes were roving, but she could see how cold those eyes were, how tight the mouth. This man chilled her.

She leaned closer to Watts, who also leaned in. She could smell the wine on his breath.

'I used to think that stuff about killers having cold eyes was writers' rubbish,' she said. 'You know – poetic licence. Eyes are muscles, right? They can't possibly show emotion or killer instinct or anything.'

'But then you started seeing killers' eyes. Gary Parker maybe?'

She glanced over Watts's wide shoulder to see if Grimes was listening. She'd bet the house he would know the name Parker. Grimes was looking at the menu.

Watts said: 'The first time I looked into your eyes, I remember thinking that you would have trouble with the tough guys.'

She frowned, her guard rising.

'Why?'

'Because,' he said, his voice falling to a whisper, 'you can't disguise your essential softness.' She started to jerk her hand away. He held on to it. 'That wasn't meant as an insult,' he almost hissed. 'Your eyes reveal your emotions. That's a good thing.'

They ate in silence for the next ten minutes. Grimes ordered only a main course and was quickly tucking into it.

Gilchrist could tell by the set of his shoulders that Watts was impatient to turn round but knew better than to do so. Slightly wine-fogged, she was thinking about what he had said about her eyes. He was right, of course, but she wasn't going to admit it.

She also wasn't any clearer about what they were going to

achieve here. Bernie Grimes was a tough cookie. He wasn't going to fold when confronted. She looked again at Watts. He sipped his wine.

Grimes was a smoker. Even in France, the non-smoking rules applied. After his main course, whilst Gilchrist and Watts were lingering over their coffee, he went out into the courtyard to light up a fag.

Gilchrist and Watts watched him wander down to the canal, trailing smoke behind him. Gilchrist looked at Watts.

'And?'

FORTY-NINE

Tingley was being sick on the side of the road. Bent double, trying to expel the thing chewing his insides. Except now he didn't know whether it was the serpent or Radislav's bullet that was killing him.

He'd used the medical kit to try to staunch the blood and a couple of shirts as wads but he couldn't get the bullet out. He was dripping sweat and blood, and his mind was swirling in and out of reality.

When he had finished vomiting, he slumped into the passenger seat of his car and wiped his mouth with a tissue. He was exhausted.

He blearily wondered what to do. He knew he had to make it right with the Di Bocci family in Orvieto for what had happened with their cousin in Chiusi. Then what? He closed his eyes, just for a moment.

The wind tugged at Charlie Laker's jacket as he waited for Claire Mellon to open her door. He needed to be out of sight for a bit and nobody knew of his relationship with her. Nobody alive, anyway.

Relationship was too strong a word, but what else did you call something that had continued, off and on, for forty years? Admittedly, more off than on, but even after all these years, and with all the women he could have, he still got a thrill doing what he did to her.

Abuse her, that is. Her posture, her stupid splay-footed dancer's walk, her whole fey manner had infuriated him from the first time he'd met her. That was only a few hours after he'd shot Elaine Trumpler, John Hathaway's girlfriend, in the face. That was on the orders of Hathaway's father, Dennis, although he'd fucked her earlier off his own bat.

Claire Mellon had been in Elaine's flat when he'd gone round to clear it out. She was Elaine's flatmate. Mellon cowering against the wall had brought out the worst in him. It wasn't right and she didn't deserve it, but a few slaps and she'd done anything he wanted. Seemed to get off on him treating her rough.

It had been a revelation to him, both about himself and about posh totty. He'd discovered two things. He liked being sadistic and posh totty, when it came down to it, were skanks.

They'd seen each other regularly for a bit after Trumpler had apparently disappeared. Gone travelling was the official view. If Mellon thought otherwise, she never said.

Laker soon tired of her, packed her off and went back to Dawn. He never raised a finger to Dawn. From time to time, though, over the years, he saw Mellon. Same old, same old. She told him once he'd ruined her for other men.

'I give a fuck?' he said.

Mellon's house had always been available to him, as had she. He'd been staying with her when Finch went off the cliff. In fact, he was sitting in the back of the car when his men did it. He didn't know her cat had jumped in the boot. Bloody thing had been following him everywhere.

He had one of Trumpler's diaries from the flat clearance. Usual teenage girl drivel, but he'd hung on to it in case there was some way he could use it against John Hathaway. He'd given it to Mellon to give to the police, to help them get John Hathaway. She didn't ask why. He couldn't think of the last time she'd asked anything. Just let him in whenever he turned up, let him do what he wanted, if he wanted. Waved him goodbye when it was time to go.

The door opened. What was that look that crossed her face

when she saw him standing there? Fuck if he knew. Fuck if
he cared.

Five miles an hour now seemed pretty fast. The lock was still
half a mile away but Gilchrist could see the boats backed up,
waiting to get into it. The Canal du Midi connected the Atlantic
with the Mediterranean. These long, straight stretches went
150 miles from ocean to sea.

Here the sun glittered through the dense foliage.

She was aware how nervous her hand was on the tiller, how
sluggish the boat was at doing anything but going ahead in a
steady, straight line.

Watts was down the hatch with Grimes. In the restaurant
he'd sloughed money on to their table and that of Grimes,
then he and Gilchrist had followed Grimes out. They'd snug-
gled up together and cosied down to the canal side. Grimes,
head back, drawing fiercely on a cigarette, had glanced their
way as they'd passed him.

They'd separated and turned.

'My God!' Watts had exclaimed. 'Bernie!'

Grimes had started to turn but Watts's hug was fierce.

'Wow!' Gilchrist had said, also moving in to embrace him.
'Walk with us if you want to walk again,' she had whispered
in his ear as she nuzzled his head.

Grimes had struggled but the two of them had virtually
carried him on board the barge Watts had hired the previous
day. Watts punched him in the kidney and hurled him down
the stairs whilst Gilchrist took the tiller, cursing the mention
she had made to Watts of that long-ago barge trip.

With trepidation, Gilchrist now steered the barge over to
the bank. It was sluggish at shifting direction but she cut the
engine at pretty much the right moment. She really needed
Watts to tether it but she managed with a bit of a hop and a
skip.

The barge was on the opposite side to the towpath where
a group of cyclists suddenly whizzed by. There was the odd
walker. A woman waved at her. She waved back.

Once she was sure the boat was securely moored, she went

down the stairs. She was surprised to see Watts and Grimes sitting side by side on a sofa bench.

'So who the fuck is she?' Grimes said, gesturing at Gilchrist.

'A colleague,' Watts said. 'All that matters is that she knows who you are.'

'You want anything from me, you better give me names.'

'Frankly,' Watts said, 'names are the least of your worries.'

'Oh yeah? Why's that?'

Gilchrist watched Watts lean against Grimes. Watts really was a big man.

'Because you're stuck on a barge with me.' Watts brought his hand up and gripped Grimes's face. Hard. 'And I'm at the end of my tether.'

Grimes tried to jerk his head away but Watts held firm. They were too close to each other for Grimes to do anything with his hands. Gilchrist knew Watts was digging his finger and his thumb into the nerves at the hinge of the jaw. It would hurt like hell.

Watts released Grimes. Grimes worked his jaw for a moment, giving Watts an intense look.

'What the fuck has your state of mind got to do with me?' he said through gritted teeth.

Gilchrist didn't see Watts do anything but Grimes grunted and doubled over. Watts grabbed him by the scruff of the neck and jerked him upright.

'OK,' Watts said. 'I know you're a tough guy with a sawn-off in your hands but you don't have one here.'

'What do you want with me?' Grimes rasped.

'I want you to tell me about your relationship with Charlie Laker. I want you to tell me about your relationship with William Simpson. I want you to tell me everything you know about the house in Milldean where police officers shot and killed four people in their search for you.'

Grimes tilted his head to look at Watts.

'Why the fuck should I tell you anything?'

'Because otherwise we'll take you back to England and leave you flopping like a fish on Dover dock so the police can pick you up for all the lousy things you need to be punished for. And if we do that, you won't be seeing French sunshine ever again.'

'I was nowhere near that house,' Grimes said. He looked from one to the other of them. 'Who are you with?'

'We're on our own,' Watts said. 'We just want to see justice done.'

'Sure,' Grimes said. 'I hear that every day.'

He looked back at Gilchrist. His eyes widened.

'Wait a minute – I recognize you from a photo in one of the English papers. Startled look on your face, hugging a bath towel to you – jugs spilling out. Those paparazzi are the pits, aren't they? You *are* a bloody copper – which makes this very dodgy for you.'

He leaned away from Watts to scrutinize him.

'So, if I had to guess, you're going to be Bob Watts, disgraced chief constable. This screws you too.'

He started to get up. Watts restrained him with an arm across his chest.

Gilchrist leaned forward.

'Your daughter tells me you'll make sure her attackers suffer.'

'What's my daughter got to do with anything?'

'Everything is connected,' Watts said. 'Surely you know that?'

Grimes looked from one to the other of them. Gilchrist couldn't decipher the look on his face. Shifty, certainly; calculating too. But calculating what?

'How do you know Charlie Laker?' Watts said.

Grimes was wary now.

'Who said I do?'

'My intuition tells me.'

'I don't have to say anything to you two.'

'This woman saved your daughter's life.'

Gilchrist bowed her head. Grimes didn't even look her way.

'And she thinks she can trade on that?'

'Depends what kind of a father you are.'

'I'm seeing them right, believe me.'

FIFTY

When Tingley woke, his head and his left hand throbbed. He looked at his hand. It was swollen to about twice its usual size and was coloured purple-red. Those ant bites. He looked down at the shirt wadded at his stomach. It was soaked in blood but he sensed that the bleeding had stopped.

He opened the glove compartment and took out his medical kit, dosed himself with antihistamine for his hand. He slid across to the driving seat and turned the engine on. He set off for Orvieto.

Williamson didn't really know why he had a bee in his bonnet about Lesley White's two names. He checked and cross-checked anyway, following his own rule that coppers never knew what was going to be important and what wasn't.

After half an hour it looked as if Lesley White was simply her professional name. Punctilious as ever, he did one final check. He trawled the Land Registry for ownership of her house.

He sat back. He was having a Jeremy Kyle moment.

When Williamson was not working mornings, he would sometimes watch *The Jeremy Kyle Show* with Angela. She'd get cross at him shouting at the morons on the programme washing their shabby laundry in public. At some point, looking at DNA results to decide who was telling the truth about fidelity or parenthood or theft or whatever, Kyle would say: 'Well, well, well.'

'Well, well, well.'

The previous registered owner of the lighthouse, although only for a matter of days, was a certain Charles Laker.

He was pondering this when his phone rang.

He reached for it as Chief Constable Karen Hewitt tapped on the open door and stepped into the room. Williamson left the phone and started to get to his feet.

'Ma'am . . .?'

'Don't – don't get up, Reg.'

She came and stood in front of his desk. Williamson noticed her hands were clasped so tightly in front of her they were entirely bloodless.

'Reg, we've had a call. I thought I should tell you myself.'

'Ma'am?' Williamson said, his eyes fixed now on her scarlet mouth, his heart in free fall.

'It's about your wife.'

The phone rang on.

'Have you got kids?' Grimes said to Gilchrist. He sneered. 'No, you look like you'd break some guy's balls before you'd let him fuck you. So how could you have?'

Before Gilchrist could respond, Watts had backhanded Grimes so hard he fell off the sofa and actually skidded across the floor.

Rubbing his face, he looked at Watts with glazed eyes.

'Forgot – you've been up there, haven't you?'

Gilchrist moved to block Watts.

'I can defend myself,' she said, quietly but fiercely. She looked down at Grimes. 'Try acting like an adult for the first time in your miserable life. Try doing the right thing for the first time. Morons like you use "family" as some kind of badge of honour – as if there was anything impressive about you having sperm. Getting a woman pregnant doesn't make you a man, you moron – any idiot can do that. And they do. Standing by the child and bringing her up right makes you a man. And on that count you're a miserable failure.'

'I keep them,' he mumbled, still rubbing his face.

'In Milldean?' Gilchrist laughed. 'The scummiest place in Brighton? Congratulations.'

Grimes looked up at Watts.

'You going to let me get up?'

'When you've apologized,' Watts said.

'Leave it,' Gilchrist hissed at him. She didn't know how she felt about Watts coming to her rescue. First, because as a general rule she didn't need anyone to rescue her. Second, because, even when she did, Watts, who had rejected her, wouldn't be her first choice. Unexpectedly, she smiled to herself. Not that she had a first choice among older men outside of George Clooney.

'I'm so sorry, Reg,' Karen Hewitt said.

Williamson nodded and glanced towards the phone. All the time she was telling him the ruddy daft, fucking devastating thing Angela had done, it had rung and stopped, rung and stopped.

'I need to take this call,' he said.

Hewitt shook her head.

'No, you don't. You need to go home.'

'What's at home now?' he said, picking up the phone. 'DI Williamson.'

'Reg, it's DS Fairley down at Newhaven. The customs boys have a truck here looks a bit dodgy.'

'And that's news?'

'The truck belongs to one of Charlie Laker's companies. We know Brighton division has an interest in him.'

Williamson was blinking, conscious of Karen Hewitt standing in front of his desk, staring down at him. He looked at her. She looked like shit these days. He'd always been impressed that, despite the pressures of the job, she used to look glamorous as assistant chief constable. Her long blonde hair, her care over how she presented herself.

But since she'd become chief constable, all that had gone to pot. Her long hair was lank, framing a tired, narrow face. Her make-up was caked on dead skin. She seemed to have lost weight but not necessarily in the right places. She suddenly looked old.

'Laker. Yes.'

He heaved himself up from behind his desk, keeping the phone at his ear.

'I'm on my way.'

Karen Hewitt sighed.

'At least take a bloody driver,' she said. 'And that's an order.'

FIFTY-ONE

Maria di Bocci was leaning over Jimmy Tingley, enveloping him in her heady perfume. He was lying in bed, a drip attached to one arm, blankets pulled up to his chest. He closed his eyes for a moment, but when he opened them she was still there. She smiled.

'What happened?' he croaked.

She shrugged, incomprehension on her face. He closed his eyes again.

The next time he woke, Guiseppe di Bocci was standing by the bed, a solemn look on his face.

'We found you in your car in the square outside the hotel. You were unconscious. We brought you in and sent for our doctor.'

'Why?' Tingley said. He felt himself drifting away.

Di Bocci looked puzzled.

'You were ill. You have been shot.'

Tingley focused again.

'Your uncle . . .'

'Betrayed the family.'

'I didn't kill him.'

'We know. The doctor has given you morphine. Sleep now. We will talk tomorrow.'

Williamson sat in the back of the patrol car, thinking about Angela leaving him alone forever. Thinking about how she had brought herself to commit her suicidal act.

The Downs glowered down on him. The driver, a nice enough young copper, kept glancing in the rear-view mirror with the idea of starting a conversation. Williamson wasn't up for that so he kept his face sour – not hard to do as he got older – and turned to the window. The car reached Newhaven in twenty minutes, the orange lights of the decaying town looming abruptly out of the pitch dark of the Downs.

At the lorry park the lights were cold white. Williamson thanked his driver and struggled out of a back seat not designed for a man with a belly. He made up for that by striding with great purpose to the Newhaven police and customs officers milling around a container truck.

Introductions made, they looked at him and up at the rear door of the vehicle. He looked at the rear door and back at them. He nodded.

Kate Simpson rubbed her eyes and walked away from her laptop. She'd read Victor Tempest's notebooks and immediately set about trying to discover the identity of Tony 'Baby' Mancini's brother-in-law. She thought she knew but she wanted to be sure.

She was working on the assumption that Baby Mancini was the Mancini she had found in the archive who was born in Holborn in 1902 and that his sister was called Maria. However, she could find no wedding certificate for a Maria Mancini anywhere in Britain.

She'd found out more about Martin Charteris from police reports of a couple of trials for muggings – or possibly a 1930s form of cottaging? – in London. Nothing at all had come up about Eric Knowles.

She wandered over to the Brighton Trunk Murder files Watts had left with her. She had felt overwhelmed by them when she first saw them. She was excited by the treasure trove of documents but there were so many of them.

She dug through to find the file marked: 'Sightings of man with trunk'. Some of the witness statements in the folder she'd seen before. Man coming in from Worthing taking up room on a crowded train with a trunk on the seat beside him. Porter at London Bridge lugging a surly man's trunk with something sliding around inside. A statement from a couple who'd seen two men struggling to get a trunk out of the boot of a car on the road by the racecourse on Derby Day.

She remembered that last sighting from the files that had been discovered in the Royal Pavilion. When the men saw they were being observed, they pushed the trunk back in the boot and drove off. The couple had taken down the registration number. When the police had spoken to the – unnamed – owner, he said his car had been out of his possession at that time. There was nothing else in that file.

Here, there was a second sheet. On it a policeman had handwritten a note that the car had been traced to its owner, who had reported the car stolen a couple of days earlier. The owner lived in Strawberry Hill, Twickenham, London. The note gave the man's name. Bingo.

Jimmy Tingley surfaced and this time stayed afloat. He looked up at the painted canopy above his bed; glanced down at his arm where not one but two needles were attached to tubes leading to drips. One, he knew, was saline, the other morphine. Maria was sitting beside the bed watching him. She became aware of his stare and looked his way.

'Stomach cancer,' he said. 'I worry I have stomach cancer. Inoperable.' He looked down his body. 'But now my insides are really messed up.'

She shook her head, not understanding. He smiled at her.

'It's OK. I was saying it to me, not you.'

FIFTY-TWO

'About bloody time,' Charlie Laker said as he swung open the door of the converted lighthouse.

His mouth fell open when he saw who was standing in the doorway but he recovered quickly.

'DI Williamson, isn't it? I'm guessing you're not here with my pizza?'

Williamson pushed him in the chest. As Laker fell back, Williamson barged into the room and slammed the door behind him. The woman – Lesley White/Clare Mellon – was sprawled on her white sofa, naked from the waist down, her legs akimbo.

She looked up at Williamson, eyes glazed, a bruise on her

cheek. Williamson saw the white powder on the table, a flake of it beneath Laker's nose.

'Hey, fat man, fuck you and your family.' Laker's fists were going up. 'Are you mental? Laying your hands on me—'

Williamson swept the cosh out of his pocket and brought it down on Laker's collarbone. He heard more than felt it snap.

Laker howled and sagged to one side, his right hand reaching weakly up. Williamson stepped forward and pushed him in the chest again. This time Laker went down, screaming as his shoulder hit the wooden floor.

The woman on the sofa hadn't moved. Williamson caught a breath.

'Hello Lesley – or Claire – which is it?' Williamson shrugged. 'Doesn't matter. I came to question you about your relationship with Charlie Laker and to ascertain his current whereabouts. Looks like I can skip down quite a bit.'

Laker was groaning, gripping his shoulder. Williamson kicked him and got another cry.

'I've had a hell of a day, Charlie, a hell of a day. Quite aside from anything else, I've been wondering could I have done things differently, done things better? So if I'm a bit tetchy, blame it on the fact there's a lot gone on today. Oh, and I've just been at Newhaven with the customs boys, opening one of your containers bound for Dieppe. Expecting, you know, rotten meat or some other scummy thing you were intending to offload on our European Community friends. Know what we found?'

Laker moaned, hugging himself.

'You broke my collar bone – I can't fucking believe it.'

'I'm going to do worse than that,' Williamson said, his belly wobbling as he raised the sap.

Laker had taken beatings before. Dennis Hathaway had beaten the shit out of him when he'd discovered Laker had made his daughter, Dawn, pregnant. The Mexican in prison who'd sliced his face had damned near punched a hole in him first. But all that had been a while ago.

This cop was old school. He knew how to lay it on with minimum effort. A flick of the wrist rather than putting the arm and shoulder into it. He knew where to hit, too. He could do this all day and not break a sweat, despite his weight.

As Laker thought this, Williamson brought the sap down on his elbow. Laker roared. He'd never espoused the idea that keeping shtum when you were taking a beating showed what a tough guy you were. Screaming your nuts off frankly made it more bearable. That way he could take it and survive – and then he'd see about this fat fuck.

'I'll beat you to death, you don't talk to me,' Williamson said. 'Then I'll throw you out of the window and say it was hara-kiri. Think anyone will give a shit?'

The rage was on Williamson all right. He wanted to kill Laker. Williamson's life had effectively ended when his son had killed himself and Angela had blamed him. Made his life unbearable, in fact. He loved his wife and he lived in misery because he knew he could never leave her.

Instead, she'd now left him. Forever. Taken their car with her. No note. Just their car – and her – smashed to smithereens on the beach below Beachy Head. God. Yeah, God had a lot to fucking answer for.

Williamson looked at Laker and the gangster saw it in his eyes.

'Do you know the filth I've waded through these last months,' Williamson said, 'because of your sick ambitions?'

Laker ducked his head and cried out again as his collar bone shifted.

'Do you know what we found in the back of your container? Do you?'

'I don't know what you're talking about,' Laker gasped.

Williamson bent and hit him on the knee joint. It wasn't a good strike but Laker grunted. Williamson turned to the woman on the sofa, who was blearily trying to sit up.

'Five young girls we found,' Williamson said. 'Trussed like pigs, lying in their own piss and worse, scared out of their wits. Snatched off the street in Milldean.' He turned back to Laker. 'That's what we found in your container. Headed where, Mr Laker, sir?'

FIFTY-THREE

aker believed Williamson was going to kill him. His bowels spasmed. Williamson seemed to guess. He leaned over him.

'Scared, Charlie? You ought to be. Even if I don't kill you, I can guarantee you'll be shitting in a bag for the rest of your life.'

Laker's face burned. His breath was coming in laboured puffs. God, his collar bone hurt. His right arm was useless from the blow to the elbow. He was finding it hard to think straight as the pain washed over him. He'd done some lousy things in his life but did he want to go down for doing this stupid fucking favour for Bernie Grimes?

'Let me make a phone call,' he gasped.

'Fuck that.'

'No, really. To stop something.'

'Stop what?'

'There are supposed to be ten.'

'Some slimy Sultan's special order? Ten young English girls for his harem?'

Williamson raised the cosh again. Laker shrank back.

'It's not like that.'

'What then?'

'Bernie Grimes.'

Williamson laughed mirthlessly but lowered the cosh.

'Bernie Grimes. Now that name is music to my ears.'

'I need a doctor.'

'You need a microphone and a tape recorder, which I just happen to have.'

'Won't be admissible as evidence.'

Williamson smiled again.

'Let me worry about that.'

* * *

Gilchrist's phone vibrated in her pocket. She took it out and looked at the screen. Reg Williamson. She moved down the boat and took the call.

'Sarah? It's Reg.'

'Reg. How is it going? This isn't a particularly good time.'

'I'm realizing the beast is in all of us.'

Gilchrist looked back at Watts.

'You got that right. Are you OK?'

'Charlie Laker is in a gabby mood. In fact, he's like a water spout. Can't shut the fucker up – excuse my French. Oh – except you are in France.'

'You OK, Reg? You sound a bit hyper. Have you arrested Laker?'

'Not in so many words.'

'What does that mean? Reg . . . ?'

'We found five girls locked up in the back of one of his containers, no doubt headed for a brothel somewhere. Snatched in Milldean. Five others targeted for later dispatch. You'll never guess who they are.'

'Where exactly are you, Reg?'

'They are the girls you rescued Sarah Jessica from.'

'What?'

'I know. Imagine that. The very girls she said her father would make pay for what they'd done.'

'Laker is working with Bernie Grimes?'

'Apparently so. And if you think about it, that makes a lot of sense for the Milldean thing. He's copped to that too.'

'He admitted all this?'

'Oh yes. And more. Much more.'

'How? Why was he so willing to talk?'

'Got to go now.'

'Reg. You're worrying me.'

'You've long been a worry to me but I've always been proud of you. Now think on, Sarah. Make use of what I've told you to get Bernie to grass on Charlie.'

'Reg. Stay on the line a minute, will you?'

'Got to go, lass. You take care now.'

Gilchrist realized she was gripping her mobile so tightly her fingers were aching. The line went dead.

Reg Williamson had seen a film a couple of years earlier. Made in the sixties in Brighton. A B-movie but it had been on at the Duke of York's in a retrospective of Brighton-based films. He couldn't remember how he'd ended up there. The Odeon was more his sort of cinema. In one scene they'd sent a car over Beachy Head for real. He'd expected it to soar – like Thelma and Louise's convertible over the Grand Canyon – but its head had dipped and it had kind of rolled down the cliff face. He'd guessed they'd had to roll it because there was no stuntman foolish enough to drive it at speed towards the edge then jump out.

He didn't imagine his wife had soared. She wasn't the soaring type, especially after David's suicide.

He looked at Laker beside him, gaffer-taped to his seat, in loop after brown loop, more tape round his mouth, his eyes bugging. Williamson was pretty sure the gangster had fouled his pants. He'd probably be doing it again soon.

FIFTY-FOUR

'Laker's not going to help you with those girls,' Gilchrist said to Grimes.

Watts gave her a questioning look.

'What do you mean?' Grimes said.

'We know the whole story. How you wanted those kids sent out to some brothel abroad. God, you're sick.'

'I'm sick? What about what those girls did to Sarah Jessica? Did you see what they did?'

'I'm the only one who did see,' Gilchrist said. 'I was there, remember. What they did was dreadful but what you planned in revenge was a thousand times worse.'

'Do unto others as they do unto you,' Grimes said. 'Only twice as much.'

Gilchrist shook her head.

'Anyway, Bernie, your mate Charlie Laker has landed you right in it.'

Grimes stood up and this time Watts let him.

'Why would he do that?' Grimes said, seeming genuinely perplexed.

'Well, let's just say the scales weren't weighed very heavily in your favour,' Gilchrist said.

'If you've got him, what are you asking all these questions for?'

'Peace of mind,' Watts said, smiling at Gilchrist.

'Look, everybody could gain from this,' Gilchrist said, holding Watts's look. 'We could get answers we need. You can cut a deal so that you won't be held to account for some of your scumbag past. And whilst you're beyond redemption for what you wanted to do to those girls, well, nothing actually did happen to them.'

She looked back at Grimes.

'So, what's it going to be?'

Grimes tugged on his chin.

'You got booze on this boat?'

Gilchrist nodded.

'There's a minibar.'

'Well, I'm sure the sun is over the yardarm somewhere in the world,' Grimes said. 'But it's too hot down here to drink. Maybe we can go up on deck?'

Gilchrist and Watts just looked at him.

'Tell us about you and William Simpson,' Watts said. He saw Grimes attempt to deny he knew the name. 'Don't.'

Grimes shrugged.

'I've known Simpson since I was a kid. He was on the scene.'

'A crook?'

'A bum bandit.'

'You knew his father?'

'Do I look that old? I knew *of* him. Philip Simpson. The corrupt chief constable.'

'Pray tell,' Gilchrist said.

'Get me a drink and I will.'

*　　*　　*

Williamson revved the car. He thought he'd do it at an angle rather than dead on. Kind of like Steve McQueen trying to jump the barbed wire in *The Great Escape*. Dicky Attenborough was good in the film too, though not as good as when he played Pinky in *Brighton Rock*. That *was* a film.

He'd pick up some speed going one way, turn on the broad swathe of grass in front of the converted lighthouse, where that snooty woman was probably still sprawled on the sofa with her knickers off, then power downhill and over the edge.

'Look,' said Grimes. 'All I did was let slip to a grass that I was going to be staying in this house the night before I went over to France. Charlie gave me the address. He didn't say why. He said he'd do the rest. He just wanted the favour and I was happy to oblige.'

'How do you know Laker?'

'We've done a bit of business from time to time. More than I realized. I helped him when he took over the Palace Pier.'

'Helped him how?'

'I had a word with a few people. Eased negotiations.'

'What a world you live in,' Gilchrist said, shaking her head.

'What – you think legitimate business doesn't do the same stuff? Just because the chief executive doesn't personally break legs and kill people? Grow the fuck up.' Grimes spat on the floor of the cabin. 'Jesus.' He looked up at Gilchrist. 'What world do you live in?'

'Was that it?' Watts said. 'The extent of your involvement?'

'That was it.'

'But you'll testify against Laker?'

'In court? I don't think so.'

'A statement then,' Watts said.

Grimes swigged his drink.

'I'll think about it.'

Gilchrist drew Watts away.

'Let's leave him for ten minutes. He isn't going anywhere. And I'm worried about Reg. I want to make a couple of calls.'

'Who's that?' Gilchrist said, the moment her call was answered. 'Sergeant Mason – DS Gilchrist here. Yes, I know I'm on suspension. I just wondered if you could tell me if everything is OK with Reg Williamson? Has anything happened in the past couple of days?' She growled. 'If he'd told me, I wouldn't be asking.' Gilchrist listened, then with a whispered 'Thank you' ended the call. She turned to Watts.

'Reg Williamson's wife drove their car off Beachy Head.'

Watts clenched his jaw.

'Jesus. Poor guy.'

'I think he's about to follow her example. Taking Charlie Laker with him.'

FIFTY-FIVE

'Reg, it's Sarah. Have you booked Laker into the station yet?'

'We're en route but we're in no hurry. Going the scenic way.'

'Reg? What are you doing?'

'It's been all go since you went off to France. You can't imagine. More than one person can cope with really.'

'I know about your wife, Reg. I'm really sorry. But please don't do anything foolish.'

'Bit late for that, I'm afraid, Sarah. But, look, I must go. I don't have a hands-free in the car so I'm driving one-handed. Aside from being illegal, it's a bit dodgy up here.'

'Where are you?'

'Beachy Head. Me and Charlie are going to visit the missus. Well, not really visit. Share a moment.'

'Please stop the car.'

'I'm here now. I dropped the interview tape off at the café down the bottom. They're keeping it for you.'

Gilchrist's voice dropped to a whisper.

'Please, Reg . . .'

'Can't take it any more, sweetheart. But at least I'll do something right.'

'Let me talk to Laker.'

'No can do – he's a bit tied up. Remember how Finch got it? He was a dumb bastard but he didn't deserve to go like that. Apparently, Laker was in the back of the car. Watched his men do it – though he didn't see the cat jump into the boot. Oh, that snooty cow in the lighthouse – cat-woman – is mixed up in it too – he's been her bit of rough for years. Very rough but it seems that's how she likes it. Anyway, this is a bit of poetic justice to pay for Finch, creep though he was.'

'You've got a confession. You don't need to do whatever you're planning. Stop now and when I get back we'll go out, have a few beers and laugh over this.'

'No laughs left, darling. And I don't think the confession would stand up in court. Taken under duress, they'll say. Kick the case out and he'll get off scot-free. So, everything considered, this is the way to go.'

'Reg, I'm begging you. You're one of the few friends I've got.'

'Nice of you to say but we hardly know each other. Both private – too private, mebbe.'

'What would your wife think of what you're doing?'

'I'll find out soon. Goodbye, Sarah.'

The phone went dead.

Gilchrist went up on deck.

'Bob,' she called, looking down the length of the barge for him.

'I'm here,' he said from the bank several feet below.

'Reg has lost it,' she called before she scrambled off the barge.

Bob Watts frowned.

'Tell me.'

'He's got a confession out of Charlie Laker – everything, according to Reg. But I think he might have beaten it out of him.'

'*Reg?*' There was disbelief in Watts's voice.

'Back in the day he was a tough customer,' Gilchrist said. 'He always carries a cosh. Old-fashioned wooden thing with a lump of lead sunk in the top.'

'*Reg?*'

'Yes, Reg,' Gilchrist said impatiently. 'Tubby Reg Williamson. But it's not just that he's got the confession like that. I think he's going to kill Laker – and himself.'

Williamson over-revved when he started up the slope so skidded and fishtailed, and then the turn was too wide so it slowed him. Still, as he put his foot down on the return run, he could see the lights of Eastbourne glittering just a little way down the coast. The pier was a poor thing compared to Brighton's but it looked good from here: a brilliant, jutting finger pointing at France.

He aimed for it.

Charlie Laker was not going gentle into that good night. Behind the tape that was choking him he was raging. How could this be happening to him? He had big plans for the future. This fat fuck cold-cocking him. He'd tried to reason with the man but Williamson had just coshed him, again and again.

Was the mad fuck humming to himself as they skidded up the hill? Laker saw the fat man glance his way at the turn before they started back down.

'Fuck!' Laker screamed but, even though he felt something tear in his throat, no sound came through the gaffer tape.

The car bumped and slithered over the flints beneath the grass. Williamson's eyes were focused somewhere in the distance. Laker was watching the lip of the cliff surge closer and closer.

He was wondering what he should be thinking about. Should his life be flashing in front of him? It wasn't. He wasn't thinking of Dawn or of John Hathaway. Or of his brother, Roy. His parents. The women he'd had, in every possible combination. People he'd hurt, or killed or had killed.

He wasn't thinking any of this, or of all the things he still wanted to do, as the lip disappeared beneath him and the car flew into the air four hundred feet above the sea. He was seeing bitter blue sky and a seagull; he was sure it was a seagull. And that part of his final journey – the flying – didn't seem to go on a long time or a short time. It just was.

Then gravity grabbed them and the car dipped. He glanced

across at Williamson who was not looking where the car was headed but still up, off somewhere in his own head.

Laker saw the white-lashed sea approaching more rapidly than he expected. The car rolled and he was looking at the chalk cliff face and then up at the sky and that bloody seagull again. His body was trying to tear free of the tape that held him to his seat, though he wanted the car to keep him safe from the enveloping air.

And he cried in frustration because all he was thinking at this final moment in his life, as the car pitched a second time, was about his favourite fucking penny slot machine in Dennis Hathaway's amusement arcade on the West Pier in the sixties. The glass case in which all the ghoulies and ghosties and creatures of the damned popped out of cupboards and drawers and coffins behind an old miser counting his money in total ignorance of them. And all the time these things were happening, the clockwork mechanism of the machine whirred down until the penny ran out and the car hit the water and everything stopped.

FIFTY-SIX

Tingley was delirious. Drenched. He tried to turn, slick as an eel, but sodden sheets weighed him down. He groaned. His arm was free of needles now. He reached his hand up and wiped a slop of sweat from his forehead.

He stared at the canopy above his head, lost in muddled thought, until Maria came in. She wiped his face with a cloth and handed him his mobile phone. It was Bob Watts.

'Jimmy – relieved to have got hold of you. You OK?'

'I'm fine,' Tingley croaked, sounding anything but.

'Job done?'

'Done,' Tingley said, looking at Maria's watching eyes as she dabbed his face again.

'Where are you?'

Tingley knew Watts could detect something in his voice.

'Orvieto.'

'Not the Balkans?'

'They were both here. I got Kadire first. Just the way it fell out.'

'Have you taken a hit? You don't sound yourself.'

'It's nothing. Just echoes.'

Tingley took a ragged breath.

'Echoes? Jimmy, you sure you're OK?'

'Dandy. What about you?'

'Sarah and I are in France with Bernie Grimes. Got a statement from him, though it looks like we're not going to need it. You know Reg Williamson, Sarah's partner? Drove Charlie Laker off Beachy Head.'

'Jesus,' Tingley said. 'We're done, then.'

'Still got to get that slippery fuck William Simpson but I'm guessing that's somewhere further down the line. Jimmy – do you want me to come across and join you? I'm probably only a day's drive away.'

'Negative. Listen, Bob, I'll call you in a day or so.'

Tingley passed Maria the disconnected phone and sank back on the pillow.

Sarah Gilchrist scarcely spoke on the flight back from Toulouse. Watts assumed she was in shock about Reg Williamson. He wasn't sure what he felt. Nothing new there, then. He had Grimes's statement in his pocket and he'd made a call to ensure that Met Police Transnational crime officers would be on his tail pronto.

Watts was pragmatic about the death of Charlie Laker. In some ways, it was the neatest solution. Getting him legitimately would have been a bugger. He didn't really know Reg Williamson so couldn't honestly grieve about his death, though he regretted one good man less in the world.

He was worried about Tingley. There had been something about his old friend's tone of voice. He didn't know him well, despite the number of years they had been friends, but he did understand nuance. Well, a bit.

'Do you want to get something to eat somewhere?' Watts said when he and Gilchrist came out of Gatwick.

'I think I'll take some time alone,' she said, giving him a perfunctory hug, hoisting her bag over her shoulder and striding away across the concourse. Watts watched her go. The longer he knew her, the less he knew her.

He took the express train up to Victoria and the tube along to Hammersmith. It was raining again but still he walked along the towpath, lugging his bag. By the time he reached his father's house his suit was a sodden mess; water dripped from his wet hair down his face and on to his shoulders.

He'd been hoping for some kind of cleansing from the rain. At one point he'd turned his face up and let it drench him. All he'd got from that was stinging eyes.

He stripped off and showered and changed into jeans and jumper. He phoned Tingley but the phone went to voicemail. He didn't leave a message. He poured a brandy – he'd drunk all his father's whisky – and sat in the wingback chair, his head thrown back, his eyes closed.

Kate was standing on the balcony, holding the handwritten note from the Twickenham policeman, when she heard the flat door open and close. She looked over her shoulder. Sarah, a gloomy look on her face, passed through into her bedroom and firmly shut the door. Kate walked into the sitting room.

'Sarah?'

'Leave me,' Sarah called through her bedroom door.

'OK,' Kate said in a small voice. She stood in the middle of the room, a little lost. She looked down at the handwritten note. It was the name and address of the car owner. The name of the Brighton Trunk Murderer. Mr Eric Knowles.

It was raining heavily again when Watts sat down and phoned Jimmy Tingley. This time his phone was answered.

'*Pronto?*'

'Who is that?'

'Guiseppe di Bocci. You wish to speak to Signor Tingley?'

'Please. But first: is he wounded?'

'Signor Tingley is not well.'

'Wounded?'

'Let me give him to you.'

Watts looked out of the long window up into the sky. The rain falling from the roof of the world.

'Bob?' Tingley's voice weak but recognizable.

'What's happening, Jimmy? Are you injured?'

'Poorly.'

'Are you safe?'

'I think so.'

'I'm flying over.'

'No need for that.'

'What kind of poorly, Jimmy? You told me you hadn't been wounded.'

'I lied. Shot in the stomach.'

'You need to be in a hospital.'

'Negative. My carers know what they're doing. If anything can be done.'

'Jesus Christ. James . . . ?'

'I'm here. James – rarely hear that. I guess that's what my parents might have called me. Or maybe not. Thank you. You know, Robert, there's a weird dignity in names.'

'I know it. Though if my mother ever called me Robert around the house, I knew I was in trouble.'

Tingley rasped a laugh.

'And your dad?'

'My dad?' Watts looked into his brandy glass. 'James, you're gonna get through this. Hang on.'

'For another weary winter? Robert. Things are what they are.'

'I know that.' Watts forced a grin down the line. 'The only true account is the thing itself.'

Tingley's laugh didn't really start before it was cut off by a cough.

'James?'

'I gotta go.'

Watts was welling up.

'No, you don't.'

'Yes. I do.'

Watts heard Tingley's raw chuckle.

'What a ride, eh? I wish I'd known my mum and dad. One or the other.'

'It's not over yet, James. But if the time comes, I'll give you your mother's kiss, I promise. But not yet.'

No response.
'James?'
No response.

FIFTY-SEVEN

K ate was on the phone with her father when Sara Gilchrist came out of her room. When she'd seen the Notting Hill number come up, she'd hesitated before she'd answered. Now she wished she'd hesitated longer.

'Your mother has left me,' he said without preamble.

'Not before time,' Kate said, before she could stop herself. 'Where has she gone?'

'No idea, but I'm sure she'll be in touch with you in due course.'

'She's gone off with somebody else?'

'Not at all.'

'Have you?'

'It's nothing like that. Your mother had . . . there's this man – Charlie Laker—'

'He's dead.'

'What?'

Gilchrist wandered on to the balcony.

'He's dead. He died yesterday.'

Her father was effusive.

'But that's wonderful news,' he said.

Kate looked at Sarah's long back as she leaned over the balcony.

'Not for Reg Williamson,' Kate said quietly. 'Or do you mean because Laker can't dish the dirt on you?'

'I must phone your mother and let her know,' Simpson said and hung up.

Kate looked at her phone in surprise.

'That was sudden,' she said, as Gilchrist came back into the room.

'What was?' Gilchrist said, walking into the kitchen and opening the fridge.

'My father hung up virtually mid-conversation.'

'That's men for you,' Gilchrist said, putting a bottle of white wine and two glasses on the coffee table.

Kate Simpson looked at her.

'Sarah – I'm really sorry to hear about Reg Williamson.'

'Me too,' said Gilchrist, sitting on the edge of the chair on the other side of the table.

'But you've been able to get a few things clarified?'

Gilchrist nodded as she poured two generous glasses of wine and passed one to Kate. Their hands touched for a moment.

'Just a question now of whether I still have a job,' Gilchrist said.

Kate shuddered.

'And whether I go to jail.'

Gilchrist held her glass out to chink against Kate's.

'I'd bet money on a suspended sentence at worst.'

They took their first sips. Gilchrist took more of a healthy swig.

'Finally figured out the identity of the Brighton Trunk Murderer. Bloke called Eric Knowles.'

Gilchrist shrugged.

'Should I know him?'

'No. But I think we should be able to find out more about him than we already know.'

Gilchrist nodded.

'Job done, then.'

Kate smiled.

'We still don't know who the victim was.'

'Of course,' Gilchrist said, topping her glass up. She proffered the bottle to Kate. Kate shook her head.

'I really want to find out who she is. I keep thinking: she liked music, she had a favourite food, she sighed over a favourite movie star. We know she liked the sun.'

Gilchrist nodded again.

'She was another human being.'

'Right,' Kate said.

Gilchrist gave her a tight smile.

'That's your next project, then.'

EPILOGUE

Restless still, Watts roamed his father's house. He wandered over to his father's bookshelves. His father had read widely, more widely than Watts would have expected. Organized, too. Alphabetical within countries.

He was scanning the American section. It was all classic stuff: Hawthorne, Melville, Fenimore Cooper, Hemingway, Scott Fitzgerald. There was a narrow-spined work by Thomas Wolfe called *God's Lonely Man* squeezed between John Dos Passos and some hard-boiled crime. There were signed copies of Chandler. Watts remembered his father telling him he'd once gone on a bender with Chandler and Ian Fleming.

On the shelf below were photo albums. An old cigar box was acting as a bookend. Watts took it down. He sat at the table by the window and slid the lid open. The box was filled with papers. He took out his father's birth certificate. Three First World War medals lay beneath it. Watts smiled.

He knew the slang name for these medals were Pip, Squeak and Wilfred, sarcastically named after a long-running strip cartoon that had begun 1919. Pip was a dog, Squeak a penguin, Wilfred a rabbit with very long ears. They went everywhere together, as did this trio of medals. You got one, you got the rest. Though it didn't mean you were alive.

Watts picked up one of the medals. The British War Medal, issued in 1919 to anyone, dead or alive, who had fought in the Great War. It was silver with George V's head on one side and a naked St George mounted on a horse on the other. The sun of Victory shone down on St George trampling the Prussian shield beneath his horse's hooves.

The second was the four-pointed Mons Star made of bright bronze, with a crown on one side and crossed swords on the other. It had a wreath of oak leaves beside a scroll inscribed 'August 1914'.

The third was an Allied Victory medal, also issued in 1919

to all those who had been awarded the other two medals. This one was bronze lacquer. Winged Victory on one side, 'The Great War for Civilization, 1914–1919' engraved on the other.

His grandfather would have been awarded them post-humously. Watts knew he had been in the Royal Sussex Regiment, 2nd Battalion. He'd gone over with the first division of the Expeditionary Force in August 1914 and been killed at the battle of Mons.

The Great War. He had seen a TV drama about Rudyard Kipling and his son Jack recently. Kipling, gung-ho about the war, had pulled strings to get his severely short-sighted son into the Irish Guards. He had fought at the Battle of Loos in torrential rain. With his glasses on, Jack Kipling wouldn't have been able to see anything, especially not the bullet that killed him.

Watts had visited his grandfather's grave once at St Symphorien cemetery, near Mons. It had been created by the Germans for both the Allied and German soldiers who fell in the battle. Well, some of the ones who fell.

He'd stood on a mound beside a tall obelisk and looked down at the five hundred or so grey granite headstones laid out in neat rectangles on every side. The man he was named after was somewhere among them.

He spent the next thirty minutes looking for him. It was quiet in the cemetery, although a breeze occasionally shivered the branches of the trees.

Some graves were unidentified. He found the grave of Private John Parr, killed on 21st August 1914, believed to be the first Commonwealth soldier killed in the Great War. Nearby was the grave of the Canadian soldier, Private Gordon Price, believed to be the last.

He found his grandfather's grave in a secluded patch of the cemetery. Private Robert Edward Watts, Royal Sussex, 24th August 1914. It didn't state his age, though ages were listed on some of the others. A rosemary bush had been planted in front of the headstone. He took out his pocketknife, bent and sliced off a clump. Put it to his nose.

He ran his hand over the rough granite of the headstone. A little self-consciously, he saluted his grandfather, the clump of rosemary still between his fingers, then turned and headed for home.

In the box there was a faded, creased black-and-white photograph of a pretty young woman. Nothing written on the back but Watts was sure it was his grandmother, Jenny. Robert's wife. He hadn't known her either. She had died a decade before Watts was born.

He picked up the photo albums he had found earlier. He was surprised that his father kept something so sentimental. He went slowly through the albums, page by page.

He found a photograph of his grandmother standing beside a short, broad-shouldered man with a walrus moustache and dark hair scraped back from his forehead. It had been taken in a studio with a rural scene on a painted backdrop behind them. Both were standing erect and neither was smiling, though there was a glint of humour in the man's eyes.

Watts went back to the cigar box. There was a thin envelope addressed in faded copper plate to Mrs Robert Watts at an address in Haywards Heath. He extracted two sheets of flimsy paper, one wrapped in torn tissue. He carefully removed the tissue paper. There was a crumpled, muddied, sheet inside it. A note in faded pencil. It had been folded twice and on the back the same pencil had written: 'For Jenny'. Not all the words were legible. Watts wrote it out on a sheet of paper, filling in words as best he could. It read:

Dear[est?] Jenny,

I don't know if this will ever get to you. They tell us the post from here only takes a day although I feel a world away from hearth and home and my beloved family. If you are reading this, however, that will probably not bode well [for me?]. A big surge tomorrow and I'm over [the top?] again. I pray all goes [well?]. I carry your picture at all times in my breast [pocket?] and [your?] last words and kisses to me forever in my heart. If this is to be Adieu then God bless to you and the little ones. I pray your father will find it in his heart to forgive your strong-headedness in marrying me and take you back in. Other[wise?], I [fear?] how you will fend.

I love you until death do us part – and forever
thereafter.
Your loving husband,
Robert

There was something written in brackets after 'Robert' but
Watts couldn't make it out. He placed the note carefully on
the table and took a few slow breaths.

He looked in the cigar box. There was another photograph,
face down, in the bottom. He turned it over.

Four men in uniform with 'Somewhere in France' written
in chalk on a blackboard in front of them. All had muddy
puttees and boots. Four men, four different moustaches. Three
wore peaked uniform caps. Robert Watts was bareheaded.

He looked on the back of the photograph. Nothing written
there. He put the photo down and picked up the second sheet
of letter-paper. It had the same neat handwriting as the
envelope. It was addressed care of a hotel in Brighton and
dated 25th February 1915. He read it slowly.

Dear Mrs Watts,
I understand that you have by now received news from
the War Office of the sad death of your husband, Robert
Edward Watts. (We knew him as 'Ted'.) I was with him
when he died. He and I were firm friends. He was a fine
man who spoke of you and your children in loving terms
every day. I have some few small items of his possessions
and a note he wrote to you the night before his death
that I hope you may allow me to bring to you. I am
spending some days leave in Brighton. Perhaps you would
be good enough to let me know if a visit would be
welcome.
I am most sorry for your loss. My best wishes to you
and your children.

He looked at the photograph of his grandparents in the album
again. He ran his hand through his shock of blond hair. His
father had been blond in his young days. Watts couldn't see
any family resemblance between himself and the man in the

photo, although he thought there was something of his father in the woman's features.

He picked up his father's birth certificate. Robert had his occupation listed as 'Soldier'. Jenny was listed as 'Teacher'. The birth was registered at Haywards Heath, Sussex.

Watts looked at the date on the birth certificate and frowned.

He had always believed, as the obituaries had stated, that his father had been born on 27th November 1913. The birth certificate had a different date. 27th November 1915.

He pondered this, then walked over to his father's book-shelves. He double-checked the date of the Battle of Mons.

He returned to his seat. Robert Watts last saw his wife at the start of August 1914. He was dead by 23rd August 1914. His son, Donald Watts, aka Victor Tempest, was born in November of the following year.

Some fifteen months after Robert had died.

Watts steepled his hands under his chin. Looked down at the photo of his grandmother. He could see how it might have happened. It was almost a cliché. The grieving widow. The wounded soldier who had fought alongside her beloved husband delivering his final note to her. Misplaced emotions. A sense of gratitude. Sorrow. Loneliness.

In those days she would need to hide the fact of a child conceived after the death of her husband. Especially if she was to get help from her father.

Did his own father, Donald aka Victor Tempest, know? Perhaps Jenny confessed it to him, her son, when he was grown-up. Perhaps he figured out from his birth certificate that his father couldn't be his father.

But did he know everything?

Watts looked again at the photo of the four men. Only one of them had a blond moustache and blond hair. The tallest of them. He looked straight into the camera and Watts could see his father in the cold eyes and pursed lips.

He picked up the letter and looked at the name carefully printed out below the indecipherable signature. It was a name he now knew. The name of his true grandfather.

Eric Knowles.

AUTHOR'S NOTE

Eric Knowles is entirely a product of my imagination. Martin Charteris/Castledene flits tantalizingly through the police files dealing with the second Brighton Trunk Murder at the Sussex Records Office and the National Archives, and even in several news reports in *The Times*. Tony Mancini/ Jack Notyre/Cecil Lois England did the things I attribute to him.

There is confusion in the newspaper reports and police files about his villainous past and it looks as if acts committed by Antonio 'Baby' Mancini were attached to him. 'Baby' Mancini was executed in 1941, by Albert Pierrepoint, for murdering Harry Distleman in a Wardour Street club.

For information about the British Union of Fascists I once again (as I did with my novel *Foiled Again*) turned to Richard Thurlow's *Fascism In Britain* (I. B. Taurus); Nicholas Mosley's *Rules of The Game* (Fontana); Robert Skidelsky's *Oswald Mosley* (Papermac); and an unpublished memoir by Nellie Driver in the Nelson library about her time as a member of the BUF in Colne and Nelson in the 1930s.

I am indebted to Joanna Bourke's *Dismembering The Male* (Reaktion) for information about and fascinating insights into attitudes to dismemberment and disfigurement in World War One and after. I have put some of the phrases and sentiments she quotes from Great War soldiers into several of my characters' mouths.

To inform the account by Victor Tempest/Donald Watts of his police days I used Clive Emsley's terrific *The English and Violence since 1750* (hambledon continuum).

Above all, though, this is a work of fiction in which historical fact was just the starting point for my own inventions.

Peter Guttridge